# The Traders Club

## by

# Jim Dreis

# DISCLAIMER

This book is a work of fiction.

Names, characters, places, and incidents are the product of the author's imagination, or are used fictitiously.  Any resemblance to actual events, locales or persons, alive or dead, is purely coincidental.

Written by Jim Dreis

Member, Real Estate Solutions, LLC

An Arizona Limited Liability Company

Dedication

To my family

Acknowledgment

I want to thank my daughter Shelly, her good friend Leann Sasek, and our neighbor Hazel Hatch for reviewing the book and sharing their thoughts.

I want to extend a special thanks to Marguerite Wainio for correcting the many grammatical errors I sent her way, and for offering words of encouragement and ideas during my moments of writer's block. Margi's a terrific editor.

Welcome to The Traders Club;

The Traders Club is a sequel to two books, The Traders and Trader Among the Flock. Only two characters remain from those books, Ivan Schmidt and his pet macaw Peety; the rest have retired from the Trader series or lie dormant in the author's mind, ready to emerge when the urge strikes.

In the first book, The Traders, readers learned that Ivan was an only child who had a rough childhood. A loner, he had a difficult time relating to other kids so spent a majority of his time in his room reading and fantasizing. Because he was bright and well read, learning came easily, and he excelled in school. But loneliness and a desire for companionship ate at him, and played a role in his being abused. Enraged over being violated, he withdrew more. His parents were unaware of what had happened; they just worried that his isolation and anger would forever impair him, so decided they would find a companion for him, and bought Peety.

At first, Ivan hated Peety. The thought of having to take care of and share his room with a damn bird was not to his liking, and he told Peety that. And he told Peety more. For that matter, every ill in life that frustrated him, he told Peety. Unbeknownst to him, Peety became his analyst, his outlet. He could rant and rave and Peety never rejected him--instead sat on his perch and listened, and because he did, in time Ivan's attitude towards him changed. He began looking forward to coming home because Peety was always there to hear him out. He could rant and rave about whatever, and Peety always listened.

Because Ivan was so involved with himself, he never learned that he had one sharp bird on his hands. Through high school, college, law school, and on into business, Ivan shared his woes with Peety, and did the same when he got involved with the drug lord, going so far as to share information about his drug dealings. When he was hauled off to jail, and Peety was carted off to a caretaker, it profoundly affected both of them --Ivan for being incarcerated, and Peety for being abandoned, which he was none too happy about.

In short order, he warmed to the gal taking care of him, as she not only talked to him but also listened. She listened to the point wherein she realized that Peety was a font of information about Ivan's drug dealings, so she contacted the police. Soon Peety was spilling the beans about Ivan's drug activity, only to have the detectives realize they'd look like idiots if they put him on the stand.

When Ivan found out that Peety had ratted on him, he was not happy. But because no one would testify against him, he was released from jail. So in the second book, Trader Among the Flock, Peety and Ivan are reunited, though their relationship is very strained. Ivan toys with wringing the little bugger's neck, but realizes that if he did that, he'd have no one in his life, so decides against it, electing instead to watch what he says around the bird. Because of his drug dealings, he's financially set for life. Nonetheless, he returns to the Traders Club in hopes that he can put his money to work. Soon he comes across a church in need of a first mortgage. Realizing it's a safe investment, he lends the money, then becomes concerned when they have a change in ministers. Unsure about the new minister, he gets involved in the church--which is a recipe for disaster.

Whereas "The Traders" will cause you to shake your head,

"Trader Among the Flock" will cause you to double over from laughter.

Freud reasoned that the mind is composed of an Id, Ego and Superego. The Traders, those lovable profiteers, couldn't care less about the Superego because that is our conscience. The Superego carries a sledgehammer called "guilt," and the Traders can't let guilt get in their way. How would they ever make any money? Nothing can get in their way, so the Traders are happy to push the Superego aside and let the Id reign. The Id is their ego. Many Traders have a huge ego and believe that ethics are optional. Why would they need ethics when they can simply hire an attorney when they are caught being naughty? Furthermore, ethics usually just get in the way of the Traders' goals. Plus, ethics just make people appear soft. A person definitely does not want to be soft around the Traders, because that will make them an easy target for some of the vultures.

Psychotics think two and two is five. Neurotics know that the correct answer is four, but they are so involved with themselves that they are too afraid to answer out loud. People with character disorders don't really worry about either the question or the answer because not much worries these types anyway. These people often believe that behaving responsibly applies to everyone else but not to themselves. That being said, let me introduce you to a group of really colorful characters. Julius, Windy, Gilbert, Hadley, the Critter, Gomer, Buttercup, Ivan, Peety…and the list goes on. I hope you enjoy reading about them and their adventures.

# The Traders Club

Reading this book comes with a warning. Fits of laughter and somber moments of shaking your head are sure to occur, as the book is chock-full of characters and situations to keep the most discriminating reader amused.

Imagine if you will: an immature, wealthy male chauvinist weasel; a paranoid schizophrenic who functions well when he's on his medication but not when he's not; an overweight fixer-upper whom clients rave about; a sleight-of-hand mortgage broker; a wealthy do-gooder who gets his pockets picked; a devious guy with a pet macaw named Peety; a multi-tattooed hard-ass; a naïve young agent just off the farm; a Southern belle; and a character named The Critter--all packed into one book.

A more colorful group of real estate practitioners you won't find, though unfortunately, their quest for wealth is often waylaid by their idiosyncrasies, which add notably to the humor and drama.

Enjoy. I enjoyed writing it.

Jim Dreis

## Chapter 1

Julius Stern is a spoiled jerk. He is about as insecure as they come, but he comes across as arrogant, controlling, and a male chauvinist. Women hate him. It comes as a great surprise that he actually made it through adolescence without getting the crap beaten out of him by some woman whom he pissed off. Julius thrives on putting any women down who shows the least bit of confidence or competence. His favorite mode of insult is to tell as many off-color jokes as he can. When he is on a roll, he will usually end up aggravating everyone around him, including men.

Julius needs to feel like he is in charge. He needs everyone to think he is a dominant man. The thought of being seen as vulnerable is totally unacceptable.

Julius had a miserable childhood. He was an only child. His parents were Senor Milquetoast and the Queen of Guilt. He was destined to have mental and emotional troubles. His mother never wanted children but felt she had to go through with her pregnancy because of religious and familial beliefs. Somebody had to pay for her suffering and that was Julius's father. She constantly put him down with disparaging remarks and other castrating comments.

She thrilled at telling Julius's father that he never measured up to what she deserved. She would tell him she only married him because he got her knocked up. To this day Julius still doesn't know why his father stayed with that woman. Julius vowed that he would never be treated like that by a stupid woman. Julius learned at a young age that he would never let a women get close to him, because women can hurt you.

Julius stood 5'5" and weighed 125 pounds, with an attitude of someone much larger. For that matter, he saw himself as a real tiger. He was very wealthy. He inherited a fortune from some rich relatives, and lived the part. From his designer clothes to his Rolex watch to his million dollar home to his $100,000 convertible--everything reeked money. His license plate said "Julius." In other words, "Look at me--I'm successful." Standing next to him you inhaled expensive cologne. One sensed that he bathed in it. Everything had to be perfect.

After inheriting millions, Julius severed ties with his parents for the most part, partially because his mother kept badgering him for money. He didn't mind giving his father a few bucks now and then because he never asked for any, but his mother threw one guilt trip after another at him. She was forever pointing out how fortunate he was to inherit so much money, and how unfortunate they were that they didn't get it. She went so far as to add that since they had sacrificed so hard to get him into the best schools and have the nicest clothes, he owed it to them to at least split the inheritance with them, because the million dollars he gave them wasn't enough. In her opinion, he should have been far more generous. So to avoid her constant haranguing, he stayed away.

He didn't really need to work but he got bored just lounging around, so he bought a quality apartment complex. The place had forty-eight units and was run by fantastic on-site management. Julius, of course, had to be in control, so he micro-managed and caused all kinds of turmoil in the running of the place. He irritated everyone, so turnover was huge, both in the staff and the residents. Sylvia Goldsmith had had her fair share of confrontations with Julius in the past. He had once threatened and made her pay a late penalty on her rent because she was a day late. He thought that he was going to collect another late penalty from her. Little did he know what was about to come.

"Sylvia, you've fallen into the nasty habit of paying your rent late and I want my money!" said Julius. "I will call the Sheriff and have you evicted if you don't produce your rent check right now."

"You blood-sucking weasel. I paid my rent the first of the month. I even have the receipt from the office manager!" Sylvia had a good five inches and twenty pounds on Julius, so she was a bit of an intimidating figure, not that Julius would admit that. Sylvia was only getting started, though. "You are such an idiot. If you don't start showing your staff and your tenants a little respect, we are all going to walk out on you!" The commotion caused quite a few residents to open their doors to see what was happening. Once they realized that their friend Sylvia was blasting Julius, they silently cheered her on. If anyone deserved a good ass-chewing it was Julius, and Sylvia was the right person to do it.

Julius was furious and a bit embarrassed too. He was so flustered that he couldn't even get a word in. Sylvia continued to berate him about his poor managerial abilities. He finally had enough and stormed off to his office. The office staff had been given a heads-up by one of the residents, so when he stormed in they all appeared very busy. Nobody wanted to be on the receiving end of his tantrum. To their surprise, though, he simply went into his office and slammed the door. Julius needed someone to talk to and the only person he could think of was Rabbi Goldman.

Rabbi Goldman was a wise old sage well aware of Julius's many shortcomings. He knew Julius's parents and the turmoil he grew up in. Rabbi Goldman knew that Julius was the result of PPP (Piss Poor Protoplasm). The Rabbi felt Julius was a walking example of narcissism, but today he was a badly bruised one.

Julius was not used to having a women stand up to him. How dare she do that! The worst part was that she was right. She had paid her rent on time. What should he do? Apologize? He never apologized. It wasn't in his nature. He was always right. Even when he was wrong, he was right. He insisted on it. He could never live it down. He might as well sell the place because he could never go back. No way. They would all laugh at him. His macho ego was bruised. They all saw a *woman* put him down.

Rabbi Goldman listened to him ramble for a while then assured him that he would be okay. Julius was starting to feel a little better after his tirade, but he definitely wasn't ready for Rabbi Goldman's next question.

"Has any women ever done that to you before, Julius?" asked the Rabbi.

"No!" replied Julius angrily.

"You could have sent one of your staff members to collect the rent, true?" said the Rabbi.

"I should have," he muttered defensively.

"Tell me about this lady?"

"What's there to tell, she's a tenant. What do you think, I like her or something?"

"Do you?"

"Of course not, she's just a tenant who owed me money."

"Is it possible you just wanted an excuse to talk with her?"

"Ridiculous!" was his retort.

"Tell me about your social life, Julius?"

"I didn't come here to talk about my social life. Listen, thanks for your time, but I need to get back to work." Then he abruptly walked out.

Rabbi Goldman smiled. This tenant sounded like someone who was not afraid to set Julius straight.

Julius drove back to work determined to show everyone Sylvia wasn't getting away with her tirade.

"Give me Sylvia Goldsmith's rental agreement," he bellowed at Maria Gonzalez, his most recent hire. The previous leasing agent had quit in a huff in response to his obnoxious ways.

A couple of minutes later she walked into his office and was told, "I'm going to get rid of that broad. When's her lease up? No woman's talking to me like she did!" he blurted out.

Maria had been around long enough to know that now was not the time to talk. Back out the door maybe, but not talk, because anything she said would have sent him into a rage, and a rage she didn't need because it was almost time to go home. Sticking around for another hour while he threw a temper tantrum wasn't high on her list of things to do. No, she'd stay mum and back out the door.

She was almost there when he said, "Find some dirt on her so I can cancel her lease and throw her out."

"I know little about her. Except for the one time she was late making her payment, she's been on time and a model tenant."

"Then make something up. I need a reason to get rid of her!" he ordered.

"Yes, sir," she responded and walked out, seeing herself losing her real estate license over this. Maybe she should look for another job. What a way to start a new one. Maybe everything she had heard about her new boss was true. She had elected to believe it wasn't, which is why she took the job. She guessed she was wrong. If she didn't need the money she'd walk out, but she did, as she was behind on her own rent. God, what a mess! Maybe tomorrow would be better. With that she headed back into his office to say goodnight, only to be handed Sylvia's folder with the instructions that she was to stay until she found a loophole sufficient to dump the tenant. With that he walked out. She was stuck. What was she going to do? Thank God her mother lived near her apartment so could pop over to watch the kids and get supper going. At the moment her thought about work was, "It sucks!"

Chapter 2

Julius attended the Traders meeting the next day rather than head to the office.

Walking into the Traders Club, one is immediately confronted with the sign, "No Guns Allowed." But true to their nature, and indicative of their attitude, members didn't pay a bit of attention to the sign because they wouldn't be caught dead without their guns.

The Traders Club is a place where members go to swap properties. There are tax benefits to swapping properties, and the Traders are experts at capitalizing on those tax benefits. They are also experts at seeing to it that Uncle Sam waits as long as possible to get his share of the take. The term "greed" is a term of endearment at the Traders Club, where members attend with the same goal in mind: to extract wealth from everyone, an attitude they believe symbolizes the free enterprise system, a system they're strong supporters of. It's the group where you can earn a bundle and lose your shirt too. This is why members love it when strangers show up--they're treated like a breath of fresh air, or fresh meat, if you prefer—while all the while filtering through the members' minds is the question, "How can I capitalize here?"

The Internal Revenue Service, affectionately known as the IRS, has a provision in one of its tax codes for exchanging "like kind" property: it's called a 1031 Exchange. It lets owners of income and investment property defer paying Uncle Sam by trading for property of a like kind nature. Standard practice was to sell property and then buy something else. Uncle Sam loved it; he was right there to take his share; he called it his right under the tax called capital gains.

The end result was that if you sold, you had less money to buy another property. So it didn't take long to reason that it would be great if Uncle Sam had to wait to get his portion of the take. From this grew an industry in the real estate community known as the "Exchangers," or "Traders." They were licensed real estate agents and brokers who gathered to exchange, trade, or swap, income and investment property belonging either to them or to their clients.

The Traders had their own vocabulary. Words like "equity," "in lieu of," and "alligator" became common expressions, with "equity" being right on top. It signified the difference between what was owed and the market value. If the market value was $125,000 and $50,000 was owed to a lender, then the "equity" was $75,000. Balancing equities became an art form. Sometimes it meant adding land, notes, trucks, airplanes, and other property to a transaction. Usually, it was a point of negotiation. Some investors even broke down and added cash, the word many Traders dreamed about. In the 1970s, you could find 200 agents and brokers at a weekly meeting, and more at a national convention. For many Traders, it didn't matter where the property was located as long as deals could be put together and profits made.

Over the years, attendance at the Traders meetings had declined. Some attribute the decline to tax laws, while others say it was the shift from client-owned property to Trader-owned property. Seldom mentioned was the notion that the Traders destroyed themselves from within, as more than one person described the club as, "The home of the weasel clause."

Julius wasn't sure why he showed up, but it beat facing his staff. Everyone sensed his mood was sour when he walked through the door, so stayed away from him. The president opened the meeting with a few comments, everyone stood to recite the Pledge of Allegiance, and then the marketing manager took over.

He asked, "Does anyone have a package they want to present?"

Three hands went up. They were invited to pass them out. Agents with "packages" put together information about a property they controlled, such as who owned it, why it was available for trade, and what the owner would take. As the packages were passed out, the marketing manager selected a member to lead the discussion, and when he was through asking questions, he would allow others to ask. One of the major interests to all was the motivation of the owners. How badly did they want out? The more motivated, the more likely they would receive "mini-offers," or "would you take" inquiries.

All three presenters had plain-jane-vanilla properties no one was excited about, so the marketing manager quickly disposed of them, then asked if anyone had a property that they wanted to talk about.

Julius's hand shot into the air.

"Julius, what do you have?"

"A forty-eight-unit apartment complex I want to dump."

Everyone sat up and took notice, including Ivan. They all knew Julius didn't need money, so the question was--what prompted him to want out of his apartments?

"Julius, what do you owe?"

"Nothing, they're free and clear."

"What do you think they're worth?"

"At the moment I haven't the foggiest idea."

"So why do you want to trade it?"

"Because of the damn tenants; they're a pain in the ass, and so is the staff!"

Many of the traders chimed in with, 'You got that right.'

"I got people who don't pay on time and when I question them they blow their stack." Part of the statement was true. Part wasn't--typical Julius. He distorted reality to meet his needs, and his wants too.

Ivan wondered why he was upset. He owned one of the nicest complexes in town. He was a jerk, of course, and more than likely upset his tenants and staff (which was his norm), so the question was, what was the little weasel up to?

"Julius, how many vacancies do you have?"

"Ten."

"How come so many?" a Trader blurted out. "The demand for apartments is unprecedented."

"The jerks keep breaking leases. They offer some sorry-ass excuse my rental manager falls for, and then she even refunds their security deposits. So I've dumped one or two because of it." Rumor had it that no one wanted to work for him, because he made Napoleon look like an angel.

Windy Wales chimed in with a statement you'd expect from a paranoid schizophrenic. "You kind of feel they're out to get you, don't you?"

"Yeah!"

Windy shook his head and said, "I'm with ya', partner," giving him a "thumbs up" to show his support. For Windy it was reality at its finest. If you didn't know better, you'd be convinced he actually had both oars in the water.

All the while this was going on, Ivan was thinking to himself, "Nutty bastard. Only Windy would pick up on the paranoid part." Though truth be known, Ivan was as paranoid as Windy, though he never admitted or showed it.

"Julius, you realize you've got what everyone wants. A free and clear income property! Why in the world would you want to trade it?"

"Is there something wrong with your hearing? I told you, I'm fed up with tenants and staff. I want out!" Julius repeated, frustrated and irritated.

"All right already, I hear you," the questioner responded. "So what can we give you in trade?"

"Try me. I don't know what I want. Nothing with tenants and staff, that's for sure."

"How about land, will you take land?"

"Depends!"

"Depends on what?"

"Depends on what I can do with it? If I can split it or develop it, I might be interested."

No sooner were the words out of his mouth than people were frantically writing offers. The pace increased in response to the next question.

"Will you add cash to a transaction?"

"I might."

"Let's say your units are worth a million and a half. Would you add a million and a half in cash?"

"Run it by me."

People were getting cramps writing offers. This was one of those moments every Trader dreamed about. Free and clear cash flowing income property the seller will trade for vacant land and add cash to boot. Voila! Nirvana at it's finest.

Getting offers to Julius created pandemonium, to the point where he had quite a stack when he left. He promised to give serious consideration to each one, and some actually believed him, not realizing that he had no intention of taking their offers, but instead would toss the entire batch in the trash when he got to his office. But not before telling his staff that some jerks were trying to steal the property. Word spread quickly that Julius was looking to sell.  Hoping it was true--so they'd be rid of him--they soon learned it was a hoax, and that he had no intention of selling.  So the normal melancholic state that had jettisoned to euphoria came crashing down.

 Julius decided he'd tell the Traders at the next meeting that he had changed his mind about getting rid of his property, giving as a reason that his staff was against the idea.  They'd know he was lying, of course, but would be upset nonetheless for getting their hopes up.  It would then dawn on them that they should have known better.  He wouldn't take their offers; the whole thing was too good to be true. Julius was just screwing with them.  Ivan knew it and vowed to get back at the little weasel.

Chapter 3

 Julius arrived at work anxious to get rid of Sylvia, only to be told that she had gathered all the tenants in the dayroom the night before to discuss a massive walkout.  Hearing this, he became livid.  The bimbo was trying to destroy him.  Now he would have to get rid of her.

"Where's Maria?" he demanded to know.

"Which Maria do you want?"  Betsy Whitman asked, "We have two."

"That new gal!" he barked.

"They're both new; for that matter, everyone's new around here except for me."

"The one that was here last night, you know, the one I gave Sylvia Goldsmith's file to."

"Maria Gonzalez."

"Yeah, her, where is she?"

"She doesn't get here until noon because today she works noon to eight."

"Well, get her. I want her here now."

"I'll try, but I can't guarantee it."

"Can't anybody do anything right around here? I make a simple request and all I get is mouth."

"Who's giving you flack? All I said is I would try, which I will."

"Well, get on it!" he barked.

A few minutes later she walked into his office and said, "She'll be here at eleven. That's the earliest she can come."

"That's over an hour from now. Did she say if she found anything on Sylvia?"

"Yeah, she did."

Julius was ecstatic. "What did she find?"

"She lied on her application."

"Now I can nail her," he said. "What did she lie about?"

"She put down that she's a community organizer."

"Those people are nothing but trouble. I knew she was bad news the minute I laid eyes on her. So that's not what she really is?"

"No. She was when she came here, then finished law school and went to work for the ACLU."

Julius headed to the bathroom. His stomach suddenly wasn't feeling well. Being a community organizer wasn't bad enough (he thought)--no, now the dingbat's a frigging Socialist, any attorney involved with the ACLU is, they're the most left-leaning organization in the practice of law. How come his staff didn't know this? Someone was gonna' get fired for this!

What Julius wasn't aware of was Sylvia's background. She came from a unique family, Jewish father, Arab mother, two people totally devoted to each other, as they had no one else. Their families would have nothing to do with them because they had married someone from another religion. Neither had an opportunity for higher education, so they impressed upon Sylvia the need to excel academically, and she did. Because she did, she was often the envy of others to the point where she was teased and bullied, which taught her to stand up for herself. As she did, her confidence grew and fostered a strong desire to protect others, especially the downtrodden and neglected.

The family scrimped to get by as her father's work as a tailor brought in little income. In spite of it they managed, largely because of her mother's ingenuity. She could turn little into much, and do it with a smile. Her warmth bonded the family. Her father loved her for it, commenting often how fortunate he was to be married to her. Home was a wonderful place.

The eldest of three girls, Sylvia was often called upon to look after her sisters. Because of this, she developed a nurturing, protective side, which came greatly in handy after her mother suddenly died, devastating the family and slamming her father into a deep depression. With her father unable to handle a forty-hour workweek, the family's income dropped. So to make ends meet, Sylvia took part-time jobs while assuming more of the role of mother to her two sisters. This left little time to study.

As her grades dropped, so did her chances for scholarships, but Sylvia didn't care, figuring she'd struggle through and come out stronger for it. In time, her father's depression lifted and so did his income. With the family on sounder financial grounds, she began working less and hitting the books more, which reflected in her grades. They bounced back, and because they did, she set her eyes on college. Fortunately for her, her sisters inherited many of the same nurturing skills that she had, and they soon were able to start looking after their father, which was a huge relief to her.

Sylvia lived at home while attending college, but spent considerable time in the school library, which paid off, as her grades qualified her for the dean's list every year. After graduating, she decided to get experience before pursuing an advanced degree, so she went to work for an agency helping low-income families. There she developed a strong distaste for the well to do, especially those who flaunted their wealth.

Chapter 4

"Rabbi, this is Julius. Do you have a few minutes? I'd like to stop by."

"Of course, Julius, I always have time for you. Let's make it an hour from now. Will that give you enough time to get here?"

"I'll be there."

Rabbi Goldman watched Julius pace back and forth. Whatever was going through his mind had his total attention, as he was obviously obsessed.

"Julius, you're unable to sit down. Something's eating at you. What is it?"

"It's that dumb tenant. She's nothing but a pain, she causes total mayhem in my apartment complex and now I find out that she's a damned attorney with the ACLU."

"You're obviously very worked up over this. Is it affecting other parts of your life?"

"What do you mean?"

"How's your appetite? Are you sleeping all right?"

"I can't sleep. I lie awake trying to find a way to get this bimbo out of my life. Excuse me for saying this, Rabbi, but that's what she is. I have no appetite and I'm not getting along with my staff. For some reason they don't do anything right. I think she's got them upset too. This lady's bad news. I need to get her out of my life."

"You seem quite preoccupied with her. I'm wondering if it might be wise for you to meet with one of our new members. You haven't been coming to Shul lately, so you haven't had a chance to meet Dr. Goldfarb, but he's quite competent. Psychiatry is his specialty. I'm not saying you need psychiatric help, but you are having difficulty emotionally and psychologically when it comes to this young lady. I think Dr. Goldfarb could help to sort out some of these issues. As you know, sometimes we can't see the forest because the trees are in the way, so having someone trained in these matters can help us clear up what's going on. I think it would be worth your while to speak with him. I would be happy to introduce you if you'd like?"

"I've got to do something. This bimbo is causing havoc in my life. Maybe I should see an attorney instead. Get a nasty one to get rid of her."

"Why don't you discuss that with Dr. Goldfarb. I think he can help you come to grips with that issue, and more."

"Yeah, what have I got to lose? Maybe he can give me some pills to sleep at night and something to settle my stomach. It's constantly in a knot. I'm nervous, edgy, confused, frustrated. I don't know what to do."

"Dr. Goldfarb specializes in addressing those issues. I think you'll benefit from talking with him. Can I arrange a time for you?"

"Go ahead. If I don't like the guy I'll drop him."

"I think you'll find him quite helpful. Are you free tomorrow?"

"I am in the morning."

"Thanks for coming in, my friend. I'll call you later. Keep me appraised. Salome."

The appointment was set for ten the next morning. Rabbi Goldman gave Dr. Goldfarb a brief social history then added his sense of what was going on between Julius and Sylvia Goldsmith.

The next day, Dr. Goldfarb and Julius settled into comfortable chairs in a private office to discuss his issues. Julius immediately recognized him from an article in the local paper that had included his picture.

"Rabbi Goldman said you've been having difficulty with a tenant."

"She's impossible. She challenges everything I do. On top of that she has the tenants up in arms and my staff too. My staff loves me, but she's got them convinced that I'm someone to be despised."

"I see. What caused you to have such differences with this lady?"

"She lied on her application and I want to get rid of her, but now she's an attorney, and blocking everything I do."

"How did she lie?"

"She put down that she was a community activist. Then I found out she's an attorney."

"Is it possible she started as a community activist, then went to law school?"

"It's possible, but nobody told me that was taking place, and I want to know these things."

"What do you like about this lady?"

"What a stupid question! There's nothing to like about her. She's bad news."

"I see. What do others see in her?"

"The damn tenants like her because she stands up for them."

"What do they need standing up for?"

"Tenants want everything and don't want to pay. They want the best of this, the best of that, plus they're constantly asking for more, which bothers me to no end. I hate tenants. I expect them to pay on time but many don't, which infuriates me, just like that wicked witch does."

"How long has this lady been a tenant?"

"Five years."

"Tell me about your dreams?"

"I don't have dreams. I have nightmares. This dingbat causes them."

"So she's in your thoughts night and day?"

"Whatever."

"If you had one wish what would it be?"

"That this woman was out of my life?"

"Who does she remind you of?"

"My mother."

"Let's continue this discussion next week. Can we set a time?"

"I suppose so, but we need to talk about this dingbat, not my mother."

"Here's my card. Call if you would like to come in before Wednesday."

Julius stuck the card in his briefcase out of fear that someone would see it and think there was something wrong with him.

Returning to work, he asked if Sylvia had given her notice, only to be told, "No, she hasn't, instead she told us that she'd be willing to sign an extension on her lease if you're selling, then added that quite a few other tenants will do the same."

Julius stormed into his office and slammed the door, all the while muttering, "What's my mother got to do with this?"

Julius hated Sylvia. If there was ever a thorn in his side it was Sylvia, and proving her wrong had become an obsession. Occupying his thoughts day and night, he couldn't get her out of his mind. What was so maddening about it was that she was often right, which he hated to admit. He preferred pointing out deficiencies in women as it made him feel superior, but she was strong, while he preferred someone weak. Why couldn't she admit that she was wrong once in a while; why did she always have to be right? Why did he care? He didn't know, but something about her drew him back to her. He certainly didn't like her. How could someone like someone he couldn't control- and he couldn't control her-which was maddening.

After a number of sessions, Dr. Goldfarb felt that he was getting nowhere with Julius. Words like immature, spoiled, irrational, paranoid, and passive aggressive jumped out at him. Of course, Julius believed he was just the opposite. Saw himself as well liked, reasonable, fair, unbiased, and misunderstood, though he did admit to being a bit nerdy, which was a huge admission. Julius was truly screwed up. Due to his gross narcissism, it was nearly impossible to get through to him, especially when it came to his feelings toward Sylvia and his mother, where he had absolute blinders on. Realizing his own feelings were coming into play while treating him, Dr. Goldfarb decided he would give Julius a few more sessions before dropping him as a patient, as dealing with the little weasel was maddening.

Chapter 5

Windy Wales was a member of the Traders Club, and had been
for years. How he ever got his license, God only knows, and
how he managed to keep it was even more surprising. Of course,
he didn't represent anyone, because he knew he was a certified
nut case, a legitimate card carrying "wacko." What helped was
that he knew he was off his rocker, but could function as long as
he stayed on his medication, but he also knew that it was when
he quit his meds that his paranoia ran amok. The Traders saw
him as a blow-hard capable of making no sense, though they
didn't know that he was a legitimate paranoid schizophrenic. In
their minds he fit in, as he was convinced the government
intended to take everyone's properties which, considering his
mental makeup, met the benchmarks of his diagnosis. The
property rights advocates loved having him attend meetings, as
he would go off on issues related to eminent domain with
tremendous passion. He could be very convincing provided his
medicine didn't wear off--when it did, he'd go a little far afield.
But they were prepared for that as they'd been around him
enough to know that when he started getting balmy, they'd step
in, but until that time he could be an absolute whirlwind.

Windy was a tall, wiry guy who might reach six feet tall if
required to stand up straight. Weight-wise, he touched the scale
at 150 lbs. What helped keep his weight off was a metabolic
system that burned calories quickly. His appearance wasn't a
major concern to him—no--clothes from second-hand stores
worked just fine, though his mother saw to it that he also had
nice duds to wear if the occasion called for them.

Windy was caught off-guard when Dr. Goldfarb was introduced at the meeting, as he never expected a shrink to be invited to the Traders Club, so immediately he shut his trap and went into "safe mode." He'd been around enough docs to know that this wasn't the time to get off on one of his tangents, as this doc would soon become alarmed and start asking questions. No, he'd sit there, take in what was said, and get the hell out as fast as he could. He knew now why no one had told him that a shrink was showing up for their meeting! It was because of him. They were onto him.

The more he thought about it, the more paranoid he became, to the point where he had trouble keeping the lid on. Here he thought he had them all conned, that the medication covered up his mental issues, but apparently not. Totally engrossed in his thoughts, he ended up not hearing a word the guy said, then made a fatal mistake by scratching his head. Thinking he had a question, the moderator called on him, which jettisoned Windy from "safe mode" to "panic mode," as he thought everyone was watching him. Filled with paranoia, he shot out of his chair and raced for the exit, soiling his pants in the process, thereby guaranteeing that he wasn't coming back.

"Is he all right?" Dr. Goldfarb inquired.

"Couldn't be better," Mark Grayson chimed in. "Probably forgot the books. He's our treasurer."

"I'll leave my card if it turns out to be something worse."

Mark thanked him for coming, escorted him out the door, then promptly threw his card in the trashcan. Windy wasn't going to a nut doctor--no, Traders don't go to nut doctors because it isn't manly. Only goof-balls in residential go there, commercial guys don't; and that included them.

When Windy showed up for the next meeting, he muttered that he left early because he had a sudden onset of the flu. Of course, no one believed him, which meant everything was copacetic at the Traders Club.

The president reminded the members that there was a board meeting after the regular meeting, which prompted Windy to panic again because he had forgotten the books. For that matter, he hadn't balanced them in a month, so he shot out the door, again convinced they were playing with his head, only to realize that the meeting was written in his day-timer. Scooting home, he grabbed a shot of bourbon and headed back armed with an excuse, only to be met at the door by Ivan, who smelled the booze.

"A little early for that stuff, don't you think, Windy?"

"I've got a bit of a cold," he replied, not interested in discussing it further because he despised Ivan, the guy made him feel creepy, and when you're nuts, feeling creepy doesn't help. So they exchanged pleasantries, then looked for a reason to end the conversation, with Ivan walking away convinced the guy was off his rocker. Of course, had he known he really was, he would have filled his drawers, but Windy made sure no one knew.

Windy could function reasonably well as long as he took his medication, but it was when he quit that his problems started. Paranoia would ratchet up to the point where he became convinced that someone wanted to break into his home and commit mayhem. Unable to put the idea out of his head, he wouldn't sleep, wouldn't eat, and prowled the house with a gun, waiting for the intruders to break in, which could go on for days.

Luckily he lived alone--of course, no one in their right mind could live with him because he was so goofy. Part of his illness was that he was obsessed with cleanliness to the point where he kept the place sterile for fear it would become invested with bugs. Luckily his mother and brother lived close by, so when he didn't respond to their calls, they would check on him, making sure they identified themselves first, because they didn't want to become a casualty when he was off his rocker, which was a definite possibility. Thankfully, he had no deep-seated hatred towards either of them, so when he heard their voices he would unlock the door and let them in so they could talk some sense into him like, "You're off your rocker; you need to go to the hospital to get your medication adjusted."

Normally that was enough to get him to drop his gun and agree to the trip, because he knew he'd only be there until the medication kicked in and he got some rest. By then he would be anxious to return home and get back to the Traders Club, because the traders were his bond with reality. Their hard-nosed bottom-line approach made him think, which was what he needed most. Convinced that they accepted him, he was not aware that the only reason they kept him around was to handle the books.

Chapter 6

Ivan Schmidt charged through the door of his condo, frustrated
that he had forgotten the document. A long-time member of the
Traders, Ivan had a checkered history. A disbarred attorney, he
had obtained a real estate license only to lose it, but not before
talking the Traders into letting unlicensed people attend the
Traders' meeting.

If members hadn't been so afraid of him, they would have throw
him out, but fear stopped them from doing so, as they knew he
had no compunctions about making their lives miserable. That
he wasn't in prison was amazing, but his attorney got him out of
the drug-dealing charges he was facing by claiming that they
couldn't rely on what Peety said--Peety being Ivan's macaw.
The one Ivan now refers to as "big mouth."

His relationship with Peety was better than it used to be, though
he could never forget that Peety had once ratted on him. Of
course, Peety had been equally upset because he had felt
abandoned. But Peety had grown accustomed to the
constant company of the lady who took care of him while Ivan
was in jail. She was nice. She talked to him in civil tones,
kept his food and water dish full, and cleaned his cage daily--
something Ivan never did. She was great, and Ivan was a
grump. Didn't used to be as a kid but had grown up to be one.
Plus he had left him--the dirty rat. "I had every reason to rat
on him,"Peety thought to himself, "And the Feds thought I was
some 'bird brain.' They were the birdbrains."

Though Ivan had just left when he walked back in, Peety uttered,
"Praise the Lord," just to irritate him.

"Shut up."

"Oh, isn't he touchy?" Peety thought. *Guess I better keep my bill shut before he rations my food.* Peety and Ivan had been together for years. Forty-two to be exact, so he wasn't totally worried that he'd be starved to death. Nonetheless, he knew that when Ivan was testier than normal, it was best to leave him alone.

Losing or misplacing items drove Ivan up the wall as it played with his sense of control and, being a control freak, that wasn't good. Asking Peety for help was akin to opening Pandora's Box. It was bad enough that he uttered, "Praise the Lord" every time Ivan came through the door--so to admit that he needed help would empower Peety to the point where he'd never shut up. No, he'd just keep looking.

Peety watched Ivan's frustration grow. He wasn't going to help him locate whatever he was looking for--no, he'd wait until Ivan asked or blew his top (the likelier of the two). Ever since being cornered by the church, he'd been particularly edgy. He was furious that they caught him. Of course, he gave them their money back; he had no choice. They called the bank and put a hold on transfers, causing all kinds of havoc, so what could he do?

When you take pride in screwing others, you hate being caught--it's the principle of it all. Ivan was so angry he was tempted to leave the state, get out of Dodge, if you will. He even told Peety that he might move to the Caribbean. When he heard that, Peety thought, "Of course he'd take me along, but then again, if he didn't, he'd probably leave me with that nice lady who let me watch reruns of Oprah and Dr. Phil all day long."

Ivan wasn't aware as a child that his parents worried about him. They viewed him as moody, angry, and definitely a loner. Because he had no friends, they bought him "Peety." At first he detested the thought of having to take care of a damn bird, but soon Peety became his friend, his confidant. He could rant and rave about the injustices in life, and Peety would cock his head as if he were listening. He soon came to feel that Peety would always be there for him, that he was the one thing in life that Ivan could count on.

Both Ivan and Peety were deep in thought when the doorbell rang. Ivan reacted, as few people knew where he lived. Looking out the peephole he spotted the mailman, which was strange, as normally his mail was put in a P.O. box. Opening the door, he was presented a registered letter from the church he held the note on. Inside was a check for $400,000. The "bastards" paid him off. Though he wasn't surprised, he was furious none the less, as now he'd have to reinvest it.

Spotting the missing document stuck in a chair, he grabbed it and headed to the bank, after which he'd go to the Traders Club. Though he didn't trust the Traders, he thought it was possible that one might have a safe haven for his money, though he doubted it.

Most people would feel good depositing $400,000, but not Ivan, no. In his mind, he was being ripped off. Putting money in a bank wouldn't draw enough interest, so he was in a surly mood.

The president opened the meeting by asking if anyone had cash to lend or was a buyer.

Ivan raised his hand.

"Ivan, are you a buyer or lender?"

Ivan replied, "I've got $400,000 I'd like to put to use." One would have thought he had passed gas the way some reacted. Oh, they'd love to get their hands on the money, but it was dealing with Ivan that they didn't like. They'd prefer licking snot on a pogo stick to dealing with him; nevertheless, he had money and they had needs.

Horace Stoneman said, "I've got a free and clear commercial building on Twentieth Street and need to put an addition on for a tenant. What kind of interest do you want?"

"Fifteen percent," he responded.

"Forget it."

'You asked. I told you."

"I'll get it someplace else."

Another member raised his hand, said he had $100,000 to lend, and the meeting took off.

Opportunities were never better at the Traders Club. Foreclosures, bankruptcies, and jail sentences were at an all-time high. Rather than fight lenders, Traders were turning over deeds while others were scurrying to avoid prosecution because of minor irregularities like lying on loan applications. Of course, the only reason they lied was to acquire the property and then flip it, not live there. In their mind there was a difference. Convinced that they were in the right, fudging on the application was okay.

What wasn't okay was getting screwed by the people you trusted to make payments, who didn't. Imagine that, place trust in somebody and they let you down. Anyway, since they were in no condition to save the properties, they were in a pickle.

Complicating matters was the fact that the mortgage companies were in no mood to be benevolent, especially after finding out that they'd been hoodwinked on the application. So to save their bacon, they were coming up with all kinds of excuses, some very creative because the last thing they worried about was saving some dumb old property. Keeping their butts out of jail was their top priority, but unfortunately for many, excuses were no match for facts, so some ended up in jail anyway.

The market was bad, so bad that banks and mortgage companies were calling Traders to bail them out. Now that's bad! Normally Traders are at the bottom of the call list, but lenders were desperate to unload properties, so would listen to anyone. There's something about vacant, vandalized properties that will do that. Seeing value depleting in their portfolios meant every option was being pursued. They even considered vacant land, reasoning that it was better than what they had, as there was less chance for breakins.

The Traders were ecstatic with the new thinking! Looking upon the smorgasbord of properties, they wondered how they could profit at the expense of the lenders. God forbid they be required to make mortgage payments, because most were strapped for money. Finding tenants wasn't a problem, but finding tenants who made lease payments was! Many offered barter credits, but barter credits were worthless--for that matter, no one would take them. Then there were those who offered items for trade, items that had been pawned off by the Traders years before, so they certainly weren't taking them. No, they'd figure out some way to put money in their pockets at the expense of the bankers, though it would take some ingenuity.

When the president got around to asking if anyone had properties to present, Gilbert Humphrey raised his hand and passed out his package. Gilbert was considered an idiot in the club. Luckily he had a pension coming in, and money he inherited, because his theory of "going against the grain" was costing him a bundle. The general theory in real estate is to buy the least expensive home in the most expensive area, but invariably Gilbert got talked into buying the most expensive house in a run-down neighborhood because it needed fixing, and he fashioned himself a "fix up artist."

Invariably, he created a castle surrounded by junk, then wondered why his real estate deals cost him a bundle. Talk as people might to get him to change his ways, it didn't sink in, because invariably some good looking babe convinced him that his artistic talents were exactly what her listing needed and soon he was signing on the dotted line. Though a likeable marshmallow, he was lonely and an absolute sucker for big eyelashes and smooth talk. On top of that, he didn't have the resolve to say no, though if truth be told, he enjoyed being chauffeured around by the knockouts as it did wonders for his ego.

Gilbert did draw the line when it came to acquiring property in areas noted for violence, which is why the babes escorted him around in the mornings and early afternoons--because there was less chance of shootings taking place then. Gilbert could have driven through the neighborhoods at night to check things out, but elected not to as he preferred engaging in his two favorite pastimes--spending time with Whiskers, his cat, and being engrossed in an active fantasy world.

Ivan didn't think much of Gilbert--in fact, thought he was an idiot--reasoning that some of his purchases had disaster written all over them, though that didn't stop him from taking advantage of Gilbert whenever he could.

Unbeknownst to Ivan, Gilbert thought Ivan was a sharp dude, one he wanted to know better. Thankfully, he was a quiet, non-aggressive guy who kept his thoughts to himself, because had Ivan known how he felt he would have served him with a restraining order. The majority of people hated Ivan and he preferred it that way, so to learn that Gilbert felt just the opposite way would only justify Ivan's belief that he was deranged.

Gilbert occupied a unique position at the Traders Club-the brunt of jokes. While he thought they were laughing with him, they were laughing at him, and what they said to his face differed from what they said behind his back, which made him a welcome punching bag for one and all. Of course, it didn't help that the big dunce kept making the same mistakes. It was as though he was such a lonely moron, any response was better than none, and the members saw to it that he was royally taken advantage of.

Gilbert was a laid-back guy who wasn't ruffled easily, took things in stride for that matter, as he figured it wasn't worth getting upset over things over which he had no control. His appearance reflected his persona. Not into designer clothes, he was content wearing pretty basic stuff, as he had no need to call attention to himself. For that matter, he preferred working on a project where jeans and tee shirts were all he needed.

Hard-toed construction shoes were recommended, though tennis shoes were his preference, as they were more comfortable. If he wore them out or ruined them pouring concrete that didn't matter--his size twelves were easily found on sale some place. He didn't wear a hard hat working on site as he didn't like the feel, nor was it required since he set the rules. Wearing clothes until they qualified for the rag bin was his preference, and the looser they fit, the better. He didn't like snug-fitting clothes, though between projects tended to eat more, which frustrated him--but food was his outlet. He always felt content after eating so he found himself nurturing that need especially when he had a lot of time on his hands.

Gilbert was the oldest of three. His parents divorced when he was young, and he was raised by his mother. After the divorce, he didn't have much contact with his father, which was fine with him as he preferred being with his mom anyway as they were very close. Though he wasn't the man of the house, he learned that being responsible, working hard, and keeping his nose clean made her life easier. The thought of letting her down kept him awake at night. She told him often that she was very proud of him, and he made sure she always was.

Because he was called upon to look after his younger sisters, he didn't socialize much with other kids, especially boys, so wasn't up to par with others when it came to sports. And because he wasn't, he tended to be the last one called when he had a chance to participate. His inactivity and propensity to dream lead to another problem--weight issues. He easily gained weight, to the point where it became a constant battle.

When his mother came home from work she encouraged him to play with others, but he was content to draw and fantasize about building different things. Teachers mentioned that he had a

fantastic imagination as well as creative side. Whereas most of
the boys in school weren't interested in colors, designs, and
materials, Gilbert was, though it came at a cost. Many of the
guys chided him for it. Some went so far as to bully him, calling
him a sissy.

He relayed it to his mom and she told him to tell his teachers,
which he did, but it didn't do any good, so he withdrew further
into himself. He did well academically which didn't set well
with some of the kids either. They picked on him for that too.
Of course, they felt jealous not being able to rack up high scores
in math, science and reading like Gilbert did. He didn't flaunt
the fact that he did well academically – in fact, he acted just the
opposite way; he was quite humble about it all, which set some
kids off too. So Gilbert received a lot of attention from other
kids and not much of it was positive. None the less he kept his
nose to the grindstone, thinking he'd soon be away from people
who would deride him not being aware that it wouldn't happen.

Gilbert couldn't afford to attend a major university, but could
afford the tuition at a two-year college, provided he worked part-
time. And that he did, in the school's cafeteria. Though it
probably wasn't the best place for him because of his appetite
for food and the fact it was free, he figured eating there cut
down on the expenses at home for his mom. Unsure of what to
do with his life, he reasoned math, drawing, and design were
areas he enjoyed, so he took a course in drafting and loved it.
He excelled so highly that a prominent architectural firm offered
him a job at the end of his first year. Twenty years later he
retired. With the security of a steady income, he decided to
pursue an area he knew something about, and enjoyed--real
estate.

Gilbert's mom passed away a number of years before he retired, and his two sisters married and moved out of town, so he was essentially alone.

Gilbert's break at the Traders Club came at the urging of Mindy Bork, a not-so-attractive real estate agent new to the Traders, who had heard that Gilbert liked fix-up properties.

Mindy was a down-to-earth, responsible, hard working gal who knew her looks weren't going to open doors for her, but what would was a willingness to go the extra mile to do things right, a pleasant personality, and a sharp mind. On top of that, she was comfortable with herself in a way few people experienced. She liked herself but didn't flaunt it because of her humble nature.

She breezed through high school with a 3.8 grade point average, was on the honor roll four years and was vice president of the student council her senior year. Everyone knew that if something needed to be done to give it to Mindy and it would be, and would be with done with a smile. Her plate was constantly full, but she never complained. Instead she displayed a mild dogged determination to get things done and get them done right, reasoning it was better to do things right the first time than have to do them again.

Mindy didn't put on airs, but at the same time, sneaking up in the back of her mind, was the question, "Why pretty myself up when it's not going to matter?" Call it a mild form of depression. Whatever it was, it didn't hold her back. Often she said to herself, "I am who I am; if others won't accept me, I'll accept them in spite of it."

Her father was a small builder. He was a perfectionist and a bit on the gruff side, and Mindy's older brothers stayed away from him because they didn't always do things right, and heard about it. Mindy, on the other hand, could do no wrong. She didn't care what his attitude was, she'd assess what needed to be done and pitch in. Before long she'd have him out of his salty mood and into one that they both could live with. She liked her dad, and he liked her. Summers and school breaks were spent helping him.

Pounding nails, handing him lumber, holding a ladder for him, and being his "gopher" weren't chores because they were fun. On top of that, he paid her, which didn't always set well with her brothers, but he would have found work for them too if they had wanted it, but they preferred being off with their buddies instead. Mindy knew that when she graduated, she'd have to find a full time job, but wasn't sure in what. Academically she qualified for college, but she didn't have the funds for tuition nor did her family. She could have taken out a school loan but hated the idea of being saddled with debt so passed on that idea. Looking through the want ads, she came across one that caught her eye. "Successful real estate broker needs an apprentice." So she called to make an appointment.

Barbara Reynolds was a polished, sophisticated, smart, successful broker who could spot a con a mile away. Many applied for the position but only one was hired, and that was Mindy. They hit it off right away. Mindy's task was to get her real estate license, polish up her appearance a bit, and become Barbara's shadow. Mindy, paid a salary plus bonus, was soon working with appraisers, title companies, buyers, sellers, inspection companies, attorneys and other agents. Sixty to seventy hours a week were common. Barbara was absolutely convinced she had hired the right person--and then tragedy struck. Barbara died of a massive heart attack, so Mindy was on her own.

Barbara would have nothing to do with the Traders Club, so Mindy had never attended. Now with Barbara gone, Mindy decided to check it out because many found the Traders to be a talented group who came up with creative ways to solve real estate problems.

Seeing the abuse Gilbert took after just a couple of meetings, she felt sorry for the big oaf, so approached him with a fix-up property she had just listed that had profit written all over it. After hearing the location and the fact that no one else knew about it, he wanted to see it immediately, so they left to take a look, talking in generalities along the way, yet finding genuineness in each other which created a sense of calm for both.

Driving in the neighborhood where the home was located, Gilbert was immediately impressed. Many of the homes could easily fetch half a million dollars, which was a far cry from the neighborhoods in which he normally found his fix-ups. Thankful that Mindy's sign wasn't out, he could immediately see why the sellers agreed it needed work. Apparently when they lived there, it was impeccably maintained and continued that way with the first tenants, but it was the second ones who were the tenants from hell. Now the beautiful home needed substantial repair.

The problems for the owners started with the belief that everyone deserved a second chance. Instead of giving an eviction notice when their first check bounced, they took the tenants' word that things would get better. They didn't know that the tenants reasoned the owners were responsible for their ills in life, so felt justified in lying to them while taking their frustration out on the house. They caused so much damage that there was no way the owners could return and undertake the work, so after getting them out, they accepted their loss and offered the property for sale "As Is."

Gilbert knew that the asking price was a bit high, but being a softie, he reasoned he had no need to try to beat them down, though many fixer-uppers would. He offered their asking price and they accepted. With his excellent credit and income stream, he had no difficulty getting a loan on top of that. Mindy earned the full commission, which pleased them both. Upon taking title, he brought in a dumpster and gutted the house. In short order, he was up to his eyeballs in renovation, which pleased him to no end. For a big overweight guy one never would have known he was so industrious; underneath his marshmallow image was a workaholic with a creative side. Months later he finished renovating, and invited Mindy to handle the sale.

Driving to the home she was impressed with the outside and the landscaping, but that was nothing compared to what she found walking through the door. The busted-up, decrepit, urinated-on place had been turned into a masterpiece. The glass bubble chandelier looked stunning towering over the black leather-finish granite floors. Making her way to the kitchen, she was awed by the Italian white marble with gray and gold veins, as it set the tone for a truly contemporary look. Immensely eye-catching was the massive oak cooking island topped with granite.

Wolf and Sub-Zero appliances gave the sense that no cost had been spared. Entering the master bedroom, she was impressed with the plush carpet, only to be overwhelmed when she spotted the bathroom with its black marble floor accentuated by green granite walls and a river rock ceiling border. Equally stunning was the shower itself, with multiple sprays, rain shower overhead, and a steam machine. It was like having one's own spa. Walking back into the living room, she found Gilbert waiting for her.

"What do you think of the place?" he asked.

"It's absolutely gorgeous! I've never been in a home so stunning. You're incredible. You did all this work by yourself?"

"I had to hire a tile guy to help and an electrician, along with a few day laborers, but for the most part I did it myself. I prefer doing things myself. For that matter, I prefer working alone. Once I get a picture in my mind of how I want the home to look, I make a list of the materials I'll need and how I want everything to flow. I hate waiting for sub-contractors to show up. I find it very distracting. Normally, I become totally engrossed in my project to the point where I often sleep on the job. Once in a while I have to remind myself to head home to make sure Whiskers has food, water, and a clean box."

"If I can ever help in a situation like that let me know. I get along with cats."

"I'll keep that in mind."

"You've turned an eyesore into an incredibly gorgeous home, easily the most appealing home in the subdivision. Even though the market's slow, you'll have no trouble selling. You might even have multiple bidders, something unheard of in today's market."

"That's good to hear. I spent more time and money fixing it up than I expected to but I really like how it looks. Do you mind if we price it on the high side so I can try to recapture some of the funds?"

"I was going to recommend just that."

"You know what I paid for it, so why don't I get you a list of expenses and we'll add a bump on top of that."

"Do that, and I'll prepare the listing documents."

Both felt good walking out the door. They were a good match for each other.

After itemizing expenses, Gilbert called to say that $168,000 needed to be added to what he bought it for to break even. "I'd like to add a hundred thousand on top of that to cover your fee, closing costs and any negotiating I might have to do. Do you think I'm asking too much?"

"No, for that matter, I recommend you add another hundred thousand to that. Make it $200,000 over what you bought it for and your costs."

"Do you think anyone's going to pay it?"

"I'm going to prepare an eye-catching flyer, plus really promote your home at MLS. In two weeks, I bet you're going to have people bidding against each other for this house."

"I'm willing to drop the price if I have to."

"I don't think you will. I see many homes. You have no idea how impressive yours is."

A week after the listing went on the market, Gilbert accepted an offer that would put $200,000 in his pocket after expenses. Three parties submitted offers within hours of the home being put on the market. One tried to steal it, but the other two kept bidding against each other, as they wanted it badly. Finally one party reached the limit of how high they could go, and the other won out.

Oh, was he proud walking away from closing with $200,000 in his pocket. He was finally experiencing success.

Mindy felt good too after he gave her a large bonus, big hug, and promise that he'd only work with her. Her task was to find more fix-ups.

When the Traders got wind of the fact that Gilbert had netted $200,000 on a fix-up property, they were sure they had heard wrong, because they knew the guy was incapable of experiencing that kind of success.

"Gilbert netted two hundred grand?" Mark Ramirez said to his buddy Joe Castro. "How in the hell did he pull that off?"

"The jerk got lucky," Joe replied.

"The guy can't walk and chew gum at the same time," Mark replied. "He must have hired the work out."

"Apparently not," Mark interjected, "I guess he wore out the knees in many pairs of jeans getting it done."

"We're talking about Gilbert here. His head's usually in the clouds if not up his ass. He's not capable of pulling that off."

"This real estate babe says he's a creative genius."

"Genius, my ass!" Mark replied.

"The people who bought the house are raving about him," Joe responded.

"That's too bad," Mark replied.

"What do you mean," Joe responded?

"We won't be able to take advantage of him anymore," Mark said in frustration.

"What're you worried about? The Traders Club's loaded with people like Gilbert. Just look at Windy. You know his oars aren't totally in the water. "

"Did you see his response to that shrink when he was here? He filled his drawers."

"Big deal, who needs the crap those guys toss out anyway?"

"You weren't worried he'd catch on to you, were you? Maybe put you on the couch?"

"Stick it."

"Don't worry, he wouldn't waste his time--you're untreatable-- most of us character disorders are. Remember the picture he painted of psychopaths."

"Do I ever. My armpits started to fill up with perspiration."

"Well, the fact that they did probably means you're not one, otherwise you wouldn't care. But some of the guys who show up once in a while I'm not so sure about. His statement that they tend to be bright, charming, gregarious, impulsive, and dishonest, with little empathy for others, hits pretty close to home with some of them. And when he said they'll slap you on the back, give you a big hug, and tell you whatever you want to hear while picking your pocket really struck a nerve. But you and I are safe there, my friend. Though we're a little screwed up, we aren't that bad."

"The doc also said that Traders have a higher degree of competitiveness than psychopaths."

"Do you think he was referring to us?"

"Nah, I think he was referring to guys on Wall Street."

"You're sure now?"

"Why would he be referring to us?"

"Because he was at a 'Traders meeting' when he said it, that's why I was wondering if he was referring to us!"

"Well, maybe he was. But hey, you're a good guy; I'm a good guy; you trust me; I trust you; it's just everyone else we have to worry about, right?"

"You got that right, buddy. Let's get the hell out of here before we create doubts in that theory." Then they walked out the door.

Chapter 7

Hadley Evans III was a mortgage broker known for his ability
to "put deals together!" He often referred to himself as the
"Mortgage Doctor," with the mantra "Bring your sick, ailing
clients to me and I'll doctor them up so they qualify for a loan."
It didn't matter how he put deals together, just that he did, as he
operated on two theories: "Throw enough shit against the wall
and some will stick"; and "Get paid now, worry later." He was
also known to say, "Trust me! Let's just close the deal so we
can get paid, and I'll have my attorney work out the details later.'
A strong believer in "time is of the essence," he constantly
pushed clients to close. When he wasn't in closing, he was
bragging about the money he had to lend--though many were
afraid to ask the source—and when pressed to disclose it, he
invariably had a legitimate name, such as a teacher's retirement
fund or something like that. It didn't matter to the Traders where
Hadley got his funds as long as he did though, to cover their
behinds, they purchased Errors and Omissions policies on every
deal he was involved with, and sometimes took out two policies
depending on the intricacies of the deal.

Hadley was the youngest of five children. A "surprise" baby, he
arrived on the scene ten years after the next youngest. Being a
bit precocious, he was smothered with attention to the point
where he soon reasoned that the world centered on anything he
did. His father was a doctor and his mother was worn out after
raising four older ones, some of whom were in college, so little
Hadley was given considerable freedom and few restrictions.
The word "no" wasn't heard often in his upbringing, which was
dutifully noted by his older siblings, who reasoned that he could
literally get away with whatever he wanted.

Though he wasn't an angry child who threw temper tantrums and challenged authority, he was often in considerable trouble, but he had a gift for gab so was able to talk his way out of most any situation. To say he was a budding psychopath might be an overstatement, but between his smarts and personality, he charmed people easily.

People liked Hadley and he knew and took advantage of this, which strained his relationships once in a while, but he was sufficiently disarming that he usually won them back. From early on, he looked at rules as obstacles rather than deterrents, to the point where he became convinced that if he wanted something badly enough, he should go for it, then figure out later how to get out of any mess he created.

Hadley skated through high school, had lots of friends, partied often, and put in just enough effort to qualify for college. He often operated outside the rules of acceptable behavior, as did his buddies, though they were seldom caught. Climbing fences at the local zoo to taunt the animals was a favorite pastime, as was sneaking into the city's auditorium to watch anything from sports events to the home shows, even the circus. They were so adept at sneaking in that the even the police shook their heads, wondering how they did it. Since they were already in, though, the police could do nothing about it. With bottles of lemon extract in their pockets, they often headed to the concession stand for soda, knowing they'd have a buzz on pretty quickly.

Afterwards, they often headed to someone's watermelon patch or orchard for a late night snack. Caught one time and thrown in jail, Hadley convinced the judge that it was an honest mistake and was let go. His buddies were standing by to bail him out if need be, but it wasn't necessary as no charges were filed because Hadley talked his way out of the mess.

Hadley and his buddies didn't spend much time studying, so devised a number of ways to cheat, which they became very good at. So good that they successfully passed a number of tests for which they had no idea what the correct answers were, let alone the subject matter itself. Feeling quite proud of their achievement, they were convinced it was all a precursor to success in the world of business.

Though his parents weren't rich they were comfortable, so were able to help him with tuition which was great, because it allowed him to spend more time partying. Whereas other students were holding down jobs to pay their way through school, Hadley couldn't be bothered for fear he'd miss out on a good time. Plus, he had his parents buffaloed into believing that they had a responsibility to get him through school, since he was deprived of a normal upbringing, being so much younger than his siblings. And they bought it, not being aware that he came across the idea in a psychology course. He thought it was a great line, so decided to add it to his repertoire of excuses for keeping his parents on the hook.

His sophomore year in college, he took an aptitude test to help him decide what his skills were and where to focus his education. Two areas stood out: socialization and math. He immediately ruled out being a teacher because he knew he wasn't cut out for that. So he asked the instructor who reviewed the test results with him, "So what does a guy with a finance degree who enjoys hobnobbing with people do?"

"Have you considered being a mortgage broker?" the instructor suggested, and the light bulb went on.

Hadley loved schmoozing with the Traders as they were his kind of people. He could BS with the best of them. His repertoire of jokes was outstanding, and that he remembered so many was impressive. Invariably one led to another, to the point where he could keep listeners in stitches for hours. The only one he didn't tell stories to was Ivan. They didn't trust each other. Word in the club when their names were mentioned was, "Proceed at your peril." One savvy member went so far as to take a couple of unsuspecting clowns aside to share his long-held belief about the Traders Club--"Don't trust anyone here--especially those two."

In addition to being a smooth operator, Hadley was one sharp dresser. Though the temperature outside was often over a hundred, that didn't stop him from donning a three-piece suit with a silk tie. On other occasions, he wore western outfits consisting of black cowboy boots, black cowboy hat, western shirt topped off by a black western frock coat—all of which combined together gave the impression that he was one "macho man."

Women found his appearance stunning. One gal was so turned on by him that she was overheard telling her husband, "Don't worry, honey, but if you get run over by a truck this afternoon, I'm going after that cowboy." Hadley also loved wearing his cowboy boots made of rattlesnake when he wasn't wearing the pair made of 'gator belly. Today he wore a suit and tie with patent leather shoes. Kibitzing with one of his buddies, he was approached by Tom Jorgenson, an agent who'd been around for awhile. Hadley's buddy sensed that Tom needed to talk to Hadley, so bowed out.

"What's up?" Hadley asked.

"I got a client who's having a helluva time getting a mortgage."

"So what's the problem?"

"His credit's not so good and he doesn't make enough, but his wife's on his case to get the house. It appears he got a little frisky with a gal at work and momma found out, and he figures getting the house is the only way she's going to let him off the hook, so he'll do pretty much anything to get it."

"So why didn't you ask me to help this guy right away? It sounds like you've taken him elsewhere without success."

"Because you're a crook!"

Hadley laughed then said, "One who gets the job done, I might add. Just so you know, since it's going to take some creativity to get this done, I might need a little bump from your commission."

"That's illegal."

"Do you want me to help this guy or not?"

"How much do you want?"

"Forty percent of what you get."

"That's highway robbery."

"I'm good at what I do."

"If you deliver, I'll pay it."

"Have him call me."

57

With that, Hadley went to find Norm Hickman, his client.

"Stormin' Norman, I haven't seen you for a while, are you still flipping houses?"

"That's where I'm spending a majority of my time."

"How you doing?" Hadley asked, slapping him on the back.

"Terrific, there are bargains out there galore. You just have to make sure you buy right. I've got an ad running constantly and get a lot of calls. The more desperate people are, the more interested I am. I don't waste my time if people aren't motivated."

"With the market being what it is, how long have you been hanging on to these houses?"

"That's the key. I look for vacant houses, but if the seller's still there, I get them on contract with the understanding that I can show the house any time because they know I'm not going to live there, then I drag the closing out until I find a buyer. So both closings take place on the same day. It's gets a little hairy some times with sellers moving out and buyers moving in but I don't care, I got my money. I even have a contingency in the contract that I can walk away if I don't find a buyer."

"Are you still doing fix-ups?"

"Yeah, if I can steal and fix I'll do that. I've got some illegals that do damn good work for peanuts. I get the materials, turn them loose in the house and check in once in a while. If they're not working fast enough, we discuss their immigration status. I find that that usually does the trick. When they're done, I pay them in cash and list it."

"Where do you get your materials?"

"I buy used stuff that's dirt cheap from secondhand stores. I then threaten the illegals that if they don't make it look new, I'll dump them. You should see what they turn out."

"So you don't have a lot invested in the houses you fix up?"

"Of course not, otherwise you're wasting your time."

"Are you still using that appraiser?"

"You mean Slick Willie?"

"Yeah, Willie. Is he still hitting the bottle pretty hard?"

"Willie is constantly looking for a way to make a buck as he's got all kinds of problems, booze being one of them. So I pay him a hundred dollars and he gives me an official-looking appraisal that stinks to high heaven because he grossly inflates the value. Then I list the house for less and have my agent show the buyers what a terrific deal they're getting. You'd be surprised by how well that works."

"What lender are you using? You're not coming to me, what a jerk!"

"I let people get their own financing. I don't want to be bothered; furthermore, I don't want to act improperly."

"Yeah, sure," Hadley said with a grin.

"If I get someone I know will make payments, like a doctor, I'll carry the note myself."

Then he looked at Hadley, grinned, and asked, "You still bullshitting people?"

"Every chance I get."

"You still running ads for mortgages?"

"All the time!  People call thinking I have an inside lead to low rates, so I get them signed up, then take them to any bank or mortgage company they could have gone to on their own, and pick up a commission in the process."

"When you going to put a deal together for my note?"

"I might have something soon.  See ya'."

That afternoon he received a call from Louie Sarafoli, Tom Jorgenson's client.  They set a time to meet.

Louie arrived late though didn't apologize, which Hadley promptly noted.  After introductions he said, "Tom says you've got your eyes on a house but are having trouble qualifying."

"The damn mortgage brokers we've gone to haven't done a thing for us, so Tom recommended I see you.  My wife's got her eye on a house she really wants.  It's a little pricey, but what momma wants, I try to get."

"How much are they asking for it?"

"$400,000."

"How much do you have to put down?

"About $20,000."

"How much do you make?"

"Between the two of us we make about $60,000."

"Let's pull up your credit report here to see how it looks. Well, I've seen worse. I think if you write a letter explaining some of this stuff, we might be okay."

Hadley concluded that between their credit history and income, they weren't qualified to buy a $400,000 house, but Louie seemed to be the kind of guy they could work with, so he threw him some bait.

"I think I can get you a loan if you're willing to work with me."

"How's that?" Louie answered.

"You could benefit by having more income. To achieve that, I know a guy who has a note he lets people use."

"What are you talking about?"

"He'll let you claim you inherited a $225,000 note that pays $2,500 a month which, coupled with your salary, will be more than enough to qualify you to buy the house."

"Sound's good to me."

"Once we get through closing, you transfer the note back to him, it's that simple."

"Yeah, so what's the catch?"

"You understand a guy like this isn't Santa Claus, right?

"So, as I asked, what's the catch?"

"You're going to need extra income to make your mortgage payments, right?"

"True, so what does that have to do with him?

"He'll have a job for you, maybe a couple."

"What kind of job?"

"I don't really know."

"So how do I find out about this job?

"He'll contact you after you're in the house."

"So what happens if I don't want to do this job?"

"Hey, c'mon, you want the house right?"

"Yeah, but I don't know what I'm committing myself to."

"I can try and put this deal together some other way if you want, though at the moment, I'm at a loss as to what that would be."

"Oh, all right. Whatever it is he wants me to do can't be that bad. I've done my share of stupid things in the past."

"So you're interested?"

"Yeah! This guy's not going to cap my knees if I don't, will he?

"I'm sure he won't, though it's interesting that you brought it up. Why don't you tell momma you have a good shot at getting her the house."

"Oh, there's one small thing. The guy gets a little nervous letting people use his note so wants some collateral, if you know what I mean?"

"What kind of collateral? I don't have much in the house and I don't have any other assets. So what am I supposed to use?"

"You got kids, right?"

"Yeah, what about them, they're not worth anything!"

"While you're using the note he'd like a $500,000 life insurance policy secured against your youngest. When the note's returned, the policy's cancelled. No big deal, right?"

"So what happens if I don't return the note?"

"Let's not even go there, okay. You'll return the note. I've got confidence in you."

Damn right he'd return the note. The bastard would probably kill his kid.

Though Louie's stomach was in knots, they shook hands and left.

Chapter 8

Hadley was on a roll. Deals were going together and money was pouring into his pocket in spite of the poor market. Feeling good, he walked into the weekly meeting of the Traders, and was approached by Mark Ramirez.

"Hadley, remember that loan you got for my client?"

"Yeah, that liar loan where he put nothing down and we did some creative finagling to help him qualify?"

"Yeah, that one, anyway he called to say their interest rate just went from the teaser rate to something they can't handle, and he's pissed because I talked him into buying the house. I told him values always go up, so you're always taking a risk. Now they can't afford the payments, the values dropped because of all the foreclosures, and they owe more than what the home's worth."

"So what's the problem?"

"He wanted me to check to see if you can get him a new loan."

"A new loan; no, forget it. He needs a shrink, not a mortgage broker. Tell him to call Dr. Goldfarb, because there's not a damn thing I can do for him. He took a chance when he bought the house. Things didn't work out for them, so their problems are mental, not financial."

"The mortgage company's hounding him for payments, he's fallen behind on other bills, his wife's sick with worry, so he's turning everywhere for help. What should I tell him?"

"Tell him to picture what the owners of the mortgage company that's hounding him would do. Think of them as the 'big boys.' Let's say they bought his house under the terms he did. Nothing down, liar loan, doctored evidence, and now they find themselves with payments they're having trouble making. They realize they owe more than what the home's worth, so are faced with a moral dilemma--keep their word and pay, or hand over the keys. What do you think the 'big boys' would do?"

"They'd not make payments, live in the house until forced to leave, then hand over the keys."

"That's how the big boys make money. Tell him if he does that, to save up enough for a down-payment on another house, then come see me, as I know people who will carry a note. Oh, yeah, make sure he has enough money so there's a commission for you too."

"I think the 'Mortgage Doctor' just solved his problem."

"I'm always here to help, my friend. Do you have any other clients who need loans?"

"Not at the moment, but I'll call if I do."

"Remember, 'bring your sick, ailing clients to me and I'll doctor them up so they qualify for a loan.'"

"You're smooth, that's for sure."

"Always try to help."

"Some of the stuff you do doesn't always seem on the up and up, if you don't mind my saying so, so what happens if you get caught?"

"First off, I resent your implying that I'm less than kosher, but let's say I am. What I'd do is get a nasty attorney who will claim that I'm a victim, file bankruptcy if I have to, or change the name of my company."

"It's that simple?"

"It'll cost a few bucks for an attorney, but I'll recoup the money. In the process I won't admit to anything, just like the big boys do when they get caught with their hand in the cookie jar. When they get caught you'll read 'they neither admitted nor denied wrong-doing.' How slick is that? They don't admit to anything. I love watching how they operate."

"You've got it all figured out, haven't you?"

"See, the big boys focus on money. They don't allow this other crap to get in the way. That's why they come out on top."

"What other crap you talking about?"

"That gobbledy-gook the self-righteous talk about."

"So, focus on money, forget the rest, and a person should get ahead, right?"

"You got it."

"Do you ever get bothered by some of this stuff?"

"Nah, everyone does it. You just have to stay one step ahead of everyone else."

"Sounds pretty simple."

"Listen. If everyone didn't cheat, I wouldn't either. But I figure they all do it, so I just have to do it better, which I do, though will deny it if asked by the wrong person."

"Who's that?"

"A judge."

"See ya' later…

"Hey, Norm?"

Norm Hickman, his old buddy and client, was about to leave. "Did you get that house?"

"No, the deal fell through. I had it in the bag until the title company found another lien on the land I was trading in."

"So who put the new lien there?"

"Me, but I didn't think they'd catch it because if they didn't, it'd be their problem. But once they did, I was willing to move it, but the guy I owed the money to wouldn't agree to another collateral, so the whole deal fell apart. Which is too bad as I liked the house. It kind of screwed the people up I was dealing with, but hey, that's life. Got any deals for my note?"

"I'm working on one."

"How's that collection business of yours going?"

"It's going well!"

"You're ingenious. Put loans together, then provide collection services too."

"My specially trained assistants are very adept at encouraging people to pay."

"How many bones have you broken so far?"

"I've lost track."

"See ya' later."

Chapter 9

Windy Wales was having trouble getting the Traders books to balance. Convinced someone was screwing with them, he checked and double-checked to find out what was wrong. It wouldn't balance. Surely someone had stolen the money. The more he thought about it, the more worked up he got, to the point where his paranoia was kicking in. How did they get their hands on it? Did someone sneak into his house? Did they steal checks and forge his signature? Why was the account $10,000 short?

Where did the money go? How was he going to explain this to the members? Surely they would understand that he didn't take it.

Or would they? God forbid they should find out he was a certified wacko on medication, because that would really complicate matters. They'd be forced to decide if they should call the police, but then again, Traders don't call police on other Traders as that's not how the group works. God forbid one of them got tossed in the slammer, because then there'd be less people to attend meetings. In his case, one of them would have to take over the books and none of them wanted the job. No, they'd mildly rebuke him and set up a payback plan--either that or everyone would toss a little in the pot until they figured out who had heisted the dough.

Obsessed with the missing funds, Windy grabbed his gun and set it on his desk in case the forgers came back, though before going back through the books, he got up to lock the doors and windows. Upon returning to his desk, he thought he'd better take his gun and check the doors and windows again, because he wasn't sure he had. This went on for two hours. After every walk-through, he had this overwhelming urge to double-check the doors and windows again.

Lucky for him, Mother Nature intervened. Forced to sit down and think of something else, some degree of sanity set in. Unlocking the bathroom door, he wondered what in the hell he was doing with his gun, then realized it was time for his medication. Gulping down the pills, his head was spinning and his thoughts were running rampant when the phone rang.

It was his mother. "Have you taken your medication today?" she asked.

"Yeah, just did."

"Are you okay?"

"Someone broke in my house and stole the Trader's money."

"Should I call your Doctor?"

"I don't have time, mom, I got to find the money. The whole thing's driving me nuts," then he hung up.

His mother jumped in the car and headed for his house to determine what was going on before he flew into a full-blown psychotic episode.

Windy returned to the books. Using the last bank statement, he started reviewing what checks were written and to whom. As his medication kicked in, things began getting clearer. Someone had written three checks totaling $10,000, forging his signature to do so. A sense of rage came over him. Someone was going to pay for this. Suddenly the doorbell rang. He grabbed his gun.

Could this be the forger coming back? Determined that they weren't getting any more checks, he didn't care who it was--he was going to blast them--but luckily his medication had set in enough so that he decided he'd try to find out who it was before pulling the trigger. Hearing his mother's voice, he opened the door, grabbed her, and pulled her inside, scaring the devil out of her.

"What's going on?" she asked

"They're coming to steal more checks!"

"Who's coming to steal more checks?"

"I don't know, but they've stolen three so already!"

Realizing that Windy was near panic, she asked for the gun, then told him to start from the beginning, to tell her about the checks and missing money, figuring that with her bookkeeping background she could help him. He showed her the books, the last bank statement, and the three checks. She verified that they weren't his signatures, then asked if anyone had access to the books. He said, "Yeah, members of the Traders Club."

"I think you have a crook in your midst," she offered.

No sooner were the words out of her mouth then suspicion set in, and for a paranoid schizophrenic, that's not good because it leads to sleepless nights. Knowing this was the case, she told him to change his clothes as they were going out for supper in the hopes that some food in his stomach would fend off his nutty thinking.

She worried constantly about Windy and checked on him often. Why he had turned out the way he had, she didn't know. Her other son wasn't that way and the doctors couldn't explain it— instead told her that she wasn't responsible, and it wasn't her fault. It was just the way he was. They explained that the medication would slow his mind down to the point where he could deal with things better, though wouldn't keep all the nutty thoughts out of his head.

Assuring her that, "He's bound to come up with some real soupy ideas," she needed to be prepared for it, especially if he got the idea in his head that he didn't need his medication. Because when he did, and went off it, she could expect all kinds of fun and games, with a trip back to the hospital on inevitably on the top of her agenda.

Trying to get a better grasp of what was going on with Windy, she asked many of the psychiatrists for an explanation. One psychiatrist said, "Our impulses and thoughts pop up from our unconscious, go through our defense mechanisms, and enter our conscious mind. In the case of healthy people, most of the impulses and thoughts are watered down by the time they get to the conscious level, so they're not a major problem. But in Windy's case there is no watering down, it's as though there are no defense mechanisms. The thoughts are goofy when they start out and goofy when they enter his head--for that reason he needs medication to slow the process down. Make sure he takes his medication and he'll function okay--for that matter, can be a productive member of society."

She thanked the doctor for his explanation though, unbeknownst to him, he had just scripted her life. She would make sure that Windy took his medication.

Chapter 10

The president opened the meeting, made a couple of announce-ments, then turned it over to Windy, who was very nervous as all could see. No one knew why he was nervous because it was not uncommon to see him agitated, but this time he seemed especially on edge and they soon learned why.

Shaking as he stood Windy said, "I have bad news. We're broke. Our money's been ripped off."

Many became furious immediately. All demanded to know what had happened.

Windy told them, "Someone forged my signature on three checks, thereby wiping out the $10,000 balance."

"Did anyone else lose money or was it just us?"

"Who cares about other people's money!" one spoke up, "That's their problem! I'm only interested in ours. This looks like an inside job to me."

"Let's call the cops. We need an investigation," one offered.

"No, no, no, don't call the cops," many argued, "We don't want the cops involved, we'll handle it ourselves."

All agreed.

Ivan turned to Windy and said, "How do we know you didn't rip us off? You showed up with booze on your breath a few weeks back after you shot out of here because you 'forgot the books.' You probably knew all along the money was missing."

Windy responded defensively, "I had a cold that day so I took a little swig to coat my throat, and it wasn't until this weekend I noticed the money missing."

"You're nuttier than a fruitcake, I suppose you expect us to believe that," Ivan replied.

Believing that it wasn't time to delve into his medical history, Windy let the comment pass. Feeling under the gun, he said, "I think someone in the club stole the money."

"How insane!" one member responded. "You can't expect us to actually believe one of us would stoop to doing such a thing, do you?"

"You've all heard the saying 'Don't trust anyone here!' "

"So some crackpot made a goofy statement like that, that doesn't mean it's true. Guys have been doing business here for years, there's love in this group!"

Members roared. For someone to believe that proved he was an idiot.

"Let's form a circle, hold hands, and sing 'Kumbaya,'" one responded, and huge laughter ensued.

At least they were able to laugh about their predicament.

"Does anyone know who started that stupid idea?"

"No, no one's ever 'fessed up to saying it', but chances are they dropped out years ago, probably never made it in real estate anyway."

"'Don't trust anyone here, what a stupid statement to make,'" one said, while suspiciously looking at everyone, thinking maybe the guy wasn't so stupid after all. Nah, Christ, it was probably some dumb broad who had said it.

"Let's back to the subject at hand. I recommend we form a committee to look into the matter," one proposed.

A committee no one wanted to be on.

"I don't think we need a committee, I think the president should appoint a guy to handle it," one offered. Most were in favor of this. The only one who wasn't was the president himself. In his mind, the idea had disaster written all over it; nonetheless it was dumped in his lap, so what could he do? Racking his brain to think of someone dimwitted enough to take on the job, he settled on Gilbert.

Gilbert wasn't enthralled by the idea of having to figure out which culprit was responsible for the missing funds, but accepted the challenge as a favor to the club. Then he started investigating.

At the next meeting, he shared that the heist appeared to be an inside job.

"Boo!" was the response. He didn't know if they were booing him for claiming it was an inside job, that someone would resort to such devilish behavior, or for his bringing the matter to their attention.

Finally Norm said, "We don't have time for this, let's get on with the meeting." Which meant that he was probably the guilty party, but since he scared the crap out of people, many agreed with his suggestion. Soon it was determined that Gilbert needed to handle the investigation in a manner that wouldn't upset the normal meetings, which was just fine with him. Though, truth be known, there'd be no real investigation. No. Everyone would have their suspicions, but nothing would probably come of the matter; instead everyone would eventually throw a few bucks in the kitty, vowing to pass the loss on to someone else.

The president then said, "Does anybody have anything they want to share before we call a halt to this meeting?"

"Yeah, I do," Mark Gonzalez said.

"What is it, Mark?"

"What can we do about that guy who's posting all those nasty things about us on the Internet? They're not real, of course, but they give us a bad reputation."

"What's he saying?" another asked.

"Stuff like 'God forbid these Traders be symbolic of America-- our thinking, our moral fiber!' Another one is 'The organization where greed is a term of endearment.' "

"What else?" another chimed in.

"Yeah, here's another one; 'Traders aren't pillars of society— instead, architects of a shaky foundation?' And another is, 'Why tell the truth when it's only going to be used against you?' Stuff like this. We need to stop it."

"Does anyone know who this guy is?"

"I guess he was in the club years ago then dropped out. Apparently he's got a wild hair up his ass about something that took place with another member," one suggested.

Another chimed in and said, "Don't pay any attention to him. That's all he wants anyway, attention. I'm sure in time he'll go away."

"That's good advice," the president proclaimed. "We have enough issues to deal with here anyway."

"Yeah, let's forget the jerk. He says us Traders have taken the place of attorneys, to where we're the ones on the 'hot seat' now and not them. Go figure."

"Anybody have anything else they want to bring up?" the president asked.

"Yeah, I do," Mark Grayson said.

There were a couple of responses posted to this guy's website in our favor. One said, 'Good grief, expecting us to believe real estate agents would engage in unethical behavior is beyond words. I know the real Traders and they're model citizens, pillars of society, good church-going people who'd no sooner do something illegal than eat turnips with ketchup,' which is a far cry from the way this guy's carrying on. Another wrote, 'I know people in the Traders business, and they're dang gum good people.' So, as you can see, there are a lot of people who appreciate what we do."

"I've heard enough," Mark Gonzalez chimed in, "Let's call it quits."

"Sounds good. "Meeting over." Then the president walked out.

One of the older members shook his head at what was going on
—but then again, he shook his head at everything since suffering
a traumatic setback in the club years earlier. At the time he was
known to criticize others for bringing in packages with less than
a certain amount of expenses he believed essential for an honest
picture of the operating statement. But he got himself in trouble
when he turned up with a package on one of his own properties
where the expenses were far less than what he preached. Only
to have it brought to his attention, accompanied by a few
catcalls, which didn't set well with him!

Rattled, he promptly blamed his secretary for the error, only to
have that backfire too when he was reminded that he was a
control freak who wouldn't allow his secretary to put anything in
writing without his permission. Frustrated, and at a loss for
words, he promised to bring in a corrected package, then meekly
walked out rather than stay to argue with an old auctioneer
buddy he argued with every week. Arguing for them was pure
joy. Invariably they whipped themselves into a lather thinking it
would sway the other, but it never did though. What usually
saved them was that one had to pee, which put their argument on
the back burner for a week. Convinced the subject was worth
returning to, they vowed to take it up when they met again.

Getting members to vacate the room after the meeting presented
a challenge to the cleaning crew because, besides the two who
were arguing, another member cornered anyone willing to listen
in an attempt to convince them that nobility was in his blood.
Another banged his tennis racket trying to drum up a game,
another argued that his French ancestry warranted more respect.
Another used it as a weekly reminder to put tape on his briefcase
to hold it together, another's girth prevented him from doing
*anything* quickly, another was constantly grooming himself

while another was on the lookout for a liberal to argue politics with.

Then there were those who got out as soon as the meeting was over, because God forbid they be forced to talk to anyone, as it might take the edge off their normally cantankerous mood. Such was the make-up of the Traders Club, the club with an 85% divorce rate, exceeded only by the audacious belief that they were normal.

After Louis and his wife finalized the purchase of their home, Tom Jorgenson used his commission to buy two Error and Omission policies from two different insurers, figuring the deal had disaster written all over it. So bothered was he that he dropped out of the Traders Club after forking over a good portion of his commission to Hadley, and because he did, he didn't want to see Hadley either, as he'd be reminded of his exposure.

Chapter 11

Peety was bored to tears. Hopping around his cage with nothing going on did that; of course, Ivan stomping through the door would change the atmosphere dramatically. No sooner had the thought entered his mind than in walked Ivan, angry as usual.

"Someone ripped off the money at the Traders Club. The only question is which one of the crooks did it, because they're all capable. Most of them don't have a pot to piss in, though from listening to them, you would think just the opposite."

Peety bobbed his head and listened intently. Though he didn't really care, it was good to learn what was going on at the Traders Club. Even though Ivan was a scoundrel, he was his buddy, so on a certain level Peety cared about him. That didn't mean he wouldn't rat on him, because he had in the past and would again. What he found amazing was that he, a bird, had a conscience, while Ivan did not. Oh, perhaps he had one, but the holes in it were so big you could drive a cement truck through them. In essence, he had a Swiss cheese conscience. There were one or two things he felt guilty about, though at the moment he couldn't think of what they might be. Engrossed in thought, Peety was momentarily rattled when Ivan shouted out:

"What are you bobbing your head for over there?"

Oops, better start housecleaning; otherwise, God forbid, he might not feed me.

"There was only $10,000 in the checking account. Just goes to show you how desperate some of these jerks are, then again that's a lot of money for some, they don't have a helluva lot. They're not going to catch who did it. No one's going to turn them in if they know who it is because Traders don't do that, it's not kosher, if you know what I mean?"

Peety bobbed his head.

"See, the Traders are on the bottom of the real estate pyramid. They're like gypsies with no roots. When the urge strikes or heat rises, they pick up stakes and move on with no clear idea of where they're going but, wherever it is, they start mingling with natives hoping to trade trinkets, which is something they're very good at."

Peety was enthralled with the discussion. Ivan was talking to him. Or at least talking out loud which made him feel like he was talking to him. Of course, Ivan never asked his opinion about anything, because if he did he would have given it. No, Ivan was too enthralled with himself to seek Peety's advice, wouldn't listen anyway, that's the way he was. When you're egotistical, selfish, and bull-headed, you don't have time to hear others out because you're too involved with yourself.

Then Peety realized that he didn't listen to others either, that he too was egotistical, selfish, and bull-headed. Good grief, had he become Ivan? Was he Ivan's clone? No, of course not--he wasn't Ivan, he was compassionate, caring, someone who put others before himself--he was good. The more he thought about it the better he felt, then he realized that Ivan was looking straight at him and had quit talking.

"So, you think you're so damn good, is that right?"

"Oops." Must have been talking out loud. Oh, boy, that wasn't good.

Involved in a stare-off, the tension was broken when Ivan's phone rang.

"Yeah, what is it?"

"No, I don't want to buy any damn land. We're in a depression, don't you read the papers!"

"I don't care if the price has been cut in half. It's still not worth it."

"Listen, when I can buy the land for ten cents on the dollar, call me, otherwise don't bother me."

With that he hung up. "These people must think I'm Howard Hughes or someone like that because they keep trying to pawn land off on, me hoping I'll bail them out. They think I'm Santa Claus."

Not realizing it, Peety got rattled when Ivan said, "How come you're shaking your head?"

Oops, caught twice in one day—that wasn't good.

"This place is driving me nuts, I'm out of here." With that, Ivan was out the door.

"Damn, he forgot to feed me. I'll become 'Skinny Minnie' if he keeps that up. I better watch how I behave around him from now on. Yup, no more mimicking Ivan, my waistline can't handle it."

Chapter 12

Involved in a raucous property rights discussion at the city council, proponents in a last ditch effort to win their case brought in Windy. After five minutes of sound logic, he headed towards nutty thinking.

"Ladies and gentlemen, every homeowner has the right to use his property in the manner for which it was intended."

Everyone agreed.

"God made dirt for man's use."

Okay, everyone thought, where's he going with this?

"If it was God's intent for city councils to take land from law-abiding taxpayers for a purpose it wasn't intended for, it would have said so in the bible, and it didn't."

Oh, boy.

"Taking land from one for the benefit of another is downright evil. Only the devil would do such a thing."

The property rights people were getting nervous, wondering how they could shut him up, fearing that if they didn't, he would blow their case to smithereens.

Looking straight at the council members, Windy said, "If you resort to taking land to benefit another, you're evil, you're the devil, I will personally take it upon myself to see that you're removed from office, as a danger to society."

Windy was really getting worked up now, and so was everyone else. Supporters of the proposal were sweating bullets, while everyone else was sitting on the edge of their chairs waiting to see what would come out of his mouth next, not realizing that council members were sitting with their mouths wide open, taking everything in.

Finally the chairperson had heard enough and banged his gavel, shouting, "The speaker's out of order."

Startled, Windy was about to say more, when he was grabbed by a couple of his buddies and escorted to his seat. Then one said, "Ladies and gentleman, it's been a long night. I believe you can see that this issue brings out passionate responses on both sides. I know you're scheduled to vote tonight, but I recommend that the vote be put off until another date."

The presiding officer couldn't have agreed more, so motioned for the meeting to be adjourned. Everyone was for it. All the council members had a local watering hole with a private back room they'd head for, where they would discuss the events of the evening. They couldn't wait to get there, as they had a lot to talk about, yes sirree bob. Though it was against the law to hold meetings other than at city council chambers, they got around that by having their assistants speak for them while they downed their favorite beverages--and in this case, it would be quite a few.

Windy in the meantime was escorted out of the building before the press could grab him. As they drove him home, his buddies assured him that the council wasn't out to get him, in spite of his proclamation that they were. Realizing that he had gone overboard at the meeting, he knew from experience that he had better get his meds before he slipped into a full blown psychotic break, so upon bidding farewell to his mates he headed to the medicine cabinet to take his pills.

Shortly after that, his thinking started to slow down, which was good, because he realized he was pretty tired from the day's events and needed sleep. One thing about nutty people is they know that if they get off their medication, all kinds of hell can break loose, and since Windy had gone through that experience more than once, he wasn't interested in repeating it any time soon. Because when he did, he was known to engage in the kind of long outbursts that brought about his name, "Windy."

At the Traders Club the next day, all the talk was about how Windy had become unglued at the city council meeting. Hoping no reporters would show up, they were relieved to see Tom Slocum walk through the door, because Tom was the one who had invited Windy to the meeting.

"So Tom, what happened last night with Windy?"

Hoping to get a juicy reply, they were soon disappointed.

"The guy was doing great until he ran out of gas. It's that simple. He obviously hadn't eaten much yesterday, then got nervous speaking before the council. You all know he feels passionate about the subject, then might have interpreted some of their remarks the wrong way, and possibly saw where they were leaning toward our opponents, which caused him to choose a line of logic he felt bad about afterwards. I'm sure if he shows up today, you'll see he's the same old Windy."

No sooner were the words out of his mouth than in walked Windy, which prompted Tom to declare to one and all that Windy had done a terrific job on behalf of all property owners at the city council meeting. The group erupted in applause, many patting Windy on the back.

Not expecting a positive response, he was taken aback—and was, for that matter, relieved--as he had expected just the opposite. Acknowledging their response with a nod and wave of his hand, he elected to keep his mouth shut, as his medication was leaving him a bit stupefied. So instead he grabbed a cup of coffee.

After the uproar toned down over the issue of property rights, the president called the meeting to order. The first order of the day was a report from Windy about their financial situation, which was not good. Their money had not been recovered nor had a culprit been found so they were, in essence, broke, which Windy reasoned was a good time for a new start.

"Since we're broke, I think it's time the club hands the books over to a new treasurer."

An immediate pallor set over the club, as no one wanted the job. Silence set in. Everyone feared opening his mouth. Finally the president realized he had to say something.

Looking at Windy, he said, "Motion denied."

"I never made a motion. I said it's time someone else takes over the books."

"No one else wants the job. It's yours! Let's hear the secretary's report."

Windy didn't know what to say, just knew he was still stuck with the books. Part of him was outraged. How dare they dump the books on him? But another part reasoned that handling the books meant that they needed him--he wouldn't be tossed out. Fearing the latter, he told the evil part of his mind to "stick it," he was keeping the book--not realizing that he was being overheard by many talking out loud. No big deal they figured, just Windy being a bit nutty, which was his norm.

Windy headed home and dove into cleaning. A fanatic when it came to cleanliness, he vacuumed, mopped, dusted, and wiped until he was exhausted, but the place looked clean, smelled good, and all the bugs that existed, real or imaginary, were killed so he would be able to sleep well. Except for the fact that he was ruminating about the club's financial plight to point where he soon fell into despair, convinced that the club was secretly plotting to send him to jail.

The more he thought about it, the more he became convinced that it would be for life. Obsessed with thoughts of a life behind bars, he went to bed, forgetting to take his medication. Though his body was asleep, his mind wasn't, and it wasn't long before he was focused on the notion that people sentenced to prison for life should have the right to end their life by lethal injection. They couldn't be forced to, but would have the option of.

Knowing that he'd find peace through a shot, he then jolted out of bed knowing that the conservatives would object to it. They'd want him to spend the rest of his life in jail as punishment for ripping off the Traders Club, which he hadn't done. He might even be willing to donate his organs if he could, which was too much for his mind to handle, so soon he was out of bed patrolling the house, gun in hand, fearful that someone was coming after his organs.

His mother called in the morning to check on him but he didn't respond, so she immediately headed for his house.

"Windy, it's mom, let me in."

He opened the door and she found a sleep-deprived son with bloodshot eyes muttering, "They're after my organs."

"Who's after your organs?"

"Liberals."

"Let me check your medicine…you haven't taken any. No wonder you're having these nutty thoughts about liberals taking your organs. You're off your rocker again. Here, take these… Now go to bed. I'll check on you around two o'clock and we'll talk about it then. But no, no one's taking your organs. Do you hear me?"

He nodded his head and went to bed.

When she returned at two he'd just gotten out of bed.

"What's this about the liberals taking your organs?"

"Mom, people sentenced to life in prison, with no chance of getting out, should have the option of having their life ended by lethal injection, rather than being forced to serve out their term. They should have the option of donating their organs too, as many people need organs, so why shouldn't prisoners be allowed to donate theirs before they're put to sleep? It seems the humane way to do things."

"It's such a radical change that I don't know if it would be approved."

"As it is now, tax payers are on the hook to feed and house people in prison while prisoners vegetate until they die. By giving the prisoners the option of ending their lives in a humane way, everyone would win."

"Windy, the churches and conservative's will balk at the idea. It's unlikely that it's going to happen, so you might just as well put that idea out of your mind."

"But don't you see merit?"

"I do. There are a lot of things I think should be different, but that doesn't mean the churches and conservatives will go for it."

"Well, I can't put it out of my head. It won't go away. I try but it keeps popping back in."

"Try and think of something else."

I can't because this idea won't get out of the way."

"Do you think it will share space in your mind?"

"I don't think so. It's awfully strong-minded, mom. Stubborn too! It's determined to get its way. I hate it when that happens. I become a victim of my ideas."

"Do you ever think of Suzie?"

"Don't remind me of Suzie, mom. I hate being reminded of Suzie because I know what you're going to say."

"What am I going to say?"

"That I kissed Suzie, and I wasn't supposed to. That I was bad for kissing Suzie, I was a sinner because I did. God was un-happy with me. Suzie's parents were unhappy with me. That I was going to be thrown out of school for kissing Suzie. Mom, don't remind me of this. I can't handle that memory, mom, it's too painful, I was bad. I was a sinner."

"Windy, you were in second grade at the time."

"Mom, don't remind me of Suzie—please!"

"Okay; let's get a bite to eat. There's a new restaurant I'd like to try." Then it dawned on her that they had better not go there so she made up an excuse and suggested that they go to their old standby instead, muttering something about wanting to check out the new restaurant first. This was fine with Windy as he liked their old standby. She thought that taking him to the new restaurant (Suzie Wong's) might not be wise in light of the conversation.

Chapter 13

Gilbert was anxious to find a new fix-up. Unfortunately, Mindy Bork had not come across any yet, and since he trusted her, he was content to wait until she found one she would recommend. In the meantime, when all the knockouts heard Mindy was in the picture, they quit calling him. Though she was nothing to look at, she had a reputation for being honest, which is what won Gilbert over to the point where he told one and all that Mindy was his agent.

So the babes ran all their fix-ups by Mindy, hoping she and Gilbert would be interested, but not realizing that Mindy had a keen eye and a protective nature. She wasn't about to recommend anything to Gilbert unless she knew that he could make money with it, as she knew once he started a project, he would invariably invest more than what he initially intended, so there had to be room allowed for his idiosyncrasies.

Mindy ran a daily ad in the paper hoping to attract responses. Though calls were infrequent, one day she received one that caught her attention, as it was from out of state. She picked up the phone and the caller said:

"I understand you buy fix-ups?"

"I don't personally but a client does. Do you have one?"

"Yeah, I guess. I've never seen it. I live in Michigan. My old man and I were estranged. He just died. I think he died in the house, the jerk. He was a recluse. No one could get along with him. He wanted nothing to do with anyone and no one wanted anything to do with him. I haven't seen him in twenty years. I guess he let the house go to pot to point where neighbors reported him to the police but he didn't care--he told them this is a free country so he could do whatever he wanted. The neighbors got hold of me to see if I could talk some sense into him, but I just laughed at them.

"There was nothing I could do, for that matter I didn't want to be involved because I couldn't stand the guy. Anyway he's dead and now I own the house, so people are calling me to clean it up, fix it up, and I don't want to be bothered. Hell, I'm in Michigan. I hate the hot weather in Arizona. I don't want to be out there. I don't want to be bothered. I just want to sell the damn place as quick as I can."

"Though it sounds like you and your father didn't have the best of relationships, I'm sure it was painful to hear of his passing nonetheless."

"Whatever. Listen lady, do you or your client want to buy the house, or should I call one of these other jerks who want to buy fix-ups?"

"I appreciate your calling. If you'll give me your name, phone number and the address of the property, I'll drive by the property this afternoon and call you back after I do. In return, will you give me until this evening to respond before you call anyone else?"

"Yeah, I'll do that."

"Good."

He gave her the address of the property and his contact information. She promptly went into MLS to see if it was or had been listed (which it hadn't), then searched county records before jumping in her car to see the place first-hand. Though her caller's father might have been crotchety, he had good taste for neighborhoods. It was a nice area.

But driving by the home, she could see why neighbors had called the police. The yard was loaded with automobile parts and weeds, trees were untrimmed, and dogs had used the place for a dumping ground. The house was no better. It was a fix-up. If the inside matched the outside, Gilbert would spend a month just cleaning the place out. What it had going for it though was the neighborhood. The homes around it were upscale and well maintained. It truly was a pride of ownership locale. Realizing she needed a way in, she called the son.

"This is Mindy. I'm sitting in front of the home. You're right, it needs work, but it's nothing my guy can't handle. Before I call him, though, is there any way we can get inside to see how it looks?"

"My old man had this goofy fear of locking himself out, so he kept a key hid by the back door. Look above the door, maybe under a rock, and if that don't work break a window."

"Let's hope I don't have to break a window, as I certainly would fix it if I did. I'll start by looking for a key and we'll go from there. If I find a key should I call you?"

"No, just get your guy in so I can get some idea of what it's worth."

She proceeded around to the back and found a key hidden under a rock. Opening the back door, she looked inside and found quite a mess. He had never cleaned; that was for sure. Gilbert would need two dumpsters because of all the junk. To prove it to the seller, she'd take pictures when Gilbert walked through. She then called Gilbert and arranged to meet in an hour. Then she headed to the office for her camera.

Upon returning, she found Gilbert walking around the outside.

"The place is going to need work, Gilbert, but as you can see, it's in a nice neighborhood."

She filled him in about the seller as they walked through, taking pictures as they went. Gilbert couldn't contain himself. He wanted the house. He saw potential. She told him comparables in the area showed homes in the $400,000 range. This one had an assessed value of $260,000, but it had never been challenged, so she was sure it wasn't worth it. Then Gilbert asked, "What's it worth?"

"Considering the condition, I think $180,000."

"I'll offer $240,000. I can turn this place into a beautiful home."

"I know you can. I also know you'll spend more on it than what you plan, so I don't recommend offering any more than $180,000, maybe even less."

"I don't want to lose it. I want you to get it for me. I'll pay more."

"Gilbert, slow down. Let me handle the negotiations."

"Okay, okay, I'll do that. I'll pay your commission too, don't worry about that."

"I won't Gilbert. I represent you, remember? I'll do my best to get the house for you."

"I'll pay cash."

"Let's go write up the offer."

The offer was for $180,000 with the seller paying a five percent commission. Gilbert feared the commission would queer the deal, but agreed to Mindy including it.

When the seller got the pictures and the offer for $180,000, he couldn't sign fast enough. The five percent commission was a deal as far as he was concerned. Mindy opened escrow and

Gilbert spent hours lying awake at night, planning the renovation. He was ecstatic.

As soon as the deed was recorded, Gilbert had a large dumpster moved onto the property. In short order, he was cleaning the house, yard, garage--you name it. Neighbors were thrilled. Many came with pitchers of margaritas, which Gilbert declined, as he was on a mission and he didn't have time to drink. Which made the neighbors all the happier--so happy, in fact, that they organized a block party to celebrate his efforts. Already he was a neighborhood hero and all he'd done was begin cleaning up the place, though his dogged determination had many convinced that he'd turn the dump into a gem. Arriving early and leaving late, he toiled long and hard.

One dumpster was filled and a larger one brought in. Soon it was filled with sheet rock, carpet, tile, linoleum, windows, toilets, and vanities. Gilbert was stripping the home to its bare bones--even had a plumber in, as a water leak was discovered under the concrete pad. Soon the kitchen and bathrooms were torn apart to reroute the water line, as he was intent on doing things right.

The neighbors marveled at his work ethic. The guy was a workaholic. Many complimented him on his efforts, though he didn't spend much time soaking in the praise, as his obsessive mind was too focused on what needed doing. The neighbors began to worry because Gilbert never took a break, so they started stopping by with food. He thanked them for their generosity, stopped long enough to enjoy their faire, then headed back to work.

Neighbors were convinced he was a decent guy, and that hunger pangs took second fiddle to the job at hand, though his size said just the opposite. For sure, they admired his tunnel vision to the point that they got out of his way when lunch was over, which was usually pretty quickly, as he inhaled his food.

Much of the neighborhood had a southwestern appearance, and the structural design of the house called for something similar, so Gilbert replaced the shingled roof with red clay tiles after supporting the roof so it would hold the extra weight. He put stucco on the walls, installed sweeping archways, put wrought iron on the windows for safety reasons, and installed wrought-iron railings which added charm and romantic appeal. He laid saltillo tile on the floor throughout the house, putting back splashes up the walls to give a finished look.

For the kitchen, he had an impressive oak center island built which held a hand painted Talavera sink. To give the home a Mediterranean touch, he put in toffee-colored cabinets with an embossed concrete back splash. In short time the home became quite stunning. The inside was really taking shape but the outside wasn't, so he elected to cover the shabby looking concrete with broken Saltillo tile, making sure to add animal imprints wherever possible.

He thought he might bring Whiskers over when he grouted, to have his foot imprints in there too, but that would require time, and he was running out of it. He loved the mosaic look of the broken Saltillo tile as it resembled a puzzle, but regretted the amount of time it took, which was considerable. Nonetheless, the outside was taking shape. Wherever possible he put in mosaic tile, using porcelain, glass, and metal, especially liking the glass tiles because they contained earth oxides like copper, cobalt, and chromium.

Mindy checked on Gilbert often during the four months of arduous labor, though she didn't stay long at any one time as she didn't want to get in the way. So when he called her to list the home, she wasn't swept off her feet walking in, as she'd seen the process unfold—nevertheless, she was most impressed with the finished product.

Neighbors were in awe watching Gilbert turn the festering, termite-eaten home into a sparkling gem. Jettisoning it from an eyesore to a trendsetter, one they could point at with pride, at as it made their own homes more valuable. So for them, it was a sad day when Gilbert loaded up his tools and equipment for the last time before the "For Sale" sign went up.

Back at the Traders Club, Gilbert was mocked when word got out that he had finished his renovation, though not one member bothered to walk through—instead, they shared their long held belief that Gilbert was a lucky klutz, incapable of doing anything right.

Mindy had no sooner put up the "For Sale" sign, than offers came pouring in for more than the listed price. Buyers no sooner showed up, than neighbors introduced themselves. They couldn't say enough about the fantastic improvements Gilbert had made in the house. They were his best sales people.

Gilbert and Mindy were very pleased with the response. Though their offer was not the best, some former neighbors were very interested in the house. They were well liked but had moved a few years earlier after suffering a tragedy and now wanted to return to the neighborhood. That was good enough for Gilbert. He accepted their offer, even though it was less then others, as he wanted to make their dream possible.

Chapter 14


Mindy raved at the meeting about Gilbert's turning a dump into a masterpiece, and helping a former neighbor acquire the home even though he ended up taking less money. The Traders were convinced that he was an idiot for not holding out for top dollar.

Mark Ramirez turned to his buddy Joe Castro and said, "Gilbert better watch out. More successes like this and someone will spike his food."

"C'mon, " Joe replied, "Upset, jealous, envious, I can see, but spike his food? Do you think someone here would do that?"

"We have a few nasty people here so it wouldn't surprise me."

"Think I'll drop out."

"Just be careful who you mess with, and be especially careful who you represent. If they have an ulterior motive, and you don't support their deviousness, you're dead meat. They'll make your life miserable."

"Like I said, 'I think I'll drop out.' "

"No, you won't! You're just sounding sanctimonious. You're like the rest of us here."

"I like to think I'm above youse crooks."

'Well, you're not, so get off your soapbox."

"I took an ethics class not too long ago and passed the test too!"

"Don't give me that crap. You sat in a friggin' course for a couple of hours listening to somebody pontificate about ethics then picked up a certificate and walked out. You didn't take any damn test, probably wouldn't pass one if you had because you probably slept through the course. How many nights a week are you out now since your old lady dumped you?"

"Usually every night, though how late depends on which dolly I'm with. See, some work, so like to get bedded down real early, so I give them my best shot and bid farewell."

"I hope these babes know you're incapable of a long term relationship."

"Say's who?"

"Some of the women you've been married to, that's who!"

"How do you know? Hey, you're not doing something to these gals you shouldn't, are you?"

"I tell them I'm gay and have no interest, only to find out that that's an amazing challenge to some. I've had a number try repeatedly to help me."

"You jerk."

"Have I told you I'm in love with you?"

"You're nuts.  I'm outta' here."

Chapter 15

Mindy's cell phone rang.

"Mindy, my name is Debby Johnson."

"Hi, Debby, how can I help you?"

"I understand you work closely with Gilbert."

"I do."

"I live in the subdivision where you sold the home for him. Wow, did he do a terrific job."

"I know.  He's got a magic touch."

"Listen, there's a home next to my parents I hope he'll buy."

"Tell me more."

"They live in The Meadows."

"Nice subdivision."

"Yeah, it used to be, but a lot of the drug lords are buying up homes in nice areas thinking they'll draw less attention to themselves. Then they do just that by not taking care of the home. This is the case next door to my parents. I don't know all the details, but apparently the home has been trashed and the owners fled the country, or so people thought.

"Now it turns out that the previous people carried a large note they're going to foreclose on, but don't want to because they've moved out of state and need the money. My parents know them well and want to help. Do you think Gilbert would take over the mortgage and fix up the house?"

"I'll need more details, but he might, because he's looking for another project."

"Before I give you my parents' number, let me call them so they can expect your call. Ever since the neighbor, or tenant, moved in next door, they've been on edge and I don't want to upset them further. I'll call you right back."

"Sounds good, once I have their name and number I'll call them, then drive by the home next door."

"I'll be back in a minute," Debby said, and she was.

"Their name is George and Alice Simpson and their phone number is 432-7778."

"Thanks Debby. I'll keep you posted."

"We so admire what Gilbert did here. If he could get that house and do the same kind of thing, my parents and the owners would be ecstatic."

Alice Simpson answered the phone, thanked Mindy for calling, then she gave her their neighbor's name and phone number in Minnesota. Mindy thanked her, said she would drive by shortly, and would then call Minnesota.

Before driving by the home, she researched the property to make sure the name on the mortgage matched that of the former owners, and it did. She looked at the assessed valuation and saw that it was larger than the mortgage, then checked sales in the subdivision and discovered a number in the $800,000 range. This was outstanding, because the assessed valuation was $450,000, which is what they had sold it for two years earlier, taking a $50,000 note as a down payment, only to find out it was worthless. But by then the people were in the house.

The Meadows was a very nice subdivision in the center of town.

Driving through, Mindy was impressed with how well many of the homes were maintained, then turned the corner and saw the eyesore. No wonder Debby's parents wanted it fixed up. It was a mess. She didn't need to go inside. Walking around the house was enough. As she walked around the home, she spotted many neighbors watching her behind venetian blinds, which gave her an eerie feeling. No one came out; instead they just watched. To break the ice she waved at them, then returned to her car to call Minnesota.

Gisele and Norm Johansen were the note holders and previous owners. Gisele answered. Her Norwegian accent was obvious.

"Gisele, my name is…," only to be cut off.

"I know who you are, Mindy. We been kind of wait-in' for your call as Alice said you might. We don't know what to do because

Norm isn't so good. We're both in our eighties and thought when we sold the house a couple of years ago we'd have the income from the $50,000 note and our $400,000 carry back note but that hasn't been the case.

"It's a long story but the $50,000 note proved no good, then the buyers didn't always pay on the $400,000 note and we were in no position to come back down there to take it back. So we finally called an attorney and started foreclosure. Our attorney threatened to call the feds if they didn't sign a quit claim deed or something like that, so technically I guess we're the owners again, because our attorney recorded that deed yesterday."

"I know you're probably really hesitant to carry a note again but…"

Before she could finish, Gisele said, "We've heard so many good things about Mr. Gilbert, we wouldn't mind carrying a note for him because we could use monthly payments more than cash. We're collecting Social Security and it's just not enough."

"So you wouldn't mind carrying a note?"

"Not for Mr. Gilbert." Giselle replied.

"What kind of interest rate would you charge?"

"Six percent just like the previous one."

"Now, I haven't gone through your home, so can I do that first?"

"Of course. Alice and George have the key. Do you have their number?"

"I do."

"Good, you get Mr. Gilbert and walk through as soon as you can, okay?"

"I'll call him once I hang up."

"Can you call me back tonight?"

"I'll do my best, but if I can't, for sure tomorrow morning."

"We'll both sleep better knowing that."

Upon hanging up she called Gilbert.

He was soon headed her way.

She called Alice to get the key. No sooner had she hung up than an older lady with a key came walking toward her. It had to be Alice, and it was.

They introduced themselves and chatted briefly until Gilbert showed up. Though he made an effort to be sociable, Alice could tell he was more focused on the house next door. She bid them adieu, then watched as they entered the house, knowing they were in for a surprise.

It was apparent anger was the emotion of choice of the previous occupant, because the place was a mess. Paint had been tossed against busted-up walls, urine and fecal matter overwhelmed them, all the appliances were gone, as were the furnace, A/C, and hot water heater—plus, there was glass everywhere. Anything they could take they did, and anything they could destroy, they did too. Had they been able to get at the water pipes under the concrete floor they would have busted them up too, though that wouldn't bring them any value like the copper tubing. But they didn't care, they just wanted to send the message that they weren't happy about having to leave. Gilbert shook his head in disgust at the damage they did, but could see past it, as he saw good bones that could be refurbished.

"I can fix this place up. Get it for me."

"They're most anxious to work with you so I think it's possible."

"How much are they asking for the place?"

"I don't know. We never discussed that. They sold it a couple of years ago for $450,000. The buyer offered a $50,000 note as a down payment and the sellers carried back a $400,000 note at six percent. The $50,000 note proved to be worthless, but the sellers didn't find that out until the buyers were already in the house, and by then it was too late. The sellers sold it on their own without going through a title company, as the buyer convinced them that they all could save a lot of money that way. The buyers then made periodic payments on the $400,000 note so the experience has been a nightmare for the sellers. "

"I'll offer them $450,000."

"Wait a minute," Mindy said. "What's it going to cost to renovate?"

"I can do it for $125,000."

"You're sure?"

"Yeah."

"Then I recommend subtracting $125,000 from $450,000. Offer them $325,000 with $25,000 down, asking them to carry a $300,000 note."

"Do you think they'll go for it?"

"There's one way to find out." With that, they headed to her office to write up the offer.

Since the sellers were taking such a loss, Mindy didn't feel comfortable asking for a commission, so didn't include one in the contract, but when she called to present the offer, Gisele relayed that they wouldn't feel comfortable unless Mindy received something. And though they could use the $25,000, they owned a lot in town worth $40,000 and would give her forty-percent interest, plus would list it with her.

They then stated that they would accept Mr. Gilbert's offer, and would be pleased if he could start right away, even though they hadn't signed the contract and put it in escrow yet. Just that day their attorney had recorded a Quit Claim Deed, so the property was legally theirs.

"Apparently the people balked until he threatened imprisonment if they didn't sign, so we should have no problem with the title. Send us the contract, but tell Mr. Gilbert he has our word we'll sign. He can start clearing out the place, as I understand our beautiful home has been turned into quite a junkyard. What a shame! We took great pride in maintaining it. From what I hear from Alice and George, I don't even want to see pictures, though would love to see pictures of the finished product as I understand Mr. Gilbert is quite a magician when it comes to renovating homes."

"He does do a terrific job. And, yes, by all means we'll send you pictures when he's finished. You'll be impressed."

"I'm sure we will. Listen, dear, we're two hours ahead of you, and this old couple needs their beauty rest so I'm going to say good night. Rest assured we'll sleep well tonight, which is something we haven't done for quite some time."

"I'll mail the contract in the morning. Have a good night."

Gilbert was ecstatic to hear that his offer was accepted, and that he had permission to start on the house right away.

The signed contract was returned a few days later, and Mindy opened escrow.

When the Traders learned Gilbert had found another fix-up, the reaction ranged from disbelief to ridicule.

"He's so lucky," another fixer-upper proclaimed. "There's no way he could have come across that house without a horseshoe up his ass."

"According to Mindy, people from the neighborhood he renovated the last home in sought him out," another said.

"Sought him out, do you believe that? Mindy probably found it for him. She's homely as a fence post and probably has nothing better to do than search out gems for dip-shit."

"You're not jealous are you?"

"Of dip-shit? Of course not. Listen, I've got so much business I probably shouldn't even be here, but I needed a break so decided to check things out here."

"What's this I hear you're filing bankruptcy?"

"Don't believe everything you hear. Listen, I got to run." With that he was out the door to see his bankruptcy attorney. Seems he had gotten a little over-extended, and people were none too happy about it. The big house, trophy wife, and fancy cars were a façade, and now were about to go up in smoke, as no one would lend him money.

His world was crashing down around him, but he wasn't going to let that crush his ego—no--he viewed his difficulties as a minor glitch in a long journey. He'd come out of it, he'd get back on his feet. Those who wouldn't take him at his word would become history. He'd find people who would. He was resourceful that way. If doors closed here, he'd go somewhere else to start anew, as he was convinced there were many who not only wanted to help but needed to--it was just a matter of finding them.

Chapter 16

It took Gilbert nearly a month to clear out the house and strip it down to its bare bones. All the while he was doing this, he planned its renovation. Everything would be top-of-the-line, including putting in Wolf and Sub Zero appliances. Convinced that the bones of the house had the makings of a perfect home for those who loved to entertain, he would make it elegant and accommodating.

He reasoned the most important room in the home was the kitchen, so started there. To create a monolithic look to accentuate the dark cabinetry, he used large slabs of marble both on the walls and floor, then ran the marble throughout the house, except in the bedrooms where he put lush carpet.

In the master bath he changed the image. Using marble again on the floor, he continued it into the shower to be complimented by mosaic tile and natural limestone surrounded by a curved glass chamber, which created a very impressive look. Off the shower area was a sitting area with a flokati rug and stunning chandelier. The woodwork throughout was oak. In the bedrooms and living area, he hung dreamy curtains that were so beautiful people just had to touch them.

The hardware was top quality brass.

Running out of steam, he decided to hire a landscaping firm to remedy the outside and was glad he did, because they not only raked and pruned, they suggested ideas to make the yard stand out.

Mindy spent considerable time checking on Gilbert. Their relationship had grown to the point where he gave her a key to his house so Whiskers was always fed, had a clean box, and had human contact once in a while.

He chuckled when she said, "Whiskers and I are on good terms. I call him Whiskers and he calls me meow."

"So what do you think of the place?" he asked her.

"I'd move into this place in a heartbeat. It's gorgeous. You've done an incredible job once again. You truly have a knack for turning properties others abuse into something special."

"I enjoy doing it. I love the work, and love creating something unique. At least, I think it's unique. Since working with you, they've all sold quickly and for considerable profit. I can't thank you enough for bringing these opportunities to me. I'd be lost without you."

"I feel the same. Should I prepare a listing agreement?"

"By all means, write it up."

Soon after the home hit the market there were multiple bidders. Two people wanted the house so badly that they got into a bidding war, with the winner paying $800,000, which was a record for the subdivision.

Gilbert was so pleased, felt so blessed, felt so humbled that someone would pay a record amount for a home he had renovated, that he gave Mindy a large bonus for handling the sale.

Giselle and Norm were pleased too. They allowed the buyers to assume the $300,000 note as they had excellent credit, plus they put $500,000 down. Then they received a surprise from Gilbert. In appreciation for their allowing him to work on their home, and for the troubles they had experienced with the previous buyer, he sent them a check for $75,000.

When Mindy told the Traders of Gilbert's generosity, a number
mouthed, "What an idiot," only to be surprised when Gilbert
walked in. Expecting to hear about his renovating skills, they
were stunned to hear him say instead, "I know who ripped off the
club!"

While he was renovating the house he felt guilty for not spending
time trying to solve the Trader's problem. Then one day an idea
popped in his head, so he dropped his tools, locked the place up,
and headed home, delighting Whiskers in the process. Feeling
guilty for not spending time with him, he picked him up and
rubbed his back, all the while anxious to put him down so he
could go into his office to check his files.

Fearing calamity, the president said, "I'm calling for a special
board meeting after the marketing session," though he could
have dispensed with the marketing session, as all anyone wanted
to know was who the culprit was.

After the marketing session the president said, "The special
board meeting is called to order."

Every member could attend board meetings, but normally the
only ones who did were the board members. This time it was
different. Everyone stayed. Everyone waited for the
preliminaries to get out of the way so that they could hear Gilbert
identify the thief.

Turning to Gilbert, the president said, "Tell us who it is!"

Before he could speak, a board member spoke up and said,
"First, tell us how you figured it out."

Gilbert stood, faced the group, and said, "I uncovered the responsible party one night when I was reviewing hand-written offers submitted to me by members over the last couple of years. I compared the writing on one of them against the writing on the check, and found an identical match."

Before he could continue on, someone said, "I heard you were fixing up houses and didn't have time for this, because we haven't heard from you for a while. We kinda' forgot about it and now you're bringing it up."

"I needed a break from renovating, plus I had a nagging sense of guilt that I wasn't searching hard enough."

"Enough of this stuff," one said, "Who did it?"

Gilbert pointed at Norm Hickman and said, "He did."

"That's a bald-faced lie," Norm responded, muscles bulging in his neck as he flew red-faced into a rage, which was his norm (what a pun).

Since everyone was afraid of him, there was deadly silence until Lovie Lipscomb came to his aid.

Lovie was a long-time member who knew Norm well, having done a number of transactions with him. Members listened when she said, "He's a long-time member who's done a lot for the club, and further-more, it's not in his nature to rip people off, so surely Gilbert's wrong."

Norm pointed an accusatory finger at Gilbert and threatened, "I'll sue you and the club if these accusations continue."

Since his fury scared the bejeezus out of everyone, one member decided that Gilbert was less of a threat than Norm and made the recommendation that the board check out the allegations before proceeding further.

In spite of the overwhelming evidence, Lovie said to the president, "I recommend the accusations be dismissed, because I think Gilbert has a vendetta against Norm."

By then everyone wanted as far away from the mess as they could get, so a board member made a motion that they do just that, but no one seconded it, so the board meeting just ended instead.

Gilbert showed everyone the signature on the checks and on the offers he'd received from Norm, and they were, indeed, a dead match.

Before long everyone was so confused that many threw their hands in the air and got mad at Gilbert, as it was a helluva lot safer than getting mad at Norm--because Norm wasn't against pounding knobs on their heads and they knew it. There was something about his tattoos, firearms, and snarling attitude that sent a chill down their spines, and no one wanted anything to do with him, though no one was going to tell him to stay away either because that was a sure recipe for disaster.

In most groups there's a noted gadfly, and in the Traders Club, that happened to be Gomer Gibson. Convinced Norm was the victim of undo pressure, he approached him and said, "I believe so strongly you're being railroaded that in the event you don't have ten grand to cover the loss, I'll put the money in for you and you can pay me back down the road."

"You'd do that?"

"To help another Trader out of a jam, of course I would!"

"What a decent, liberal-minded guy."

"I do like to help my fellow man. Anyway, here's a check for $10,000 made out to the club from one of my corporations. No one needs to know but you and me."

At that moment Gilbert walked by, so Norm said to him, "Hey, jerk, Gomer's got a check for you."

Looking at Gomer and then the check, Gilbert said, "You're handing me a check for $10,000 to cover the loss?"

Before Gomer could reply, Norm said, "Yeah, his conscience is bothering him. And here you wanted to blame me. What an asshole. See ya," before walking out the door.

Realizing he'd just been conned out of $10,000, Gomer handed the check to Gilbert. Gilbert knew that he wasn't at fault; nonetheless, for the benefit of the club, he had no choice but to take the money.

Gomer was born with a silver spoon in his mouth but not much common sense. Being out $10,000 wouldn't sit well, but wouldn't break him either, because he had plenty more. What hurt was the realization that he'd be the brunt of jokes for years to come, so he might have to hire an investigator to get the goods on Norm just to prove he was innocent, which might get his money back but might cost him more too. Then he thought, "Ah, what the hell, it'd give me something to do."

Since he didn't need money, he had little reason to generate more, so hung around the Traders for something to do. Watching them conduct business mesmerized him. No sense in venturing into something he knew little about, as he'd have his pocket picked for sure. No, standing on the sidelines was safer. Wealthy, with little to do, he spent much of his time addressing his many ailments. To the medically attuned, he was a hypochondriac, but to those who knew him, he was a guy with bad luck. Get a cold, well, guess who would get one too? Pull a muscle, well you know who would pull one too.

Whatever someone had, he believed he had too, to the point where he was forever going to doctors. If one didn't tell him what he wanted to hear he'd visit another until he found one who did. If a day went by when he wasn't visiting a doctor, he would get sick over it. The Traders learned never to ask him how he was, because they knew that at least ten minutes would be shot listening to him. And when he cornered you to talk about his health, in short order you felt smothered by the guy, because his blood-sucking dependency sapped everything out of you.

Part of the reason Gomer attended the Traders Club was that his wife, Buttercup, insisted on it. She insisted on it because she wanted him out of the home. Their marriage centered on the fact that he had lots of money, which she enjoyed spending. An active supporter of the conservative religious right, she donated heavily to their cause and attended every political event because it sure beat being around home with Gomer, because he drove her nuts with all his ailments. Sending him off to the Traders meetings and his many doctors was the first thing on her agenda every morning. She planned his day. Told him where to go, what time to be there and what to do afterwards.

She kept him on a leash though there was little reason to as his brain was tethered to her anyway. He couldn't wait to get home to tell her over dinner what happened during his day. He didn't tell her he had foolishly signed a $10,000 check to save Norm because she'd berate him if he did, and might even go so far as to tell him to get the money back. Of course, she had no idea what Norm looked like or what he was like because his appearance certainly didn't fit into the conservative religious crowd she hung with, though his attitude did. So to avoid an unnecessary argument, he kept the experience with Norm and the club to himself.

Meals were prepared by their live-in servant, who also cleaned and maintained their 7,000-square-foot home. After supper, Gomer and Buttercup headed to their separate bedroom suites where he got on the Internet to research his many ailments while she closed her door as soon as she could, turned on the TV and called her buddy Suzie Belle to discuss politics and learn the latest gossip. Invariably their conversation turned to what should be done with those unfortunate souls who were unable to make it on their own. Feeling superior because of their wealth, they were convinced that our nation had slipped from one that was proud to one where everyone had their hands out.

Convinced the country was going to hell, they needed to do something, but since the hour was late they'd meet for drinks and lunch at the country club the next day, as the subject was too serious to drop. Hopefully they could come up with some ideas for their Senator, whom they loved dearly. Though he was a lifelong politician, what they loved about him was his staunch conviction that private enterprise needed to create jobs and not government. The fact he was kind of cute didn't hurt either, though they wouldn't admit to being turned on by him because conservative, religious women suppressed those feelings (most of the time).

A couple of days later, Buttercup told Gomer her political group had invited a mortgage broker to speak at their next meeting so they could learn more about the crisis in the mortgage industry.

Looking at her husband, she said, "If you don't have any appointments you're welcome to attend if you like." She didn't tell him she was in charge of getting people to the meeting.

"Well, thank you, dear. One can't learn enough these days. Who's the speaker?"

"Let's see, I've got it written down here someplace…oh, yes. Have you heard of Hadley Evans, III?"

"I don't think I'll attend."

"Why not?" she asked.

With a smile on his face he said, "I've heard his jokes."

Becoming defensive she blurted out, "Well, I don't think the mortgage crisis in our country is a joking matter. The least you can do is come listen to someone who knows what he's talking about." Then she stormed off.

Gomer smiled, thinking, "Hadley will have her thinking of something besides mortgages, that's for sure. For that matter, her fantasy world might be in for a real trip." Then guiltily admitted, "And here I am talking about my wife."

Gomer was an only child. He was pampered, coddled, and protected from day one, with his mother and grandmother being the principal culprits. His father didn't spend much time with him, as he devoted the majority of his time at the bank he owned where he raked in millions. Possessing no athletic skills, one would thought otherwise listening to him talk about the number of football and basketball games he attended, but he spent lavishly on tickets, believing it was a great way to treat clients and prospective clients of the bank. Though the family was very prominent at church, he was not adverse to hiring call girls if that's what it took to land a wealthy client. Business came first in his mind, with image a close second.

Gomer muddled his way through school. He didn't have many close friends and those he had were best described as inadequate and inept. Image was extremely important to the family, so he was always well dressed, active in church activities, and en-couraged to project an image of being genteel. He didn't participate in playground activities or athletics because his mother and grandmother were too afraid he'd be hurt, which fit his wish to a tee anyway. He had no desire to be knocked down or pushed around, so standing on the sidelines suited him just fine.

In the process though, he developed no discernible skills, confidence, or sense of achievement. Part of the reason he wasn't bullied was that his parents could be counted on to pick up the tab for any eat-outs or social activities he was involved with. The fact that they were willing to foot the bill allowed Gomer to escape a bruise or two.

Gomer managed to squeak into college. A nice contribution from his parents made it possible. His goal was to major in finance so he could someday work in his father's bank. To

further his social skills, his parents saw to it that he was
accepted into a religious fraternity, as drinking and carousing
were frowned upon. He struggled academically, but they hired
tutors to help him out, and even to take tests for him, as it was
important that he be viewed as successful.

It didn't take long for Buttercup to analyze what was going on in
Gomer's life. A member of a religious sorority, her group and
Gomer's gathered for religious discussions followed by social
events. After learning that he was an only child and his parents
were very wealthy, she cozied up to him by suggesting that they
study together as they had some of the same courses. Before
long they were spending considerable time in the library. Though
she saw Gomer as an inept clown, she kept reminding herself of
his parent's wealth, reasoning that whoever latched onto him
would lead a comfortable life. Coming from a family that just
squeaked by, connecting up with a wealthy guy had a definite
appeal to her.

At the end of their first year of college, Gomer and Buttercup
returned home for the summer. Each lived in different towns.
Buttercup dated and lived an active social life, while Gomer
moped around like a lovesick puppy, writing her often. They
started their sophomore year spending evenings together in the
library again. Because they spent so much time together,
Buttercup was slowly becoming the dominant person in his life.

In time, he gathered the strength to hold her hand while walking
back to her sorority. The fact that she allowed him to was hugely
rewarding for him. In time, she ratcheted up the interaction by
playing footsy with him in the library. There were times he got
so excited he couldn't concentrate because of it. That often led

to his squeezing her hand a little tighter on the walk home. God forbid he went any further than that because their religious beliefs didn't allow it.

Those religious beliefs didn't stop Buttercup between her sophomore and junior years, though, as she was one active girl. Had Gomer known the degree of her activity, he would have been overcome by feelings of jealousy and embarrassment so it was good he didn't. But Buttercup wasn't going to tell him; that was for sure. Though she was far more attracted to other guys, the one thing that consistently brought her back to him was his family's wealth. Other guys were much better in a lot of ways, but the major drawback they had was they would be working slobs the rest of their lives, while Gomer was destined to live on easy street. And living on easy street had a definite appeal to her.

Their senior year of college found Gomer engaging in activities and reaching levels of excitement he thought not possible, as Buttercup saw to it they went from holding hands to spending weekends in hotels. Though he was terribly burdened by guilt, Buttercup assured him this was the way it was going to be and if they tied the knot, it would get even better. So he saw to it that she got one of the biggest engagement rings possible, as he wasn't interested in changing their current ways. His parents were pleased to know he was engaged to a gal from a religious sorority. After they met her, his father was immediately sucked in as she turned the charm on, while his mother had real concerns as she saw her little boy being taken away by a little hussy.

The wedding was huge. No expense was spared. For their honeymoon, Gomer and Buttercup flew first class to Paris, spent a couple of nights at a luxury hotel, then drove to the French Riviera for a couple of days before heading to Monte

Carlo, where they spent a week before heading to Venice. There they stayed at one of the luxury hotels near St. Marks's Square, as it afforded them the opportunity to listen to the orchestras playing in the square while sitting outside enjoying brunch and evening meals. They took gondola rides, visited the glass factory, shopped at the many expensive stores, and just plain enjoyed themselves.

Buttercup told herself that since this was their honeymoon, Gomer could have his way with her, but that those days would be tapering off once they returned home. Though she was excited about the 4,000 square foot house they would be moving into, so maybe she'd have to rethink cutting Gomer off too soon. In the meantime, she was getting quite a sexual charge spending money, as there seemed to be no limit to the money available to her. She didn't know how many thousands she'd racked up but it was substantial; furthermore, Gomer didn't care. He was happy as a clam knowing that he was allowed to get laid once in a while, and furthermore, pops was picking up the tab anyway. He'd have to go to work in the bank when they returned but he was fine with that, as it would give him something to do.

After leaving Venice, they headed for Salzburg, Austria, as they both loved the movie "The Sound of Music" and knew they could take a tour that included a visit to the church where the wedding was held. They loved Salzburg. They spent a week there, vowing to return. On their drive to Frankfurt to catch their flight home, they discussed what they had seen and experienced on their travels, what they enjoyed and what they hadn't, what they wanted to return to and what they were willing to not see again--both agreeing that touring Europe was special.

A year after going to work for his father, Gomer's father suffered a major heart attack and died, leaving his wife the sole heir. She knew Gomer wasn't capable of running the bank, so put it up for sale and accepted an offer that pocketed her millions. Knowing Gomer wasn't capable of doing much on his own, she gave him two million. A year later she died. The two million paled in comparison to what he picked up next. He'd never have to work a day in his life, nor would Buttercup! She would be able to lead the life she wanted, which pleased her to no end.

A few weeks later the meeting was held and Hadley spoke.

The conservative, religious organization reserved a room at one of the finer hotels in the city: for that matter, it was very upscale, which suited Hadley just fine. He liked hobnobbing with the well-to-do. Dressed in his Giorgio Armani suit with patent leather shoes, he turned heads walking in. Buttercup nearly peed in her pants when she was introduced to him. "Oh, my," she thought, "What a gorgeous man."

Hadley was invited to sit next to her at the head table. There were about a hundred people in attendance. Buttercup had done well. The president started the proceedings by asking everyone to bow their heads and hold hands with their neighbor, as Pastor Robert Schnekel would say a prayer. Holding Hadley's hand, Buttercup didn't hear a word Pastor Schnekel uttered, as her thoughts were not on prayer.

After the meal, the president introduced Hadley, saying he was one of the most successful mortgage brokers in the state, and a good Christian man. Where he got the "good Christian man" part Hadley didn't know, but he didn't care. He'd go with the flow.

Standing to address the crowd, he won them over immediately when he told them the Ronald Reagan story where Reagan stood on a pile of manure and called it the democratic platform. The audience roared. He then followed it with a couple more stories they loved as well before he turned serious.

"You've invited me to address a very serious problem in our country. Mortgage foreclosures have increased dramatically and the government and news media are after the banks and Wall Street because of it. They're casting them as the culprits, whereas, in fact, they're victims as well."

People were so stunned hearing that they looked at each other with their mouths open. They had always been told the banks and Wall Street were the scoundrels behind the mess, and Hadley was saying they might not be.

"The crisis in our mortgage industry is the result of failed liberal policies wherein banks were forced to lower their standards for fear the government would crack down on them. Required to make loans to people who didn't qualify, they set aside good conservative common sense to avoid getting sued." The crowd was on their feet clapping loud and hard. Hadley had told them just what they wanted to hear. The liberals were the cause of the mess, not the banks or Wall Street.

Hadley proceeded to speak for fifteen more minutes, giving examples of how banks made loans to people who shouldn't have received them. In essence saying, "If they had never received loans in the first place, we never would have gotten ourselves into this mess."

Hadley received a standing ovation when he finished.

After his speech, the president said, "Thank you, Hadley, for your very informative presentation. I'm sure that running through the minds of many are questions as to what's going to happen in this country because of all the foreclosures. Can we pose a couple of questions to you?"

"Of course."

A gentleman sitting close to the stage was invited to ask a question.

"Hadley, what's going to happen to the banks that made all those crappy loans they're foreclosing on?"

"Some of the small banks might not survive but the big banks will. Nothing will happen to them."

"What do you mean nothing will happen to them? If they have to take all the underwater mortgages back, they won't survive."

"Sure they will."

"How will they?"

"They're going to bring to the attention of the federal government that their failed social policies are the cause of the problem, therefore the government has a moral responsibility to ensure the banks don't fail."

"But they caused the damn problem. Why should the government be stuck with it?"

"They're on the hook for two reasons. First, as I mentioned, because of their failed social programs; and secondly because the government allowed the banks to become too large. You've heard the statement "too big to fail;" well, the government allowed that to take place."

"But the banks merged and bought up other banks to get larger!" he countered.

"They did, but they could not have done it without the government's permission. The government could have said no, but they didn't, so they're on the hook."

"So what you're saying is that the banks have nothing to lose. They'll come out of this mess smelling like roses. I forget who the president was that said 'watch out for the banks,' but whoever it was I guess he was right?"

Many of the attendees stirred because they didn't like anyone speaking negatively about their beloved banks.

Another hand went up.

"What you're saying is, if a guy owned a small bank, now might be a good time to sell."

Hadley replied, "If you had anything to do with mortgages, I would sure look at it."

The guy said, "Thank you," then walked out the door.

The president said, "We have time for one more question. Yes, sir."

"Hadley, with foreclosures mounting, property values falling, 401 Ks dropping, and the economy in god awful shape, what's going to happen to the middle class?"

"I'm not an economist but I fear the term 'middle class' is a term we'll hear less of in the future. I'll go so far as to say that it's a dying breed. The poor will be taken care of because of good hearted folks like yourselves, but I'm afraid your burden is going to get worse because more folks are falling into poverty every day."

"We can't afford to take on the burden you're talking about. The equity in our homes and other properties dropped 30.9% the past decade, which is worse than during the depression, when it dropped 30%, so what should we do?"

"I have a couple of suggestions. First, require anyone who receives welfare or help from the community to pay it back. They can write a check, sign a note, or perform community service."

"That's a great idea," one said.

"Then I would change the judicial system too. There's absolutely no reason you should have to pick up the tab for someone going to jail or prison. It should be their responsibility. The policy in our country is 'the irresponsible go to prison and the responsible pick up the tab' and that should be changed."

The crowd was on their feet expressing their approval. They loved his ideas. The meeting broke up, but not before many came up to pat him on the back, shake his hand, or thank him for coming. Hadley's ego had never been so massaged.

Buttercup and Suzie Belle waited in the wings while others surrounded Hadley. They were convinced that he should be first in line to replace their beloved Senator, so waited until everyone else had filed out, and then Buttercup approached him with the idea.

"Have you considered running for office?"

"No, I haven't. I've been so involved with running my business, I've never given thought to it."

"We need successful business people to consider public service because some of those in office now have no common sense. These do-gooders and their failed social programs are driving this country into the ground. We need good conservative people like you in there instead."

"I'm quite flattered that you see in me qualities suited for public service. Can I think about it and perhaps call you to discuss this further?"

"Here's my number. I have a private line so you can leave a message if I'm not there."

He held her hand and said, "I'll be in touch with you. By the way, I don't know if anyone's ever told you this, but your name is very feminine." Her knees went weak.

After he left, she turned to Suzie Belle and said, "I could use a drink. If I'm around that man too much, I'm afraid my resistance will wear down."

"Sweetheart, between you and me, I wouldn't offer any resistance. So let's have a double!" Suzie Belle giggled as she grabbed Buttercup's hand and they headed to the bar where they spent the afternoon talking politics, focusing specifically on what it might take to convince Hadley to run for office.

When Gomer got home he was told that "Miss Buttercup" would not be joining him for supper, as she had had a late meal at the club and was awfully tired from her busy day. This upset him slightly, as he was so looking forward to hearing her report about Hadley.

In the morning Gomer dressed and walked to the kitchen for his coffee where he found Buttercup sipping hers.

"Well, good morning, dear. I missed your company at supper last night, though I understand you were wiped out from your active day."

"I was, plus I ate late so I couldn't have gotten another bite down if I had to," she replied.

"So how was your session with Hadley?" he asked.

"It was fantastic! You never told me he's such an attractive man, though you don't have to worry none, but he's down right good-looking. On top of that, we loved what he said about the mortgage crisis. He really knows what he's talking about." She started to show signs of coming alive.

"What did he say that y'all loved?"

"He said liberal policies are behind the crisis, not the banks and Wall Street like we read about all the time in the papers, which just goes to show you can't believe everything you hear on TV or read."

"Hadley said that?"

"Yeah, plus the stories he told were very appropriate for a Christian audience."

"Apparently they were a little milder than the ones he tells at the Trader's meetings."

"I don't know anything about that, I just know we were very impressed with how he conducted himself, to the point that we think he has a calling for public office. And, just so you know, I'm going to explore that option with him."

"You're going to meet with Hadley to discuss his running for public office?"

"Yes, I am. I think he would be a good replacement for our beloved Senator when he retires."

"Bring your chastity belt when you meet with him," he told her.

"Oh, what do you mean by that?" she asked sheepishly. "You don't think I'm attracted to him, do you?"

"That guy's been married two or three times and been in more women's pants in this town than you know," he said mildly, with a rebuking tone.

"Of course, I'm only interested in finding the best replacement I can for our dear Senator. I certainly have no other intentions. You believe me, don't you?"

"Yes, dear, I do." With that, he gave her a peck on the cheek and asked for his agenda for the day. She had it typed out. His first stop was the bank. Looking at his watch he realized it would soon open, so out the door he went.

No sooner was he gone than her phone rang. "I'm sorry, but this isn't whom you were hoping would call, I'm sure."

"Oh, Suzie Belle, what do you want this morning?" Buttercup giggled.

"So, did he call?"

"No, but Gomer warned me to wear my chastity belt if he comes calling," she replied.

"Does he know?"

"What he knows is that I found Hadley attractive, and thought he should be groomed to take over when our dear Senator steps down."

"So he told you to wear a chastity belt if you were going to do the grooming, is that it?"

"I guess so."

"Oh, this is exciting. What about corsets and bloomers?"

"We haven't gotten into that yet."

"Listen dear, I'm getting excited thinking about this. I'm just going to have to hang up and take a nice hot steamy bath. Talk to you later."

Crawling into her tub, Suzie Belle's thoughts strayed from Buttercup and Hadley to a conversation she had had with Scarlett, another old friend, years before. Though she didn't know why the conversation popped into her head, she had no choice but to let the reel run its course.

Suzie Belle didn't have a monetary worry in the world after divorcing her husband of eighteen years. How they stayed to-gether that long was a mystery, but after his third affair, she decided he wasn't going to change, so she got herself a piranha of an attorney and went after the thing that meant the most to him-his money. With millions in the bank and other investments, she had no need to work, so she began hobnobbing with the Christian right, reasoning that the gentleman there were sure to operate by higher standards--only to have that theory shot full of holes one afternoon in the company of Scarlett. Scarlett had been around the block a few times and saw the direction Suzie Belle was headed, so she set a couple of olive-loaded martinis in front of her and said, "Dearie, let me give you some advice."

"Coming from a southern belle like you, Scarlett, I'm open to any suggestion you want to pass on."

"Sweetheart, when you shake hands with some of these boys, and some of the ministers too, you count your fingers after-wards."

"Well, lordy, why do you say that?" Suzie Belle said, a bit taken aback by it.

"Don't ever tell me I didn't warn you!" Scarlett proclaimed.

"You mean to say some of these boys are no different than my ex-husband?"

"They all come equipped, is all I'm going to say."

"It sounds like you're speaking from experience," Suzie Belle said.

Scarlett raised her martini, laughed, and said, "I'll drink to that."

They clinked glasses, then took a big sip.

"Some of these boys are so nice. Surely you're mistaken in referring to them in that manner?"

"Honey, I'm talking to you as a friend. When those boys' hormones kick in, there isn't much that's going to stop them. They get kind of focused on having their way, if you know what I mean. Now God forbid I tell you this, but if it was up to me any male up to the age of twenty-five would be unable to get a lady pregnant, unless they were married of course. I think doctors need to come up with a pill guys would be forced to take that kept the sperm from coming out. That way we wouldn't have any abortion issues and problems like that. Oh lord, I've had too much to drink, please forgive me for rambling on like I am. As you can see, some of my ideas are pretty far out."

"Don't you worry none, and thank you for setting me straight, Scarlett. Though I haven't dated anyone, I have had my eye on a couple, if you know what I mean?"

"Sweetheart, if you've been eyeing them, rest assured they've been eyeing you too. So you be careful when they start inviting you to a prayer meeting because you're liable to end up parked next to a cemetery afterwards. You're not afraid of cemeteries, are you?"

"During the daytime I'm fine with them, but to be parked next to one at night could be down right scary."

"Why do you think they park there?"

"No, you're not serious?" she said.

"Sweetheart, just remember, that equipment is itching to be put to work. So you be careful!" Scarlett advised.

"I'm glad we had this talk, Scarlett. You're a good friend."

"Speaking of being a good friend, I think we've had enough talk and enough to drink so we best be going home before we have too much and get pulled over and find our names in the news."

"I love olives. Wait while I finish them…now we can go," Suzie Belle replied.

And out the door they went.

Why the conversation with Scarlett popped into her head she didn't know, but she'd need to pass it along to Buttercup, as she'd get a kick out of it. Then she decided she might not, because Buttercup might become offended by the notion that good Christian men would take advantage of poor southern girls.

Later in the morning, Buttercup was getting herself put together when the phone rang.

"Buttercup, God, I love that name. This is Hadley."

"Hadley, it's nice of you to call. Have you thought any more about our discussion?"

"I must apologize for my response to your inquiry, but I had never considered political office until you brought it up, so I was caught off-guard."

"Well, I think you would be a natural to step in for our great Senator when he retires."

"God forbid he has no immediate plans to do that because we certainly need his expertise in Washington," Hadley crooned.

"I'm not aware of any impending plans, but the party needs to be grooming someone to step in when he does, and I think you would be ideal for the position."

"I would very much like to discuss it with you. Since the phone is so impersonal, can you recommend a quiet restaurant where we could meet after the lunch crowd leaves?

"I know just the place. Giordano's on Fifth and Maple. Are you free about three?"

"I am," he said.

"I'll see you at three," she responded.

They hung up and she called the maître d' at Giordano's to reserve their back room.

She then called Suzie Belle. "Guess who I'm meeting at three today?"

"The tone in your voice says it all, sweetheart. I don't need to guess. I know who it is."

"He's open to the idea of running for office."

"Sweetheart, if anyone can convince him, you can."

"I'm getting hot and sweaty just thinking about it."

"You better be careful he doesn't take you to another level."

"We're just talking politics today, Suzie Belle, you know me."

"In the event that you can't make the meeting, let me know and I'll substitute for you."

"Stay by your phone tonight and I'll fill you in on how it all goes."

"I'll uncork my wine bottle when you call so we can talk a long time. I can't wait to hear."

At 3 that afternoon, Buttercup arrived to find Hadley waiting. He gave her the kind of warm greeting that nearly caused her knees to buckle. The maître d' then escorted them back to their private room.

Hadley said, "I appreciate your taking the time to meet with me."

"You have no idea what a pleasure it is," she replied.

"Would you care to join me for a drink?"

"A vodka martini about three goes down smooth."

"Good selection, I'll have one too."

He placed their order. After it arrived he offered a toast: "To our mutual success."

"I'll drink to that."

"If you don't mind my asking, your last name is familiar to me."

"You likely know my husband, Gomer."

"I do. He attends the Traders meetings."

"I'm so happy he's involved with that group."

"We really enjoy having him as he's not afraid to step up and help."

"That's good to hear. Now let's talk about what we need to do to convince you to run for public office?"

"I'll need someone who really believes in me to help me get started. Can I rely on you for that?"

The martini was taking affect and she knew she shouldn't have another, but needed something to grab onto, so said, "Can we talk about that over another drink?"

"I was thinking the same thing," he said, then motioned for their waiter.

An hour later he escorted her to her car, gave her a big hug, peck on the cheek, and saw her off.

Things were looking up, he thought. Here he had envisioned being stuck as a mortgage broker. But Senator Evans had a nice ring to it!

Supper was waiting for Buttercup when she got home, though she didn't want to eat or talk to Gomer because she wanted to get a drink and call Suzie Bell, but had no choice as Gomer was anxiously waiting for her to sit down.

"Dear, I hope your day has been better than mine because mine has been horrible," he uttered.

Though she felt like telling him to "stuff it," she didn't have the heart to, so she said, "My god, what happened?"

"My doctor thinks I'm developing hemorrhoids."

"You poor dear, that's terrible! I've heard that soaking in a nice hot bath does wonders for that issue. Perhaps you should forgo supper and do that."

"I think I will. Good night, dear." And then he left.

Buttercup was ecstatic that he took the bait, pushed supper aside, grabbed a bottle from the wine cooler, and headed for her suite to call Suzie Belle, after changing into something comfortable.

Suzie Belle was waiting for her call, though had broken her promise about waiting to open her bottle of wine--for that matter, it was empty, and as such, she was feeling no pain.

Slurring her words, Suzie Belle said, "Tell me the good news."

"Are you sitting down?"

"Oh, my, this sounds exciting. I'm doing better than sitting down. I'm in my recliner with my legs stretched out."

"Well, good, because he said that if he was going to enter the race for the Senate, he would need someone who really believes in him, and wondered if I would be that person, because if I was we would have to spend a lot of time together.

Suzie Belle passed out.

Realizing her buddy was down for the night, she filled the tub with hot water, set her wine glass close by, and crawled into the tub, accompanied by her fantasies.

Chapter 17

Computers need defragmenting and anti-virus systems to clean out viruses and related clutter, while human beings need therapy to sort out emotions and thoughts. Otherwise, the trees get in the way of the forest, which pretty much describes the Traders. Their brains are pretty cluttered, though the one who doesn't pay attention to the psychobabble is Ivan, as he's pretty focused--as most sharks are.

Years earlier, his foray into the drug business convinced him that the drug policies in this country were a welfare system for law enforcement. Legalizing marijuana and other drugs would put many out of business, so to guard against it, they filled the nation with fear of what would happen if drugs were legalized. God forbid people be allowed to use marijuana and other drugs because that would be un-American. No, it was better to keep the public afraid and their paychecks full, letting later generations address the issue in a rational manner, because God forbid the gravy train end on their watch.

Ivan's sojourn in drug trafficking had its headaches, but benefits too, as he was now financially set for life. Putting his money to work now was his goal, though that was frustrating also. Of course, he didn't have to do anything risky; for that matter, unless it was risk-free, he wasn't interested. Borrowing money from Ivan meant giving up control of your assets, which was disastrous at best, as he would make life miserable for you until you paid in full. He was no fun to do business with--for that matter no fun to do anything with--so how Gilbert saw something good in him was mind-boggling, but he did. He believed under his crusty exterior was a decent bloke, so he did his best to treat him well, much to Ivan's chagrin.

"Ivan, I was sorry to see you spend time in jail."

"Go screw yourself, Gilbert. Don't bring that up again. Otherwise, I'll sue you for defamation of character."

"Oh, aren't you being a little hard on me? I'm only trying to be nice."

"Be nice with someone else. I don't need your compliments. People who compliment usually have an ulterior motive like a need for money, and if you think I'm giving you any, you're goofier than a bedbug."

"I'm not after money. I'm after dialogue with someone I admire."

"You're nuts," and with that, Ivan walked off. In spite of his rebuff and abrupt departure, Gilbert wasn't concerned, because he vowed to keep the lines of communication open in spite of Ivan's resistance. Anyone else would have seen that Ivan wanted nothing to do with him, but not Gilbert, the eternal optimist. In his mind there wasn't a house he couldn't renovate and a person he couldn't win over; both just took time.

Gilbert looked at Caller ID on his phone and recognized it was Mindy. Hoping she might have another renovation, he took the call.

"Gilbert, Habitat for Humanity needs a hand. They've promised a home to a family, but the job superintendent and many of the volunteers have come down with the flu, so they asked if I knew anyone who could step in and I thought of you."

"Where's the job site?"

"The corner of Alameda and Western."

"I'm on my way."

A week later the job superintendent returned to a home that was nearly finished. Everyone raved about Gilbert's management skills, determination to get the job done, and his ability to work with people. The fact he paid for a number of upgrades himself didn't hurt either. The couple acquiring the home admired his passion and the hours he had invested in finishing their home.

Though everyone begged him to stay, he said, "Sorry, folks, my agent just called with a fix-up opportunity I need to look at right away. But before I go, I want you to know I've enjoyed my stay. You've been a great group to work with." Looking at the new homeowner he said, "Enjoy your home, young lady."

Picking up Mindy, they drove to the base of the Catalina Mountains where the 4,500 square foot, obviously neglected house sat.

"This baby's been neglected for years," he said. "What's the deal on the owners?"

"Three brothers inherited the house. It belonged to their mother. They were estranged from her, each moved out of town to get away from her, and now they can't decide what to do, though each has strong feelings, which they willingly share. One wants to renovate, one wants to sell "as is," while the third wants to do some cosmetic repairs and turn it into a rental. Did I tell you they're strong-minded and don't want to listen to the others?"

"You're making that quite clear."

"The one who called me went through your last renovation and was really impressed. He said we might be wasting our time but they wanted you to look at the home and make a recommendation as to what it would cost to fix it up."

"I'll do that. Call and set up a time. From the outside, the roof needs replacing, the windows should be changed from single pane to double. Well, anyway, it's going to need considerable work, which isn't going to be cheap. But yeah, set up a time."

When they arrived the next day, waiting for them were three stern-faced guys. It was quite obvious none was having fun. After introducing themselves, the brother who was interested in renovating spoke up.

"Thank you for coming. As you can see, the place needs work. Our mother, in addition to being a pack rat, went through a terrible depression after dad died. None of us could talk to her. We all live out of town and she preferred it that way. As you can see, the place is a dump and very likely has structural problems. One of us thinks if we clean it out and throw some paint on it we can turn it into a rental. One thinks we shouldn't do anything and sell "as is," while I'm of the opinion that we should renovate, or maybe find a renovator we can work with, which is why I called you. I've been through a couple of homes you renovated and I'm really impressed with your work. Now, rather than put you on the spot to see what you think, why don't you walk through and get back to us in a couple of days with an opinion. Would that work for you?"

Gilbert said, "That would work fine." With that they shook hands and handed him the key.

After they left, Mindy looked at him and said, "This place will be a challenge. Even I can see structural problems."

Gilbert responded, "Yes, it will. There's a termite problem too. Mom was a pack rat all right. Looks like she had a family of pack rats living here, see those wires over there? Some animal has been gnawing on them. She has scorpions, black widow spiders and rattlesnakes too. Hear that?"

With that Mindy grabbed on to Gilbert's arm. She hated rattlesnakes. She didn't like scorpions or black widow spiders either. She wanted out of the house, but Gilbert assured her that if they watched their step they would be okay, then added, "Critters need a home too."

Gilbert pulled out a pad to make notes, then said, "Why don't we start at one end and work our way to the other."

Before long he was scribbling away.

She said, "What do you think?"

"The roof needs replacing, and many of the ceilings are water-stained, as are the walls. Many of the adobe blocks are crumbling so they'll need attention. The walls were never insulated so that needs to be done."

"Gilbert, look--a basement."

"They're certainly rare here in the desert. Of course, the reason for it is the caliche in the soil. It's like concrete. The cost to dig it out is huge, so most builders don't bother, and of course most home owners don't want the additional expense either, which is why most homes in Arizona are built on grade."

"Can we peek downstairs?"

"I certainly want to."

As they start walking down the steps, Mindy grabbed Gilbert's arm and said, "What was that rattling noise?"

"I think we both know."

"I hate snakes. I'm going upstairs." He chuckled to himself, as he had never seen her move so quickly.

He didn't go down much farther. It was obvious that there was more than one snake occupying the basement and he had no need to rattle them any more. He jotted on his pad about the adobe walls, exposed ceiling, concrete floors, and twenty years of trash. Finding Mindy walking through the home, she saw him and asked, "Should it be bulldozed?"

"No. Gutted, yes; bulldozed no. Done right it could be a very nice home but it's going to take work. I'll work up an estimate and meet with them in a couple of days. Why don't you sit in when I do as it's possible they'll elect to sell rather than renovate." With that they locked the place up.

Gilbert's computer software allowed him to calculate renovation costs quickly and accurately. Double-checking to make sure he hadn't left anything out, he hit the total key, and $148,000 stared back at him. "Ouch," he thought. Then again, to do it right, which is what they wanted, that's what it would cost. With that he called Mindy. Told her to keep the morning of the fourth open, then called the brothers.

The three brothers were waiting for them. The one he spoke with wanted to know what it was going to cost to renovate over the phone, but Gilbert said he'd prefer sharing that in person.

The brothers knew they were looking at a fairly hefty bill but weren't prepared for $148,000. In spite of the shock, they maintained their composure, though Gilbert sensed they weren't happy, so he explained what needed to be done and why it cost so much. When he finished, they thanked him for his time, said they needed time to digest what he had presented but would get back to him in a week.

Knowing the dollar amount was their biggest concern, Gilbert said, "I've renovated a home like yours. If I could get permission from the owners to show you through, would you be open to looking?"

They looked at each other, figured they didn't have much to lose, so said, "See if you can."

He called the next day to say he'd meet them at nine the next morning at 13439 N. Ventana, giving them directions to get there.

They were awed by the external appearance, then taken away when they saw the inside. Looking at the before pictures, they asked, "Can you really make our home look like this for $148,000?"

"Yes, I can."

One of the brothers looked at Gilbert and said, "Give us a minute to discuss this."

Gilbert approached the homeowners to thank them.

"No problem, Gilbert. We're always eager to show off our home."

"Thank you. If you have any problems of any sort, don't hesitate to call me."

"We don't expect we will, but it's nice to know we can."

Walking back to his truck, he found Mindy waiting with the three brothers.

"We'll do it! We've signed the contract. Here's a check for $25,000 to get started. When can you begin?"

"In the morning."

"We're looking forward to working with you. We hope to not get in the way but while we're still in town we'll be watching and, of course, providing funds as called for in the contract."

They all shook hands and the brothers left. Gilbert promptly ordered two dumpsters, knowing his days were about to get busy. Then again, he loved it that way.

He drove Mindy back to her office. When he dropped her off, she asked, "What are you going to do now?"

"I'm going to introduce myself to the neighbors. I want to tell them what's about to take place, as they'll be full of curiosity when the dumpsters show up."

"Are you going to be there all day?" she asked.

"Just a few hours, I'll be spending enough time there the next few months. Why don't we grab an early supper? I'll tell you what the neighbors say."

"Sounds great, I'll be at the office until five then will head home."

"I'll call you."

Gilbert drove back to the house, parked his truck and found a neighbor standing in his yard looking at the house, so figured that was as good a place to start as any.

Introducing himself, he explained what was about to happen.

"What took them so long? I've been watching the three brothers walk around the place, argue, storm off, and here I thought their mother was strange."

"Did you know her well?"

"No one knew her well. She was a recluse. She didn't have time for anybody, didn't wave, wasn't friendly, and for sure didn't like anyone suggesting her place was a dump. None of the neighbors were happy with the way she allowed her house to deteriorate."

"Well, hopefully those days are over. I'm having two dumpsters delivered in the morning, and a extermination guy show up to remove rattlesnakes from the basement."

"That doesn't surprise me. Over the years we've spotted our share, though lately not many. Guess they went into the basement."

"Possibly, but tomorrow they will be transported out of here."

"Good, say, nice talking with you. Do you mind if I check in once in a while you're working over there?"

"Stop over anytime. I might not talk long but you're welcome to look about."

"I'm retired and don't have much to do, so I'm looking forward to this."

"Are any of your neighbors home?"

"You can try Joe next door. He's kind of grumpy, but you might try him."

"I will." They shook hands and Gilbert headed next door.

The description of Joe was pretty accurate. Gilbert introduced himself, told him what was about to take place, to which Joe replied "I don't want to be bothered."

"Will you do me a favor though?"

"What's that?"

"If you see any people messing around over there, will you call the police?"

"Yeah, I'll do that."

"Thank you. Do you know if any other neighbors are home?"

"I don't pay much attention to them, though I suspect most work, so probably aren't."

"In that case perhaps I'll see them tomorrow. Dumpsters being dropped off at a property have a tendency to bring neighbors out of their houses."

Then it dawned on him that he had forgotten to call the rattlesnake remover, so placed the call.

Early the next morning Gilbert arrived early to start clearing out. Though he preferred doing things himself, removing rattlesnakes was not on his list. While he was standing outside his truck sipping coffee, a truck pulled up with "Critter's" on the side.

"Are you Gilbert?"

"Sure am. You must be Dusty."

"That's me."

"How'd you get that name?"

"When you drive over as many dirt roads as I do dealing with critters, everything gets dusty so the name kinda' stuck."

"What's your real name?"

"Reginald Mc Laughlin the Third. Now you know why I prefer Dusty."

"That I do. Let's talk about the residents inside."

"We're here to do more than talk, but shoot away."

"I don't want them shot! You're not going to shoot them are you?"

"No, of course not, what I'm going to do is gather them up and transport them to the desert. You can come along if you'd like?"

"No, thanks, I don't need to drive along to get dusty."

"Now, since you pay by the varmint, you can count them after they're boxed up if you want."

"Normally I would, but you have a trustworthy face, and furthermore, I don't want anywhere near them."

"That's what most of my customers say. I'm not a wealthy guy because of it."

"Good to hear."

They shook hands and Dusty went to work. Gilbert was tempted to watch him retrieve the slithery varmints, but thought that they might not be happy being removed so decided to stay well enough away.

An hour later Dusty said, "I've got quite a load here. Want to count them?"

Gilbert's business judgment said yes, but the rattling said no, so he went with the no.

"Send me your bill."

"I'll do that."

"Before you go though, I have a question for you?"

"Fire away."

"How did you ever get involved in rounding up rattlesnakes to take out to the desert?"

"No one wanted the job and I couldn't get any others."

"That's as good a reason as any. See ya'."

With that, Dusty and his unhappy friends headed for their new home.

With the house rid of critters and the dumpsters in place, Gilbert started filling them, only to realize it would take two weeks by himself, so broke down and hired two day-laborers, figuring that between the three of them, they'd get the job done in three to four days.

Once the clutter and junk was hauled away, he turned his attention to installing support beams and posts to improve the structure. When that was done he scratched his head and said, "Now what, boss?"

Over the next four months he was a slave to the property. Fifteen hour days, seven days a week was common, but because of it the place was undergoing a remarkable transformation.

The brothers took turns flying in to check on the status of things. All were impressed. They truly believed they had made the right decision in hiring Gilbert. He kept them informed, answered their questions and had time for them when they showed up, which they appreciated. What was amazing about his relationship with them was that in spite of the fact that they were control freaks, they told him they didn't want to be involved in the design process, instead leaving it up to him to "surprise us." And surprise them he did. They were in awe when they saw the finished product, as their home had been converted to a jaw-opening, head-shaking, incredibly gorgeous abode.

The front door entry had been widened, so walking in one immediately sensed openness, followed by a feeling of awe at seeing the natural stone floor abutting walls covered in half-inch drywall sanded to a smooth surface finish, with assorted stone wall coverings. The coffered ceilings and heavy crown moldings stood out, as did the wainscoting. Single pane windows had been replaced with energy efficient double panes that were stained along with the wide casings to compliment the flooring. Draped over the windows were lush, dreamy curtains.

Walking in the kitchen you were impressed with the ceramic tile and stained hardwood cabinets, as they matched perfectly the granite countertops. The kitchen sink was plated nickel as was the hardware. The range, oven, microwave, refrigerator, ice machine, wine cooler, and dishwasher were black and fit in well.

The natural stone flooring in the master bath, and ceramic tiled shower with multiple sprays contained by a glass enclosure looked rich, as did the bedroom itself with its lush carpet, arched moldings, and wainscoting. The guest bath had a special feature: a cast iron tub that contrasted nicely with the ceramic floors. The hardwood vanity with granite top matched well also.

The snake-infested basement had been converted into a comfortable, usable area. One would have never known what it was before.

Gilbert broke down and hired a landscaping firm to spruce up the outside. The brothers' reaction was very positive; they were impressed.

The three brothers approached Gilbert, shook his hand and one said, "We didn't want to spend the money, you know that. But looking at the finished product, I'm sure we'll get it back, plus more. You've done an incredible job."

"Thank you. I've enjoyed it. I also appreciate the opportunity you gave me."

"We wish we had more houses to send you, but we don't. Now all we need to do is find an agent," and he winked at Mindy.

Gilbert said, "She's terrific. She'll treat you well."

And treat them well she did.

They were in love with the house, so listed it a little high, but two weeks after putting it on the market, they received a full-price offer. Each left town with $150,000 in his pocket, which was far more than what they expected considering the condition they found it in when they took over.

Chapter 18

Jumper Gehrig was a plodder. That's how he made it through school and how he handled his day job feeding cattle. Convinced he was going to be a farmer, that changed when some slick old salesman came by and told him, "Boy, you're never going to get ahead feeding cattle, you need a real profession like real estate."

Tired of using a pitchfork, the thought was planted and the match lit, so he plunked down money for an evening real estate course, convinced his journey to wealth was underway. He wanted to be like that smooth-talking, well-dressed salesman. Looking at him decked out in a three-piece suit and fancy shoes, you knew he was successful, and when you listened to him, you were convinced of it. What he was doing in a feed lot he wasn't sure, though he probably owned many of the cattle he was feeding. Nonetheless, the guy looked sharp and talked like a successful dude, and Jumper wanted to be the same.

He poured his heart and energy into learning real estate, often staying up late to review tests he'd taken, as he understood many of the questions would appear on the school's final exam and the state exam. Though he didn't clearly understand many of the concepts, memorization would be his ticket to success. And memorize he did. When questions were asked he knew the answers to, he regurgitated them really quickly, feeling good that he was catching on.

When it came time to take the school's final exam, he was so nervous he could barely concentrate and didn't do well; in fact, he failed. Assured by the instructor that failing was not uncommon, he was advised to get a good's night sleep as he'd likely do better next time. He promptly went home, dug his old tests out to study and spent much of the night doing it, which proved to be a mistake, as he overslept and got hollered at for being late to work.

He muddled through the school's final exam again, passed, and was approved to take the state's. Putting money down to take it, he was determined not to fail as he knew you only had so many chances to pass before they wouldn't allow you to take the test anymore. Many late nights followed, as Jumper was determined to pass--which he did--and on the first try too. Opening the letter from the state and seeing "pass" next to his name was one of the greatest days in his life. Now he just had to find a real estate company to take him on, and when one did, he would give notice at work.

Many of the larger real estate firms passed on Jumper. They couldn't see him fitting in with their more sophisticated clients. But those firms wanted to keep 60% of the commission anyway, so he wasn't overly upset, especially when he learned that there was a way that he could earn 100% of the commission, though had to pay a $300 desk fee each month to do so. Deciding that was the way to go, he signed on with a small company that unfortunately came with no training, plus he had to share a common area with ten other agents. Nonetheless, he was convinced he was on his way to success.

The feed lot was sorry to see him leave, as he was a good worker who handled a pitchfork well--a hard combination to come by, especially since he was willing to scoop stuff from the other end too. But convinced that his days of handling shit were over, Jumper was set to make his mark in real estate, where manure wasn't a daily subject.

Though he was excited to be with his new company, trying to get an appointment with his broker was a challenge because he was seldom in the office, as he owned a furniture company where he spent most of his time. That didn't bother Jumper though, as he picked up ideas from the guys in the pod, so felt he was getting ahead. On top of that, he was learning to use a computer which was something he had no experience with. Things were definitely looking up.

He was told by a number of agents that if you have no clients or limited experience, you needed to either pick up the phone and start calling people, or walk the streets knocking on doors making cold calls. Since he wasn't really good on the phone, he thought he might have better success if he grabbed a bunch of business cards he had paid for and started passing them out. So out the door he went, filled with conviction that success was just around the corner--only to learn many people didn't like having their doorbell rung by real estate salesmen. For that matter, what the cows dropped paled in comparison to the direction some told him to go. Hearing "no" became the norm, to the point where he didn't think a "yes" would ever follow, though the guys at the office said, "The greatest thing about hearing no is that you're that much closer to a yes."

Unconvinced that this was true, the next door he knocked on was answered by a guy who looked like death warmed over. About to make his pitch, he was suddenly face to face with an abrasive, snarling female who told him they didn't need a real estate salesman bothering them. Not sure who she was, she certainly seemed to be in control, so he headed on down the street. Then he decided that he had enough cold calling for the day and headed back to the office, where a few of the agents were discussing going to the Traders Club in the morning. He listened in, then asked, "What's the Traders Club?"

Horace Mann said, "You mean you've never been to the Traders Club?"

"No, I never even knew one existed. What do they do?"

"They trade properties."

"I've never heard of that."

"You ought to attend. You'll get a kick out of them. They're wild. Some will trade anything to make a buck."

"You don't have to be a member to attend?"

"Are you kidding me? Breath and you can attend. Why don't you come as my guest, I'm a member. The meeting's at ten. We'll leave the office at nine-thirty."

"I'll be here. I'm stoked. These guys sound like my kind of people."

"You're in for a treat."

The next morning Horace and Jumper headed for the meeting, with Horace filling him in along the way as to what to expect.

"When we get there, we'll grab a cup of coffee and I'll introduce you to some of the members. When the meeting starts, the President will ask if there are any guests and I'll introduce you."

"Do I have to say or do anything?"

"Whatever you want, though most people wave their hand and sit down to take everything in."

"That's what I'll probably do as I don't feel comfortable talking in front of people."

"Don't worry about it. The president will say a few things then turn it over to the guy who runs the program. That's when the excitement starts."

"What do you mean?"

"Well, if someone puts a value on a property others think is too high, they'll let him know. In some cases, it's like sitting in an AA meeting."

"An AA meeting, what do you mean?"

"Have you ever been to an AA meeting?"

"No."

"You haven't been around at all, have you?"

"Guess not."

"Well, if the presenter gets defensive, he'll likely hear about it."

"What do you mean?"

"Just wait, as the meeting's about to start."

 Jacoby Clausen stood, thanked the president for turning the program over to him, then he addressed the crowd.

"Folks, we have three written packages presenters are anxious to bring before you. Some have been presented before, and I know all of us want to help see that they don't come back again, so please do your part to see to it that the presenter has a clear picture of what he has to take back to his clients. First off is Snuffy Schultz. Tom Clayburn has agreed to lead the discussion, so take it away, Tom."

"Snuffy, you've presented these ten acres before."

"True."

"Have you had any offers?"

"No."

"Why not?"

"I really don't know.  See, it's one of the nicest parcels in the area."

"What are you asking for it?"

"300,000.00"

"Do you think that's a fair price?"

"My client thinks it's under-priced.  We should be asking more."

A hand shot up.

"Yeah, Ivan, what's your question?"

"I don't have a question.  The damn idiots aren't getting any offers because the property's $100,000 over-priced."

Jumper squirmed in his chair.  He wasn't use to that kind of confrontation.

Snuffy hesitantly said, "We don't need your unsolicited opinion, Ivan."

"Opinion my ass! There are two ten-acre parcels like yours that sold for $200,000 each. So why in the God damn hell should we pay $100,000 more for yours?"

"Because my client wants $100,000 more, that's why."

"And you're dumb enough to go along with it, is that it?"

Jumper was really getting excited now.

"If my client wants to ask $100,000 more that's his prerogative," Snuffy shot back.

"Let's hear from the next presenter," Ivan responded. "Snuffy and his client are looking for idiots. We don't have time for this."

Snuffy, caught between his client's wishes, reality, and his desire to earn a commission, grumbled under his breath, though wasn't going to share his thoughts with Ivan because of his nasty nature.

Horace looked over at Jumper and knew he was hooked. He'd be returning. He'd never been around such gruff, aggressive people--even working in the cattle business. They were mellow compared to members of the Traders Club. At the same time, Jumper was thinking, "So this is what it's like going to an AA meeting." Wow. Sitting on the edge of his seat he anxiously looked forward to the next presenter to see if he'd get shot down like the first.

Jacoby Clausen then introduced Butch Winthrop, who owned a seedy motel in a tough part of town. Cindy Blackpool agreed to moderate him. Cindy looked like she could handle a pitchfork and fit in with the cowboys too.

"Butch, tell us about your ten-unit apartment complex."

"I've owned it a couple of years and it's priced right for the area."

"What do you take in each month?"

"Well, my tax return shows $2,000 a month."

"So are these annual rentals, six month, or monthly rentals?"

"Hourly."

"Hourly, what are you renting?  A whore house?"

 Jumper nearly leapt out of his chair upon hearing this.

"Well, there are some special perks to owning these units that I'd be happy to discuss with a prospective buyer."

Cindy, who's as rough and tough as they come, said, "So somebody might not take in a lot of money but if they want to wear their pecker out, you've got the property for them, is that correct?"

 Jumper couldn't wait for the response.

"Well, I wouldn't go that far, but a few of my clients believe in the barter system, so let's leave it at that."

Cindy then said, "Is anybody writing an offer?"  No hands went up so she said, "If anyone wants, Butch will stick around to answer your questions," then sat down.

Jumper turned to Horace and said, "They never said what he's asking for the place."

"Why do you want to know? Are you interested?"

"Well, no, not really; but I was curious what a place like that would go for."

"Go talk to Butch. He might even give you a tour if you're interested. Possibly introduce you to some of his tenants too."

Jumper was toying with the idea of talking to Butch until a suave-looking dude stood and said, "While Jacoby's lining up the next package, let me tell you guys a story."

Only to have everyone bust out laughing seeing him wearing a red unisex union suit (long johns) that he had changed into. He had taken off the black western sport coat and tan pants, but kept the black cowboy hat and black cowboy boots he wore walking in. Folks roared seeing him dressed as he was. What a character! Then he told his first joke and they laughed even louder, only to have him reel off three more stories that were equally good. Everyone was in stitches.

Jumper was impressed with Hadley Evans III, because he sure could tell a good story. Everyone loved his stories except Windy, who was offended to the point that he stood, looked at Hadley, and said, "You're insulting my mother. God have mercy on you," then stormed out.

"What brought that on?" Mark Ramiriz said to his buddy, Joe Castro.

"Don't pay any attention to him. It's just Windy being Windy."

"Probably so, but the jokes weren't that bad, were they?"

"Let's just say, except for the women in this club, he's not going to tell those jokes to a lot of women's groups, because if he did, they'd likely remove those hangy thingies guys are so proud of."

"You think?"

"I'm quite confident he'd leave their meeting without a couple of jewels."

"So maybe Windy's not so nutty after all."

"I wouldn't go that far."


Jacoby Clausen then said, "Folks, I said there were three packages, but the third one withdrew his after pulling a muscle laughing so hard at Hadley's stories. Nice going, Hadley!"

"I've got more."

"No, we need to get some inventory out for people to consider. Does anyone have anything to pass on that the club might have interest in?"

An old codger raised his hand.

"What have you got for us?"

"I used to be a member years ago, and when I was, I had a client with a five point six acre parcel in Benson."

"Arizona, right?"

"Right. Anyway, the five point six acres was divided into two pretty equal parcels with one next to a grocery store. Everyone scoffed at the $190,000 appraisal we had, and no one would make offers. Finally my listing expired, the owner kept it off the market, a couple of years passed, then he called to say he had an offer of $100,000 for one parcel and wanted my opinion. I figured he was halfway home so recommended he take it, which he did.

That left the parcel by the grocery store. Anyway, he called a year later to say he was in escrow on that parcel, turns out a company was buying the grocery store and needed access for their trucks, so they asked him what he thought his two point six acre parcel was worth and he said $350,000. They told him that sounded fair and struck a deal."

Ivan leaped out of his chair and said, "I was going to trade for those parcels but didn't because I didn't think they were worth it. You mean he ended up getting $450,000 for them?"

"He sure did!"

"Damn, that money could have been mine!" He stormed out the door.

 Jumper turned to Horace and asked what it took to become a member.

"The ability to breath and $65.00."

Convinced he could handle that, he sought out the secretary of the club to sign up. He liked the Traders Club. They were his kind of people.

The president took control of the meeting and asked, "Before we call it a day, does anyone have anything they want to bring up that the Club might have an interest in?"

Mark Ramirez raised his hand.

"Yeah, Mark, what do you have?"

"We need more inventory because we're hearing the same properties week in and week out. Let's open our meetings to non-licensed owners!"

"No way!" Horace Stoneman barked out. "We don't want non-licensed owners attending."

"Why not?" asked Mark, "What are we afraid of?"

"They'll realize they don't need us," Horace replied.

"They don't need us; that's the thing! At the same time, they've got a problem. They want to dispose of their property, and would like to do so without paying a commission. "

"So how do we benefit if we don't receive a commission?"

"By trading properties we no longer want or need. Plus, it's possible they have problems we can see solutions to. So by acquiring their property, we benefit."

"Yeah, but I don't like the idea of not getting a commission."

"So who needs a commission if you're getting a good deal on the property?"

"It's the principal of the whole thing. Agents are supposed to get commissions."

"If you're getting a good deal on a property without receiving a commission, would you not do the deal?"

"Well, I might, but I'm still against the idea of these owners not paying a commission," Horace said.

Mark realized he was getting nowhere, when Windy came to Horace's defense. "What guarantee do we have that some of these owners aren't nuts or psychopaths?"

"We don't have a guarantee, but can you guarantee our members aren't nuts or psychopathic?"

"Well, maybe some are," Windy said, then sat down, as the topic was getting a little too close to home.

The president spoke up and said, "Maybe we need to put this issue on hold for awhile, as it's obvious we have strong feelings on both sides."

By then Mark had given up on the idea that the group would change their policy.

"Does anyone have anything else they want to bring up?"

Joe Castro said; "Hey, listen, the people at the real estate association are telling agents to stay away from us. Apparently some agents got their pockets picked and were none too happy, so started bad-mouthing us. The association checked and determined nothing was done illegally, then concluded the agents just got outsmarted. So to avoid future conflicts, they're telling agents to stay away. Apparently the agents relied on what they were told rather than doing their own investigation."

One of the older members spoke up and said, "Over the years we've dealt with this issue more than once. What we've done in the past is make a 'peace offering.' We've put on free educational seminars about trading. The MLS folks like free things. Usually some of our guys are trained to put on courses, so we've sent them over to sooth their ruffled feathers.

"Should we do the same thing?" another asked.

"We can't," another spoke up.

"Why not?"

"We don't have anyone to teach a course. The guys who were qualified dropped out."

"Why'd they drop out?"

"They weren't making any money. Of course, both preferred being liked by their clients over doing deals, so it was bound to happen."

Jumper turned to Horace and said, "Wow, is it always like this here?"

"You never know what to expect walking through the doors of the Traders Club."

"I can't wait to come back," Jumper offered.

Horace looked at him and said, "Welcome to the Traders Club!"

A week later Jumper attended the next meeting and once again was not disappointed. One of the reasons for his attending, though, was to speak with Hadley. After the meeting he waited for Hadley to clear his social calendar, then approached him.

"Hadley, you got a minute?"

"For you my friend, of course."

"We haven't met, but my name is Jumper Gehrig."

"Glad to meet you. I've seen you here but haven't had a chance to introduce myself."

"I like your jokes!"

"Thanks."

"Listen, I haven't had a chance to talk with my broker and you're a sharp guy so I thought I'd run this situation by you."

"Let's see if I can help."

"I came across a guy in his eighties who lost his wife, has nearly depleted his savings, and is struggling to keep his house. On top of that, he's got cancer, six months to live, no heirs, and is considering flying to Switzerland to be put to sleep. The poor guy needs help and I don't know how to help him."

"He does need help."

"He's holding off doing anything until he decides what to do with his house."

"What did you advise him to do?"

"I don't know what to do!"

"Do you have a passport?"

"No, never needed one," Jumper replied.

"I've dealt with problems like this before. I can help him. Give me his name and address and I'll make sure he knows I got it from you. I'll give him a hand."

"You'll do that?"

"His situation is very complicated and he's obviously under tremendous stress, so I'll offer to handle his estate, and if I end up with the house, I'll see to it that you get the listing. And if he insists on going to Switzerland, I'll even take him there."

"You'll go that far?"

"To help him, sure; it's a good feeling knowing we're helping someone, and you're helping him by doing this."

Relieved that he might have found a solution to the old guy's problems, Jumper said, "I'll get you the information."

After bidding him farewell, Hadley walked out the door absolutely giddy. The kid's an idiot, of course, but because he is, he was being presented with a golden opportunity."

Jumper called later to say he had spoken with Hans Brewer, the older gentlemen, and got permission for Hadley to stop by. Hadley thanked him, then told him again he was doing the right thing. After hanging up he got in his car to meet Mr. Brewer.

Hans Brewer was sitting in his recliner looking like a guy with one foot in the grave. Over the next hour, Hans poured out his soul, telling Hadley that he didn't know what to do because of his dire situation, adding that he had spoken with an attorney but didn't like him so never went back. Hadley assured him he could help even though he wasn't an attorney.

The more Hans talked and listened, the better he felt. When Hadley learned he wasn't eating properly, he called Meals on Wheels and arranged for food to be delivered, then contacted Han's doctor to get a nurse practitioner to stop by. Hans was relieved. In short order, Hadley was working his way into his life.

Over the next two months, Hadley spent considerable time consoling, advising, and helping in any way he could. Han's condition deteriorated to the point where he gave Hadley Power of Attorney to handle his estate.

Experiencing extreme pain, he knew more medication wasn't going to get him better, so he decided to hasten his demise by flying to Switzerland to be put to sleep. Hadley made the arrangements and went along at Han's request.

On the flight home, he upgraded to business class, since Hans was paying for it. Of course, making the decision easier was the fact that Hans signed over the deed to his home before taking his last breath. After a couple of drinks, his mind was working overtime. He wondered if there might be more folks like Hans Brewer who needed help making life-ending decisions.

One way to find out would be to get in good with the insurance companies or, if they wouldn't help, maybe some of the payable clerks would, because at the end of life is when seniors rack up the most medical expenses. The insurance companies might be willing to give him names of those racking up the biggest bills in the hope he might get them to move that final act up, thereby saving them money. Perhaps they'd even give him a percentage of what they saved. He'd certainly have to broach that idea with them. If the payable clerks gave him leads, he might slip them a few bucks so they'd supply him with even more leads.

Another idea would be to develop a tear-jerking infomercial to talk about how hard it was to take his good friend Hans Brewer to Switzerland, but how wonderful it was to see his suffering come to an end. Retirement communities and clubs for seniors might invite him to speak, which could be a terrific source of leads. Since he had flown one friend to Switzerland he knew the hurdles, so could be an invaluable aid to others. And since many were filled with fear of facing their demise, he might be just what they needed.

About this time the stewardess came by to see if he wanted another drink.

"Oh, yes, it's doing wonders for my mind."

"Glad to see you're enjoying your flight."

"My mind's at its creative best thanks to your superb beverages and service."

When she returned with his drink, he returned to fantasizing. He would point out the need for two things: a letter from your doc saying you have six months to live, and a passport. The more he thought about the possibilities, the more excited he became. Living in the retirement mecca of Arizona was ideal for such a program. The majority of folks he'd give cursory information to, but it was folks like Hans Brewer he'd invest time in. He finished his drink, turned his seat into a bed, and pulled his blanket up to mull the idea over, only to fall asleep.

A month later he listed the old man's house with Jumper Gehrig.

Norm Hickman approached Hadley after Jumper began pitching the house.

"How'd you get the house that idiot's pitching for you?"

"Some old guy appreciated the help I gave him and deeded it over to me."

"You aren't known for bending over backwards to help others, so there's more to it, I'm sure."

"He was in a tough spot and I came through for him. There's not much more than that, but I wanted to discuss an idea with you to see what you think, maybe you want to get in on it."

"So what's the deal?"

"On the flight back I was thinking there might be a lot of people in bad shape who want to go to Switzerland to be put to sleep."

"So that's what you did, took some guy to Switzerland?"

"He had no one else."

"So he gave you his house for doing it. Unbelievable!"

"I think there are a lot more people like him. Maybe the insurance companies will tell us who they are. Want to get involved?"

"Possibly, let's get together," Norm replied.

"Oh, yeah, there's one more thing you need to be aware of."

"What's that?"

"Something new has come up."

"I'm waiting!"

"I'm being recruited to run for the Senate."

"You're shitting me!" Norm responded, totally flabbergasted by the possibility.

"No, it's true, Gomer's wife thinks I'd be a good candidate," he responded, a little miffed that Norm didn't see it that way.

"Who in the hell would vote for you?" Norm responded.

"You should have seen the reaction I got when I spoke to the conservative, religious group. They loved me."

"Have they vetted you yet?" Norm asked.

"What do you mean?"

"Have they run a background check?" he asked.

"We're just in the preliminary stages. We haven't gotten that far yet."

"Enjoy the preliminaries and whatever it leads to, my friend, because when they start checking you out you aren't going to be their candidate!" Norm exclaimed quite strongly.

"I kind of like the direction things are going though so maybe I'll milk it as long as I can," Hadley replied.

"Yeah, milk it but don't give up on this Switzerland idea because it's got potential…Senator Evans. I don't believe it! Hey, listen, I'm out of here."

 Jumper Gehrig tried his best to sell or trade Hadley's house, but got nowhere, as every trade offer he brought Hadley was rejected, plus he refused to submit a counter. The few cash offers they received were low, and the buyers weren't willing to offer more as the market was still terrible.

In spite of that, Jumper's spirits were good though wearing down, as he was struggling financially. What few reserves he had were dwindling, so pinching pennies took on a whole new meaning. A number of traders tried to urge him to have Hadley counter their offer, but Hadley would have no part of it as he had what they wanted--a free and clear house.

Jumper grew to find dealing with Hadley maddening, as he was so inflexible. It was his way or else. Determined to put a deal together, he put a lot of time into maintaining the house so that it would show well. Of course, Hadley never paid him for this, though he told him he was doing a good job and to keep it up. Instead of maintaining the property, he should have been out knocking on doors getting new listings, but he reasoned a "bird in the hand" was better, or something like that. All his energy went into keeping the house crystal clear, per his belief that it was better to sell one listing than acquire more. Unfortunately, he spent so much time and energy working on the house, he grew to hate the place.

Agents making offers quickly realized Jumper had absolutely no control over Hadley, which frustrated them to no end. Their clients wanted the house, but they had to make sure they didn't offer too much. Hadley knew that, which is why he didn't budge, typical of the proverbial "who's going to blink first" mentality. Hadley was going to hold out until he got exactly what he wanted, not taking a penny less. Hans Brewer deserved that. Well, actually, Hadley didn't care about Hans, just the house Hans had deeded over to him.

A day after a Traders meeting, Hadley ran into Norm and asked, "We missed you at the Traders meeting yesterday, where were you?"

"I ran into a haboob in Phoenix."

"You dirty old man."

"It's not what you think. Have you ever been in one?"

"No, what is it? I've never heard it. Is it an Indian term?"

"No, Arabic. Apparently they're common in Saudi Arabia. Didn't you watch the news last night?"

"No, afraid I missed it. Why?"

"Phoenix was blanketed with a massive dust storm that rose ten thousand feet in the air and covered a fifty mile area, causing the airport to shut down and cars to pull over because drivers couldn't see, even on the highway. And if you were outside you had to cover your mouth and nose for fear dust would get in your lungs. It was just plain nasty. Strong winds toppled trees and power poles, so I got myself a hotel room and spent the night. What did I miss at the meeting, anything?"

"Nah, Jumper presented my property again but didn't come up with any decent offers. Everybody wants to steal the place anyway. I don't have to give it away. I'll wait until I get a decent offer."

"Hey, listen, I've got a pot load of things going on so might not be around for a while, but I'll be in touch. See ya'."

A month later Norm approached Hadley and said, "I've been thinking about your idea of contacting insurance companies to get leads on old folks with one foot in the grave."

"Yeah, what do you think?"

"I'm not sure I want to get involved."

"Why not? Don't you see potential?"

"I think it's possible you'll find some, but you'll have a hard time duplicating what you pulled off with this Hans character. Aren't you doing well pedaling mortgages, anyway?"

"I am."

"Why don't you just stick with that?"

"I'm always looking for opportunities, you know that."

"What you might do in that case, if you don't want to do it yourself, is sell the idea to someone, and in your agreement stipulate that you get a kickback besides the up-front fee."

"Good idea."

"And if you pull it off, you owe me."

"How much?"

"A third."

"You're as bad as the attorneys."

"Thank you. See, I almost became one."

"You're kidding me."

"No, my mother wanted me to become one, then I started rebelling against my asshole old man. "

"You weren't the first kid to do that and won't be the last."

"Thank you, Doctor."

"Go screw yourself.  So how did you act out?"

"My old man hated tattoos, so I loaded my body with them.  It was my way of showing him 'I could care less what he thought.'"

"Did he get the message?"

"Our relationship really went to hell from there to the point where he wants nothing to do with me now, which I'm fine with, though I might call the asshole and suggest he go to Switzerland.  That would get a rise out of him."

"Is he dying?"

"I don't know and I don't care."

"Oh, you do have resentment."

"Lots of it.  For that matter, talking about it pisses me off."

"So what did your old man do that caused you to hate him so much?"

"If things didn't go his way at work he'd stop by a bar on the way home, get drunk, then beat the crap out of us when he got home.  Why my mother stayed with him I don't know, 'cause you never knew what to expect from him, especially when he was drunk, and when he was he was a nasty drunk with a foul disposition.  We were all afraid of him."

"Did you ever get along with him?"

"For as long as I can remember, no. I was always afraid of him. He hit me so hard once he broke my nose, then threatened to break it again if I said anything at the emergency room they took me to. He told my mother and me to say I accidentally fell while riding my bike, and if we didn't, and the police or child protective services came to our door to question him, he'd beat my mother and me after they left.

"I saw him more than once towering over her with clenched fists. I couldn't do anything to protect her, but I'd get so angry watching this that I'd go to school hoping someone would say something so I could start a fight. And I started a lot. I was thrown out of a number of schools because of it."

"So how did you escape his wrath?"

"I stayed away from home as much as I could. You won't guess in a million years where I hung out."

"Alright, I give. Where did you hang out?"

"The public library! I could find peace and quiet there. And when I was there, I read. And because I did, school started coming easier to me. My grades started improving, but that didn't make any difference to my old man, he was still an asshole."

"So did you ever figure out why he was so angry?"

"His old man used to beat him all the time so I guess he figured that's the way you raise kids. I don't know? I'm no friggin' psychologist. I just know I didn't like getting knocked around that way. So I decided if there was going to be any knocking around, I was going to be the one doing the knocking.

"The jerk was a crook too. He'd steal anything. Hell, he stole the money from my piggy bank once because he needed beer money. I had to steal from someone else to get it back, other wise the money would have been gone forever because he'd never have admitted he stole it."

"So how did you get away from him?"

"After one of the fights I got in at high school, the football coach approached me. Guess he figured I needed an outlet for my anger. Anyway, it worked, because I was one nasty lineman, to the point where I received a scholarship to college and did okay until I was kicked off the team because I was thrown in jail and was on the news for beating the crap out of my old man. I came home, found him standing over my mother in a drunken state, so I nailed the son-of-a- bitch and the row was on. My mother called the police because she was afraid we were going to kill each other. When the police arrived he told them I was at fault because 'no son of his was having a tattoo' and I had just had one put on.

"So then I decided, 'Okay asshole, if that's what it takes to get under your craw, guess what I'm going to do?' And I've piled them on ever since. So the old man going to Switzerland for an injection or whatever they give them could be just what the country needs. It could start a trend. Rather than vegetating in a nursing home, we could start a national movement--' go to Switzerland, get it over with.' Maybe we should contact the insurance companies after all. Perhaps you're onto something."

"Think about it. The population's getting older, health care costs are rising, most expenses come at the end of life, and insurance companies are looking for ways to improve their bottom line. What better way to reduce their costs than by partnering with us? They give us the names of people standing on a slippery banana peel, and we see to it they're informed of the benefits of going to Switzerland. "

"I can see where you're going with this."

"We'll just need to hire a company to put together a gut wrenching infomercial about moving the inevitable up to reduce pain and suffering. Of course, there would be no ties to the insurance company. All they'd have to do is provide the leads."

"So, what do you want me to do?"

"Bankroll the operation."

"Before I toss any money into making infomercials, though, I want a well thought-out marketing plan for contacting insurance companies and pitching seniors."

"We can do that. I might suggest you let me contact the insurance companies, though, when we get around to it."

"Why's that?"

"Have you looked in a mirror lately? If you walk into a large insurance company, you don't see many people walking around sporting a body full of tattoos. You might stand out."

"Let me think about this more, but before I go, what's the latest on your Senate plans?"

"I'm getting together with Buttercup to talk about it more," Hadley replied.

"Buttercup, who in the hell is Buttercup?" Norm asked.

"Gomer's wife."

"You're kidding me!  Buttercup and Gomer--what a picture that presents!  Is she with him because she's in it for the money?  Why in the world would she be with that ding-dong if it weren't for the money?  The guy's a walking ailment."

"We don't talk about him. I don't know!"

"So what do you talk about?"

"Her belief that I have a future in politics."

"And you're just feeding her a line, aren't you?"

"The thought never crossed my mind!"

"I'm sure it hasn't.  See you later."

Chapter 19

Ivan was a master at extracting concessions.  Crying foul at the slightest challenge to his unreasonableness, he charged others with trying to take advantage of him when, in fact, it was he who was trying to take advantage of them. And unless he got his way, he made it so uncomfortable that people often threw their hands in the air and gave him what he wanted just to get away from him. Crying foul, threatening lawsuits, and being a downright bully were all part of his shtick.

Anyone borrowing money from him knew to pay it back on time; otherwise there were Draconian penalties built in. Grace period, forget it!  A minute late and you'd wish you'd paid days in advance. On top of that, the financial cost paled in comparison to the phone calls that sent chills down the listener's spine, as he had a unique way of getting to people where it mattered the most. He threatened to become their worst nightmare. No one was spared in his attempt to recover his money. Once you borrowed money from him, you were convinced that "once was enough."

His biggest challenge was finding people dumb enough to borrow money from him. If not dumb enough, then in enough of a need that they'd come to him for funds. His quest was soon to be answered.

Gilbert answered the phone and it was Mindy. She was very excited.

"I've come across three fix-up opportunities you can make a bundle on. "

"When can I see them?"

"All have been trashed, and all are million-dollar homes the sellers desperately want to unload as they need cash."

"This sounds too good to be true. Let's look at them now."

"Meet me at my office in a half an hour and we'll go from there."

"I'm out the door."

She drove while he reviewed comparable sales data in the neighborhood for each home. The more he read, the more excited he became.

Mindy said, "It was stroke of luck I got the leads, as I've been running ads in search of fix-ups for weeks with no calls, then to have three come in one day, it's just amazing!"

"So you've spoken with each owner?"

"Yes, and in each case they had turned their home into a rental because the market was so bad, but now regret doing it because the results have been disastrous. They're desperate to unload them. Each has given us a day to eyeball the outside and arrange a time to see the inside. Otherwise they're contacting other renovators."

Gilbert liked all three opportunities, so Mindy contacted the owners to arrange a time to meet them to walk through. Each had his own brand of woes, though the bottom line was that the tenants had decided the homes would bear the brunt of their anger, even though neither the landlords nor the homes were at fault.

One relayed that his tenant was caught stealing money from the company he handled the books for.

"When I confronted him with what I had read in the paper, he and his attorney convinced us that he was set up and just needed time to prove it. He also convinced the judge of that, so was let out of jail. While all this was going on, he fell behind on his rent, so when I told him he needed to bring it current plus pay a late fee, he was furious. The next thing I know, he's destroyed the house. I'll never recoup my money. I just want out!"

The second had a different sad story.

He relayed, "Our tenant was furious when we found out he was running a high-end whorehouse, and demanded he stop it, but when he didn't, we sent him an eviction notice to show how strongly we felt. So what does he do? He retaliates by busting the place up. Just look at what he's done! My God, he's destroyed all that we've worked for."

The third's saga was equally telling.

"We rented the home to a foreign couple who seemed decent enough, plus their credit was okay, but what we didn't know is that she was from an overprotective family. When they learned that he didn't own the house as he had proclaimed--even worse, had been cheating on her--they decided to ruin his reputation and the house too. As you can see, they tore the place apart, apparently thinking they were getting back at him. How insane. He didn't own it. Now we're stuck. Insurance won't cover anywhere near what it will cost to fix it and our attorney has said going after the tenants is a waste of time. We're just sick. Make us an offer."

All three said they called Mindy because they had heard that her client was a fair-minded guy who worked miracles--and they all needed one.

Gilbert liked all three opportunities but didn't have three million bucks in his back pocket, plus the funds needed to renovate the homes, so was in a bind. Then, when two of the owners threatened to call other renovators, Gilbert made a huge mistake. He called Ivan.

Had he called Hadley Evans III, he would have been further ahead, but he had this screwed-up notion that he could turn Ivan into a friend by borrowing money from him. Was he in for a surprise!

"Ivan, this is Gilbert."

"How'd you get my number?"

"It wasn't easy. Listen, I need to borrow three and a half million."

"Secured by what?"

"Three houses needing renovation."

"Are you nuts? Even if they were in excellent condition, I wouldn't lend you the money."

"I'll pay you top dollar. I can renovate these homes. You'll be making a terrific investment."

"I shouldn't even bother talking to you, but give me the addresses of the property, write up a business plan for what you intend to do with each one, how much it will cost to renovate and what you'll sell them for, then send it to me. My terms are tough, I'll tell you now, and don't screw with me in any way, otherwise I'll make your life miserable."

"I'll get back to you with the addresses and the rest. You won't regret this." With that Gilbert hung up, happy that Ivan had even talked to him. He'd win him over, he was convinced of that.

Ivan drove by the properties, drove through the neighborhoods, concluded Gilbert was buying them right, which meant any money he lent was very secure. Nonetheless, he intended to put the screws to him.

After Gilbert completed the detailed business plan, Ivan reviewed it then laid out his terms. Any sane person would have said, "Forget it. I'll get my money elsewhere," but Gilbert didn't question a thing, didn't read the agreement—instead, just signed it. Which convinced Ivan that he was dealing with an idiot, but his money was so rock solid secure that he handed him the check. Gilbert smiled, shook his hand, and promised he wouldn't regret lending him the money.

Gilbert didn't know Ivan was going to stop by the job sites or call him daily to check on the security of his money. Being allowed to do so was in the contract, as was the stipulation that Gilbert's retirement check would be automatically deposited in Ivan's account on the twentieth of the month, with the loan payment due the nineteenth. This meant that Gilbert was automatically saddled with a $300 a monthly late fee--all in the fine print Gilbert neglected to read.

Gilbert purchased all three properties, keeping $500,000 of the three point five million as working capital, then dove into the renovations. Renovating three properties at one time soon overwhelmed him, as there weren't enough hours in the day. Plus, Ivan was there daily to remind him of his financial obligation. Finding his presence suffocating, Gilbert started avoiding him, but that didn't work because Ivan always found him.

And he found him because, in the fine print of the contract, Ivan was allowed to put tracking devices on his vehicles and home. So everywhere Gilbert went, Ivan knew. Finally one day, Gilbert got fed up, sat down, and read the contract--then realized that Ivan was right, he didn't like the terms at all. Ivan had told him he wouldn't, but he was so tuned into winning him over that he had never read the contract, let alone the fine print.

Mindy found herself worrying that Gilbert's work-aholic ways would do him in, so she dropped in often to check on him. Knowing that he didn't take time off to eat, she surprised him occasionally by bringing food, which he appreciated and often badly needed. He got so focused on what he was doing, and had such tunnel vision, that meeting his basic needs became secondary, and Mindy saw this. She tried to suppress the festering need to nurture him, reasoning that he was a big boy who could take care of himself, but sometimes the worry became so great, she just had to check on him.

And though he told her that she needn't bother, he grew to like having her stop by--for that matter, looked forward to it. Mindy had another reason for stopping by. She saw his decline in productivity and change of attitude, so suggested one day that they go out for lunch. Leaving his truck at the job site, they jumped in her car and headed to a restaurant that she knew offered quiet and privacy.

After ordering, she said, "Gilbert, you're not yourself. Something's bothering you, what is it?"

"It's Ivan. The guys driving me nuts! I can't go anywhere or do anything without him knowing about it. He told me I wouldn't like the fine print, but I thought I could work with him, but I was wrong. Finally I read the fine print. I'm an idiot! I gave him permission to bug my vehicles, home, harass me on the job--you name it. I can't go anywhere without him knowing it. On top of that, he shows up daily. I become so distracted that I can't concentrate, to the point where I'm getting little done. I'm so far behind and so distracted that if I don't get myself turned around, I'm at risk of losing all three properties to him, which would be an incredible financial setback, but at the moment I don't care. I just need to get away from him!"

"I'm sorry I didn't preview the contract before you signed with him. I would have spotted some of the pitfalls you're talking about."

"I should have had you review it, but I thought that by not checking closely, I might win him over."

"What do you have to win him over for?"

"I don't know, but some part of my mind wanted a closer relationship with him."

"I'm not able to delve into that, though I suggest we find another lender."

"I'd love to do that but unfortunately I'm locked in."

"What do you mean you're 'locked in?' "

"If I pay him off early, there's such a huge penalty that I'd make very little money on all three homes. In essence, I'd work for nothing."

"You need an attorney to review the contract."

"We can't let Ivan know that, because in the fine print, he has the right to sue me if I do."

"Get me the contract. I'll review it and talk with an attorney friend of mine to get her thoughts. Maybe we can get you out of this mess somehow."

Hearing these words brightened his spirits. The food arrived. He'd never been hungrier. He devoured his meal and left the restaurant feeling much better.

Shortly after Mindy dropped him off, Ivan showed.

"Where have you been? I've been trying to get ahold of you for the last hour and a half. You didn't have permission to be off the job site that long."

"I didn't know I needed your permission to go to lunch."

"Read the contract, you idiot. It's in there. I want to make sure my investments are protected. I want to know where you're at and what you're doing at all times."

"Why are you so difficult to deal with?"

"I'm not your friend, jerk, and I don't want to be your friend. I want to protect my money and get a great return on it. You've known that from the start."

"Yeah, but I thought you could be somewhat reasonable. As it is, you're impossible to deal with."

"I'm devastated to hear that. Why don't you get your ass back to work instead of feeling sorry for yourself, and oh, by the way if you're five minutes late getting me my payment there's a penalty you'll be required to pay."

Gilbert was shaking when Ivan left. Adding to his fury was the fact that Ivan was laughing at him as he walked out the door.

He found concentrating almost impossible, so returning to work was a real challenge. He found himself making simple mistakes that cost him time and money. The hole he was digging in was getting bigger, so he called Mindy.

"Did you call the attorney?"

"I did. She says she can you get out of the contract."

"Good, what's her name?"

"Sylvia Goldsmith."

"There was a Sylvia Goldsmith with the ACLU a few months back. I spoke with her. She was sharp."

"That's her. She's now on her own."

"Yeah, I'd love to talk with her."

"Goldsmith and Associates, this is Sylvia."

"Sylvia, this is Gilbert, we spoke a few months back?"

"I remember. Did you get that issue resolved?"

"Thanks to you I did."

"Good. As you can see, I've started my own practice."

"How's business?"

"It takes a while to build up, but I'm in it for the long haul."

"I need your help. I borrowed money and didn't read the fine print. It contains penalties and a level of control that I can't deal with. The guy I'm paying the money to is driving me nuts, and I'd like you to get me out of the contract. Can you look at it for me?

"Of course, when can you bring it by? Just so you know, Mindy filled me in on your concerns."

"I have to be careful doing that because he monitors where I go. It's in the contract."

"We'll end that quickly. Can you come now?"

He headed home for the contract and sped to her office.

Quickly scanning the contract, she spotted numerous areas to challenge. "We'll have you out of this in no time. Of course, the simplest solution would be to pay off the loans. Do you have access to funds?"

"I haven't checked as I've been so busy with the renovations, but Ivan has a pre-payment penalty in the contract if I pay him off early."

"We'll deal with that. In the meantime, check on other financing. While you're doing that, I'll write Mr. Schmidt notifying him that if he doesn't willingly change the contract, we'll sue him. Sometimes a letter is all it takes."

"In Ivan's case, it won't work. He likely gets threatening letters every day from attorneys. Paying him off might be the best policy even if it costs me, but yeah, go ahead and write him. "

"Keep me apprised of new financing. In the meantime, I'll get a letter off to Mr. Schmidt. We're about to rattle his cage."

Gilbert signed Sylvia's agreement and was out the door.

No sooner was he back at work than Ivan showed up.

"Where have you been? What were you doing over at Vine and Southern? I want my payment. It's due tomorrow."

Gilbert wrote him a check, all the time thinking, "You've got a letter coming, jerk."

Check in hand, Ivan was out the door but not before reminding Gilbert to get back to work. But Gilbert was so angry, there was no way he could focus on what he was doing. Tempted to go home, he realized that wasn't the answer either. Nothing would get done if he did that; furthermore, physical labor had always been therapeutic for him. Seeing positive change brightened his spirits--and boy, did he need that! So he grabbed his tools and started in.

Suddenly a storm blew in, so Gilbert abandoned any thoughts of working outside, and felt put off by the rain. Rain wasn't supposed to fall that day. Normally, days in Arizona are sunny if not hot, so to have a late monsoon rain come through messed him up and played with his mind. He grumbled about the unexpected rainfall and the role it played in his plans, then chastised himself for complaining, because any time it rains in Arizona, it's time for celebration. Though he wasn't about to do a two-step, he was drawn from his work to the windows, as the furor outside was a sight to behold. The brilliant lightning accompanied by thunder and cascading rain was mesmerizing, and Gilbert sat down to watch it.

The intensity of the rain meant little would soak in; instead, the streets and washes would be rivers in no time. Though he had no washes to cross to get home, he wasn't going home for a while anyway, but he knew that many people would try to plow their way through, which had danger written all over it. The sun-baked, drought-stricken ground was as hard as rock, so water cascading through the washes changed them quickly from something you could drive through easily, to life-threatening undertakings. He learned early on that native Arizonans kept a book in their vehicle to help them wait out the rushing water rather than challenging its fury. They reasoned that an hour spent reading was far wiser than the alternative.

Gilbert then realized he was really tired, as the rain had stopped, yet there he sat, fully engrossed in ruminating about the proper way to handle storms. Returning to work, he dove in, then checked his watch and realized hours had flown by and it was nearly midnight. Realizing that the day had gotten away from him, he locked up and left for home, picking up a burger along the way.

In spite of being tired, sleep didn't come easily, which became apparent when the alarm went off at five. Whiskers jumped when he slammed the top of the clock. That wasn't Gilbert's norm. Gilbert knew it too, so apologized. Apologizing to a cat, Gilbert thought to himself. I am losing my mind. Perhaps a shower would help. Might just as well start the day out fresh, as he knew it would go downhill from there-especially if Ivan got a letter from Sylvia. That meant all hell would break loose. He then realized that he had only spoken with Sylvia yesterday; surely she wasn't that quick (though he hoped she was).

Out the door by 5:45, he was at the job site by 6:15 and made sure he worked inside until 8, as he didn't want to disturb the neighbors. More than one had told him that they appreciated that. Forgetting etiquette was playing a role in what he was doing, which bothered him to no end, as he took pride in treating neighbors well. They were often his best sales force.

Though his mind was focused on issues with Ivan, it took a break to return to the sunrise he saw driving in. As frustrated and upset as he was, he couldn't help but look in awe at the incredible view as the sun's rays spiraled through the clouds above the mountains. The majestic hues painted across the sky were breath-taking. One of the things he loved about living in Arizona were the sunrises and sunsets. They were so colorful that no matter what was on your mind, you had to focus momentarily on the picture unfolding in front of you. The pastel colors and different hues were something few painters could replicate. Thinking about it gave Gilbert pause to reason that perhaps seeing the sunrise this morning was meant to be. He hoped so.

He needed a little brightening.  Then he realized that he had better get to work.

Chapter 20

Needing a break from work, Gilbert decided to attend the Traders meeting.  One of the members asked how things were going with Ivan, as everyone knew that Gilbert had borrowed money from him (thinking he was nuts for doing so, of course).  Feeling no compelling urge to sugarcoat things, he said, "The guy's impossible to deal with.  I finally got fed up and hired an attorney."

"Who'd you get?"

"Sylvia Goldsmith" he relayed.

"Don't know her."

"She helped me when she was with the ACLU.  Now she's on her own."

"Well, good luck dealing with Ivan.  He's impossible, as you say."

With that the meeting started.

 Jumper presented Hadley's property for the umpteenth time.  Enthusiastically, he talked about its many features, pointing out that it would be a terrific home for someone, adding that his client, Hadley, was most anxious to do a deal. Everyone knew that wasn't the case, but the kid was young so they cut him some slack.

Anxious to carry on and tell them more, the moderator reeled him in by asking for a raise of hands of those writing an offer. No hands went up. Everyone knew that submitting an offer was a waste of time. Jumper was devastated. It meant his one and only listing was going to remain his one and only listing much longer.

Gilbert felt he had conveyed the message he wanted to so he left. After he did, Julius heard that Gilbert had hired an attorney by the name of Sylvia Goldsmith to deal with Ivan. Anger swelled in him, since he hated the woman. She had single-handedly riled the residents in his apartment complex to the point where they made his life miserable. He'd never forgive her for what she had done, nor forget her, because no woman had ever stood up to him like she had.

Unbeknownst to him, infatuation, jealousy, and fear of losing her to Gilbert was hidden behind his anger. If anyone had brought all that to his attention, he would have laughed, saying that they were out of their minds for even suggesting it. No, it was safer to focus on rage. To satisfy it, he needed someone to rough up Gilbert in a way that would make everyone suspect that Ivan did it. The thought excited him. Unable to contain himself, he hustled out of the room to call Hadley.

"Hadley, this is Julius. I need your help."

Hadley's stomach turned at hearing his voice, but he said, "I'm expensive, but good. Of course you know that, otherwise you wouldn't call. So what kind of job you got?"

"I need someone worked over. No major damage, just a little bruised, sore, you know what I mean?"

"It'll cost you twenty grand, and just so you know, we charge more for breaking bones. "

"Twenty grand for beating some guy up, what a rip-off!"

"Then do it yourself."

"I don't want them to know who's behind it."

"Twenty grand and he won't."

"Oh, all right. But you have to make sure he suspects someone else."

"Who?"

"Ivan Schmidt."

"The price just went up to twenty-five grand. "

"Why?"

"Ivan's nasty, he doesn't play fair."

"The money's yours."

"I'm paid cash in advance."

"I'll get you the money."

Upon hanging up, Hadley called Louie Sarafoli, who was in good stead with his wife because she really liked her new home.

"How's the house?"

"What do you want?"

"I have a job for you. I'll meet you after work tomorrow in the parking lot at Jodie's restaurant, Fifth and Vine. We won't go in. We'll just sit in my car to discuss your assignment."

Regretting that he had ever agreed to the arrangement, Louie went to bed and proceeded to toss and turn the entire night, so when he met up with Hadley, he had bloodshot eyes.

"You look like hell," Hadley greeted him.

"Tell me what you want so I can get you out of my life."

"Hey, don't be so nasty. You got a nice house, right? Momma's happy. So now all you're doing is paying me back for the right to use that note, right?"

"Right."

"That note enabled you to buy your house if I recall."

"Yeah, big deal."

"Maybe when you complete the job, the investor will allow you to drop the insurance policy on your kid."

"So what's the job?"

"You need to rough up a guy. Black eyes, bloody nose, lots of body shots, no broken bones. Got me?"

"So what's this guy done to deserve this?"

"He upset a client. That's all you need to know, but when you're working him over, tell him Ivan wants his payments on time or else it'll be worse if you have to come back."

Hadley went on, "He's renovating a house at 6641 E. Calle Fuentes. Normally he works late and is usually alone. You can get him after he locks up, as there are no lights on outside, plus the door is in a cove so none of the neighbors will see what's going on. Catch him right and he won't know what hit him. After you're done, let me know and I'll take a look at the quality of your work in a day or so."

Louie waited until dark to drive by Gilbert's fix-up, hoping to size him up. Seeing lights on, he parked his car and peeked in a window. Watching Gilbert hang sheetrock made him feel sorry for the clown, but then again, he must deserve what he was about to get, so Louie returned to his car to plan his next move.

Gilbert was so far behind that he toyed with the idea of moving in, maybe even getting help, though he was pressed financially and hated spending money. So he concluded that he'd just have to tough it out. Thank god there were items like sheetrock lifts, as it made redoing the ceiling so much easier. After screwing the last sheet in place, he decided that was enough for the night. He'd tape in the morning after taking the lift back to the rental place.

Tired and hungry, he looked at the clock. It read 10:30 PM. Deciding that was enough, he turned off the lights and locked up, never expecting the blow to the back of his head. Dazed, he turned to see what had caused the hurt, only to recoil from a blow to the jaw, then another and another, all the while being told that Ivan wanted his money on time or he'd be back. That was the last thing Gilbert remembered.

Waking an hour later, he hurt all over but managed to crawl into the house where he made his way to the bathroom. He could barely see as his eyes were nearly swollen shut, but did manage to see blood all over his face in the mirror. He was quite a sight. Thankfully, nothing was broken.

Why Ivan would do this to him he didn't know, as he always tried to make his payments on time, and thought he had. Realizing he needed to clean up, he locked up again and struggled to get to his truck to drive home. In the shower he realized why he ached so much; he was black and blue all over.

After taking pain medication, he crawled into his recliner, where he was soon comforted by Whiskers. Though it hurt to raise his arms, he proceeded to stroke Whiskers's hair, though soon that was too much of an effort too. Going to bed was out of the question, as it hurt to move, so he painfully pulled a blanket up over himself and stretched out. Soon the medication kicked in, as did exhaustion.

When he woke in the morning he was stiff and in pain, so had to force himself to get up. Finding it very difficult to get on his feet, he finally did, and headed for more medication. Going to work was out of the question. He could barely move. What he needed to do was heal. Then the phone rang but he let the answering machine take a message. It was Ivan. He was screaming in the phone, "Why aren't you on the job?"

Unbelievable, he thought to himself. The guy has some thug nearly kill me then he wants to know why I'm not at work. If I had a gun I'd shoot the bastard.

Then the phone rang again. It was Mindy. "Gilbert, I stopped by your job site but you weren't there. Then I spoke with a neighbor who said that they heard some terrible commotion last night but were too afraid to look out the window. Are you all right?"

"No, someone did a number on me last night," he replied.

"Why?"

"They just said that if I didn't get my payments to Ivan on time, they'd be back."

"I'll be right over," and Mindy hung up.

She offered to take him to the hospital but he said no, nothing was broken, he'd just have to weather the storm, though he could use more pain medication so she headed to the store. Upon returning she asked if he was hungry, which he was--starved for that matter--so she looked in the cupboards, refrigerator too, but found nothing edible, so she headed to a fast food restaurant for breakfast.

When she returned and they ate, Gilbert explained what had taken place, expressing disbelief that Ivan would stoop to such a measure. Mindy, though, assured him that Ivan was capable of such meanness.

He mentioned that he needed to return the sheetrock jack, but she told him she'd take care of it, as it was probably wise he for him to stay home and rest. For that matter, he might consider doing that for a couple of days. She said she'd also call Sylvia to apprise her of what had taken place. Gilbert felt relieved. After she left, he crawled into bed and was soon asleep.

Ivan left a message every day demanding to know where he was and why he wasn't at work. That stopped when he got a letter from Sylvia threatening to take everything he owned if it was proven that he was behind the attack on Gilbert. Reading the letter, Ivan scoffed at the notion, then picked up the phone to call Sylvia.

"What's this crap about me being behind Gilbert being beaten? I had nothing to do with it. Take your letter and stick it up your ass, lady."

"I'll have you watch your mouth, Mr. Schmidt. Gilbert relayed that the guy who beat him up told him to expect worse if his payments to you weren't on time. I think that explains things pretty well."

"I didn't hire a goon to work over Gilbert. Why would I? Beat up he can't work, and if he can't work, he can't get his project done. So we both lose."

"If he doesn't complete the project or pay he loses-you don't. So there's plenty of reason to see to it that he can't finish. Just don't think it's going to happen that easily."

"Get a life, lady!" Ivan hung up.

Filled with rage, he headed for the Traders Club. It was apparent to everyone that his mood was not good, so people avoided him.

Sensing that, he asked, "Is anyone here familiar with what happened to Gilbert?"

They all knew that Ivan held a note on Gilbert's fix-up, though no one wanted to touch that until one said, "No, what about him?"

"Someone did a number on him to the point where he has bruises all over his body but didn't suffer any broken bones."

"That's terrible; why would anyone want to do that to Gilbert?"

"That's what I want to find out. Because the guy who did it kept repeating my name."

There was deadly silence in the room.

Hadley and Julius looked at each other, then found excuses to leave, which Ivan made note of. Norm left too after receiving from Hadley a $15,000 payment on his note, compliments of Julius.

No one was in much of a mood to have the meeting or board meeting afterwards, which didn't go over well with Windy, as he was back on his medication and had the minutes for the Club up to date. "Life sucks," he thought to himself, and then wondered if the whole thing was planned, designed to play with his mind.

The more he thought about it, the more obsessed he became-- then his cell phone rang. Luckily for him it was his mother, who wanted to take him to lunch, which was a good thing because she'd see the direction his mind and mood were going, so he figured she'd make sure he had food in his stomach and was back on his medication.

Chapter 21

Ivan stormed home to ponder who was behind Gilbert's beating, then said to Peety, "Some jerk pulverized Gilbert.  Now he and his attorney think I was behind it because my name was brought up during the attack."

Peety cocked his head, eager to hear more.

"I wasn't behind it; he wouldn't be walking if I was.  I don't believe in leaving them sore, I break bones."

"Ouch," Peety thought to himself, "Nasty stuff.  Of course, Ivan's nasty so why should I be surprised?"

All of a sudden Ivan started laughing.  "You won't believe what I recently heard Gilbert telling his damn cat?"

Peety's ears perked up.

"I've got his house bugged, everything else for that matter, so I can pick up most anything he says.  The idiot talks to his damn cat, can you believe that?"

Peety didn't say anything but thought, "He's doing the same thing--talking to an animal, a very intelligent one, mind you— nevertheless, an animal.  Just goes to show you he's oblivious to his own shortcomings. But then again, he's too narcissistic to think he has any."

Ivan's phone rang. In spite of the fact that caller ID was blocked, he answered and said, "Yeah, who's this?"

"I know who's behind Gilbert being roughed up."

"Who?"

"It'll cost you."

"I'm not paying. You better tell me who it is, otherwise I'll get you too."

"I'll call back when you're in a better mood." Click went the phone.

Ivan tried tracing the call but was unable to. Enraged, he started mulling over the reaction of club members to his revelation that Gilbert had been beaten up. Then remembered Hadley and Julius leaving early, which wasn't their norm, which prompted him to wonder if there was a connection.

Peety watched quietly as Ivan's rage grew. Similar episodes over the years had resulted in his storming out the door or heading for a restless night. He wasn't sure where this one would lead, but knew enough to keep his bill shut.

Ivan quit pacing, stopped, looked at him and said, "I'll get each and every one of the bastards. They'll regret they ever crossed my path," then was out the door.

Peety thought, "Thank God it's not me he's upset with. He doesn't take kindly to people messing with his mind, and somebody is. When he finds out who it is, they'll pay dearly."

Ivan returned later very agitated. Unable to relax, he paced back and forth until he eventually went to bed, only to be revisited by his decades-old nightmare of being raped as a child. Unable to escape the fretful event, his unconscious flooded him with memories that woke him full of sweat. Sitting up and staring at the foot of the bed, he vowed that someone would pay for what happened to him as a child. He'd settle for venting his rage on those responsible for his current torment.

Chapter 22

Louie called Hadley from home.

"So who is this Ivan Schmidt?" he asked.

"You don't want to know," Hadley replied, "Forget his name. Forget you ever heard of him."

"Well, I made sure the guy knew who was behind the beating."

"Word has it you worked him over well, to the point where he can barely walk. Great! Now we need to move on. Don't tell anyone what you did because Ivan has tentacles around the city, and if word gets out that you were behind the beating, he'll get you and he'll want to know who put you up to it. So don't give him my name, or I'll get you."

"If you or that clown do anything to me or my family, I'll get both of you!" Louie yelled, then slammed the phone down, muttering, "How did I ever get myself into this mess?"

His wife pounded on the office door.

"What do you want?"

"Who are you angry with? We could hear you threaten somebody. The kids are afraid someone's coming after them. What's going on here?"

"Nothing's going on. Tell the kids there's no reason to worry."

"Well, from the tone of your voice it's pretty clear something's going on and they're scared."

"I'll take care of it."

"Take care of what? You just said nothing's going on, now you're going to take care of it?"

"Drop it, I've heard enough, go to bed."

"Is this related to your being out late the other night, and then pacing back and forth when you came home?"

"I told you to drop it. You got the house, didn't you?"

"What's this got to do with the house?"

"Nothing, sorry I ever brought it up."

"You brought it up for a reason. It is related to the house, isn't it? Why were your hands bleeding when you got home?"

"Who said they were bleeding?"

"I saw them the next morning. Did you get into a fight or something? Is that what this is all about? You need to tell me."

"Shut up and go to bed. I don't want to talk about it anymore. If you say another word I'll beat you up." Then the kids really started crying. Hearing that, he stormed out of the house and headed to the nearest bar hoping to find relief. Later, three sheets to the wind, his mind working overtime and his anger in full bloom, he called Hadley to give him a piece of his mind. Unfortunately, someone in a nearby booth overheard the conversation. The bartender did too, so cut him off, which didn't set well with him.

"I want another drink or I'll kick your ass like I did that guy the other night for that asshole Ivan Schmidt."

"Sorry, no more. You've had too much. I'll call you a cab."

"I can drive myself. I don't want any more of your rotgut booze anyway," then he staggered to his car, totally unaware that someone was getting into theirs to follow him. Weaving his way home, oblivious to anyone behind him, he pulled into his driveway and turned off the key, leaving the car halfway in his yard. He staggered into the house, unaware that the guy in the car who followed him was jotting down his address, then heading to his real estate office to pull up public records to learn his drunken friend's name.

Though he didn't like Ivan, he reasoned it wouldn't hurt to have him indebted to him, so in the morning he called him.

"Yeah, who is it?"

"Ivan, Morty here."

"Sorry ass Morty from the Traders Club. I thought you didn't like me."

"I don't. I also don't like seeing people unjustly blamed for something."

"So civic-minded Morty is calling me out of the goodness of his heart. How noble of you."

Morty was tempted to hang up but figured that would only irritate Ivan, and he didn't need the hassle that would result because of it.

"I was at a bar last night and overheard some drunk talking about how he beat the crap out of some guy and your name came up in the conversation."

"Who was he? Did you get a name? How can I get hold of this guy?"

"I got more than that. After hanging up from whomever he was arguing with, he got cut off by the bartender, which was a good thing because he was really loaded. Then got in his car to drive home so I followed him. His name is Louie Sarafoli. He lives at 232 W. Sycamore. Nice house, nice area."

"What's in this for you?"

"It sounds like this is the guy who beat up Gilbert. I like Gilbert."

"So why don't you call Gilbert?"

"I might, but thought I'd call you first." Then he hung up, as there was no sense in waiting for a thank you. Ivan didn't give those.

Morty Holcomb was a low-key guy who occasionally attended the Traders meetings over the years, though seldom did any trades, as most of his time was spent in residential sales. Well respected in the residential community, he received many referrals from former clients, which kept him busy. For that matter, most of his work came from referrals, so he no longer had to pound the pavement to get listings or clients.

Occasionally a client would approach him with an investment property they owned and he would counsel them to check with their accountant as to their tax consequences should they sell. Since many had never thought of where Uncle Sam fit into the equation, they were most appreciative, as their focus was on selling and then buying a bigger property. When they learned that they could postpone paying capital gains taxes by trading, they invited him to explore a trade. He would then list their property and gather as much information about it and his clients as he could so as to be able to answer questions the Traders were sure to ask.

When he presented properties at the Traders Club, he did so in a straightforward manner with little fluff or frills. Members quickly learned that he intended to protect his clients and get the

best deal for them that he could, which irritated many. For that
matter, people like Ivan wanted nothing to do with him, which
was part of the reason his name was never nominated to serve on
the board of the Traders--which was perfectly fine with him, as
he had no desire to be on the board. Attending once in awhile,
keeping abreast of the tax laws, and getting a feel for what was
on the market was good enough for him.

It's how he operated with the MLS crowd too. He didn't serve
on any boards or committees--just did his thing for his clients
and left it at that. Notoriety was not a necessity for him; for
that matter, the more he could blend into the woodwork the
better. Though he wasn't necessarily shy, he had no big ego
issues either. Being out front wasn't his calling, or interest for
that matter.

Morty debated calling Gilbert, then decided against it, as he
didn't want to get any more involved than he already was.
Notifying Gilbert would likely mean the police would get
involved, whereas he knew Ivan wouldn't call them. No, Ivan
would handle things on his own.

Then a pang of doubt set in as he thought that for Louie's sake,
he probably should contact Gilbert, but then again, Louie beat
the crap out of Gilbert so probably deserved whatever Ivan was
going to subject him to--knowing it might be severe. Then
Morty settled the issue in his mind by accepting that whatever
happened, happened. Louie never should have harmed Gilbert in
the first place, and because he did, now he had to deal with Ivan,
which wouldn't be a picnic.

Chapter 23

Louie Sarafoli never saw the blows coming. He had stopped at his favorite watering hole after work to unwind, had a few too many, stumbled out to his car, which was parked in a dark area, when suddenly someone whacked him pretty well. There were three of them. He didn't have a chance. He awoke hours later, blindfolded, tied up in a chair, only to have his situation turn worse.

"We need to know who was behind your beating up Gilbert?"

"I ain't telling you anything,"

Whack was the sound of the bat on his arm. Louie screamed in pain.

"Next time, I'm going to break the son of a bitch. Now as I asked, who was behind your working Gilbert over?"

Louie didn't say anything, which was a mistake, as the next blow broke his arm.

"You bastard, you broke my arm."

Whack, his other arm was hit.

Louie cried out in pain, but there was no one else in the warehouse besides the four of them.

"You will tell us or we'll break the other arm too."

"Son of a bitch," Louie said.

All of a sudden, both arms were broken.

In absolute pain, he cried out, "Leave me alone."

"Tell us or we'll start on your legs."

"No."

"Tell us, or you'll be a cripple for life--if you're lucky."

"Oh, all right, Hadley Evans was behind it. He represented some guy who helped us buy our house. I was told if I worked Gilbert over, that would satisfy my obligation for using his note. Oh, my arms."

"Who gave you the note?"

"I don't know."

The blow to his leg was gut-wrenching. "Tell us."

"I don't know who he is."

The pain from the next blow caused him to pass out. Revived, he was ordered to talk or they'd bust every bone in his body. At that point, he believed they would.

"I don't know who he is."

Thinking he might be telling the truth, they switched focus to Ivan.

"Why did you mention Ivan's name to Gilbert?"

"Because I was told to. Gilbert hadn't been making his payments on time and Ivan wanted to send him a message."

"Well, Ivan's got a message for you too. If you ever mention his name and he learns about it, we'll be back. And we'll get your kids too."

The next blow to his leg was so excruciating that he blacked out.

Ivan received a phone call from the warehouse.

"We worked this guy over pretty well."

"Did he tell you who was behind all this?" Ivan asked.

"Yeah, Hadley Evans. He said he didn't know who the note belonged to, and we believe he doesn't."

"So what this guy's condition now?"

"He's got two broken arms and a broken leg. Guess it was a little too much for him because he passed out. Do you hear him moaning?"

"He deserves it. Pounding my name in that guy's head. He's lucky he's alive."

"So what do you want us to do with him?"

"Dump him on Hadley's front yard," Ivan ordered. "That'll send a message to him!"

When Hadley saw Louie lying in front of his house in utter pain, he knew two phone calls were in order. One to the paramedics and the other in the morning to Ivan—otherwise, what had happened to Louie would likely happen to him. Louie's life took a turn for the worse. Unable to work because of broken arms and a leg, he lost his job, then lost his home because Ivan notified the mortgage company that he had obtained it through fraudulent means, citing the note and the role Hadley played in the scheme. Louie's wife filed for divorce and moved with the kids out of state, telling one and all she was afraid her kids would suffer because of some stupid thing her husband had done.

In the meantime, Louie was filled with fear that the goons would return. The only bright spot was a check for $2,500 attached to a note saying, "You handled that job well. I'll have more work for you when you're back on your feet. And, oh yeah, you can drop the insurance policy on your kid."

Chapter 24

"Ivan, Hadley here. We need to talk."

"I've been waiting for your call. You better have a good explanation and some names or you're not going to like the outcome."

"I'm sure we can work things out. Where do you want to meet?"

"Ten o'clock at Saguaro Title Company. They've got a private room we can use."

"I'll be there."

"You better."

At ten o'clock Hadley schmoozed his way past the secretaries to the private room, giving the impression that he didn't have a worry in the world, which was typical Hadley, bullshit artist personified.

Sticking his hand out he said, "Ivan, it's good to see you."

Rejecting his hand, Ivan stared him down then said, "This better be good."

"I'm sure you want to know who put me up to having Louie work over Gilbert?"

"Damn right I do."

"What's in it for me if I tell you?"

"You get to live."

"We go back a long way Ivan, don't you think that's a little harsh?"

"You know that free and clear house that new guy's been pedaling at the Traders Club for you, the one for $75,000?"

"Yeah, what about it?"

"It's now mine for the inconvenience of letting you live."

 Hadley gulped.  Unfortunately, he knew that Ivan meant it.

"It's yours."

"Now tell me who was responsible for my name being knocked into Gilbert's cranium?"

Realizing he had no options, he said, "Julius Stern."

"Why in the hell did that little jerk want Gilbert worked over?"

"He's got the hots for a babe named Sylvia Goldsmith and heard Gilbert was in close with her."

"You better tell Julius Stern that the guys who worked over Louie are going to pay him a visit. Now why don't you walk your sorry ass up to the counter and open escrow on that house, then thank your lucky stars you've getting off that easy. Next time; well, there will be no next time, you hear?"

"I hear."

After leaving Saguaro Title, Hadley called Julius Stern to give him the bad news that Ivan had found out that he was behind Gilbert getting worked over.

Julius panicked, then asked, "How did he find out it was me? You promised you would protect me. I even paid you more to do that."

"I don't know, I guess your name slipped out when the goons were busting up Louie. You know a guy can only withstand so much pain and then they break down?"

"How did he know about me?"

"I don't know, maybe one of my secretaries said something to him. The bottom line is that Ivan had some goons work Louie over pretty good. Hell, he's got two broken arms and a broken leg. He's lucky he's not dead. Now Ivan says his goons are coming for you. You better get out of town as soon as you can."

"I want my money back."

"I don't know how your name slipped out, anyway a deal's a deal." With that Julius slammed the phone down and called Dr. Goldfarb.

Dr. Goldfarb recommended immediate hospitalization, and while there was a discussion about his insane infatuation and jealousy over Sylvia Goldsmith, he heard Julius whimpering in the background, "I want my mommy." Oh, boy, he thought to himself. This guy's sick.

While waiting for a bed to open, Ivan had his goons check Julius's apartment complex, home, airport, train depot, and hospitals, which was where they spotted his car.

After admitting Julius, Dr. Goldfarb checked on him.

"You should be safe here, Julius. It sounds like you've got yourself involved with some nasty people, so limit your calls to those you really trust. You don't want anyone revealing where you are." (Julius couldn't think of anyone; for that matter, most would call Ivan, they disliked him so much.)

"Here's the picture I have in my mind, so please correct me if I'm wrong. You hired someone to rough up a guy named Gilbert because you think he's involved with Sylvia?"

"It's far more complicated than that, but it's something like that."

"Now this Ivan Schmidt wants to rub you out, and you wonder why you're paranoid? It sounds like you have reason to be paranoid. Your irrational fantasies about Sylvia have put you in a bind that might cost you big time. Though you're not insane, you're not healthy either. "

"Can you contact Ivan and negotiate a deal?"

"I'm not a deal-maker. I'm a Psychiatrist."

"I'm sure Ivan will track me down, so I need you to save my skin. There's a bonus in it if you do."

"Bonus, you mess with guys like this and there's likely going to be a funeral--yours."

 Julius curled up in a fetal position and started to cry, and Dr. Goldfarb put his head in his hands, wondering why he had ever gotten into Psychiatry. He could have taken over his parent's successful retail operation but no--he had to go off to medical school then become a shrink. Maybe he needed to see a Psychiatrist himself. It was at times like this that he thought so, something he did often after his father died.

Though his mother was immensely qualified to run the business, he regretted seeing her stuck handling everything. They talked often about his dropping his practice to join her, but she assured him she could handle it. Though she didn't share this with him, she wondered if his close relationship with his father played a role in his thinking.

His momentary self-pity was interrupted by a page from the front desk.

"Dr. Goldfarb, there's a very angry caller on the line who insists on talking with you."

Walking out of Julius's room, he said, "I'll take it, thanks."

"Dr. Goldfarb, how can I help you?"

"You tell that little weasel I don't take kindly to someone using my name in a disparaging manner because I'm perfectly capable of doing that myself."

"Who might I be talking to?"

"Ivan Schmidt."

"And you believe there's someone here you wish me to convey that message to."

"You're not stupid, doc. You know why I'm calling. Tell the little weasel his indiscretion is going to cost him. For the moment I'll settle for money rather than broken bones."

"How much are we talking here?"

"Half a million."

"Wow, that's substantial."

"Not to him. Tell him he can pay now or my associates will collect later."

"Why don't you check with me in a couple of days, Mr. Schmidt? I might be in a better position to address your issues at that time."

"I know where to find you." Then he hung up.

Chapter 25

That afternoon Dr. Goldfarb walked into Julius's room and said, "Julius, I received a call from Ivan Schmidt. Is he ever nasty!"

"What did he want?"

"Money. Or his thugs will break your bones."

"How much?"

"Half a million."

"Half a million dollars, that's outrageous. I can't afford that."

"He says you can."

"You need to talk some sense in his head. You're a Psychiatrist. Tell him I'll give him ten grand if he'll forget the whole thing."

"So you want me to Jew him down. Is that what you want me to do?"

"You're Jewish."

"I think you're wasting your time. Furthermore, you're going to have to make a far more substantial offer to settle, otherwise you might not be long for this world. And if that happens, I'll have a pretty good idea who was behind your demise, but proving it could be a challenge because I don't think Ivan Schmidt's conscience will allow him to confess. His conscience is not his strong suit! For that matter, I suspect it's riddled with holes."

"See if he'll take $20,000?"

"I'll run it by him if he calls." With that Dr. Goldfarb walked out, convinced he was dealing with someone devoid of his faculties. And if Julius continued his lunacy, he might have to transfer him out of state or even out of the country to save his behind.

Walking to the charting area he received an incoming call.

"Dr. Goldfarb."

"When can I get my half million?" Ivan barked

"My client's under tremendous stress at the moment and until he's stabilized, I won't be able to carry on conversations with him related to this magnitude of money, though he did mention he'd offer $20,000."

"Money's not an issue to him. He's got millions. And if he wants to play games like having his Jewish doctor Jew me down, I'll up the ante and ask for a million. For that matter, I might demand he give me his apartment complex. He certainly doesn't like having it, can't manage it anyway. Everyone hates him. So tell the little weasel I'm letting him off easy by only asking for half a million."

"Again, my patient's under tremendous stress. When he improves, I'll discuss with him personal issues related to business."

"I'm not a patient man, doc. You better fix dip-shit real quick." And then he hung up.

The next day Dr. Goldfarb walked in to find Julius playing hearts on his computer, giving the appearance that he didn't have a care in the world.

"Did you get Ivan to accept $20,000 to call this off?"

"He relayed that he's not a patient man, adding if you don't agree to the half million, he might ask for your apartment complex."

"He's insane. He needs to be committed. You heard his words. Get started on it right away."

"Let me take your blood pressure. Why don't you lie back and relax and we'll discuss this later."

"When's my lunch coming? They're not punctual when it comes to my food--for that matter, it's not very good, plus the service stinks. Find me another hospital."

"I'll check on your lunch and I'll check on other hospitals too, though this is the only hospital where I'm allowed to practice, so we'd have to find you a new doctor."

"Whatever, I want better service or I'm walking out."

Walking out himself, Dr. Goldfarb thought, "I hope the little weasel really wants to move to another hospital. Maybe one in Palestine might be the right place for him. God forbid I should think that."

Later that afternoon he met with Julius to assess his condition and discuss how to deal with Ivan.

"How was lunch?"

"I want it catered from now on."

"I'm not sure that's possible."

"Then find me another place."

"I haven't had a chance to check on any. In the meantime, let's talk about the outrageous demands Ivan Schmidt is making on you. I recommend that we contact the police."

"Under no circumstances do I want you to do that."

"Why not?"

"It'll make him mad."

"He's already mad. For that matter, he's extorting you."

"It's only money."

"He wants half a million dollars. Doesn't that bother you?"

"Yeah it does, see if he'll take $50,000."

"You do know what you're doing, right?"

"Of course, I'm trying to save myself $450,000. Can't you see that?"

"I see that perfectly. At the moment, we're not focusing on mental or emotional issues, we're talking money. You should probably have an attorney represent you in this matter instead of me."

"No."

"Why not?"

"They charge too much. Furthermore, I'd be as afraid of them as I am of Ivan, plus I'd probably end up with some gold digger like Sylvia Goldsmith. At least you have to be honest."

"Well, I don't know if I'm the most qualified person to represent you in this matter. So why don't we both think about it."

"Great idea, furthermore, it's time for me to order in food."

"Want me to cancel your evening meal?"

"Do whatever, I don't want to be bothered."

So he called food service and placed a hold on future meals. About to head back to the office, he received a call from Ivan.

"When can I pick up my half mil?"

"Mr. Schmidt, your demands are outrageous. They're extortion."

"Just a second doc, while I get a tissue. I'm starting to get teary-eyed."

"This is no joking matter, Mr. Schmidt. Though in a quest to end this matter, even though he's being extorted, my patient said he'd offer you $50,000 to end this tragic affair."

"Tell him he's at the right hospital, doc. He's nuts!" Then he slammed the phone down.

"Guess that means he's not interested," the doctor thought to himself. While he was hoping to have a less stressful afternoon, his pager went off.

"Dr. Goldfarb, this is Judy, nurse on Two West."

"Yes, Judy, what's up?"

"We had to break up a fight between Melinda and Lucille."

"What were they fighting about?"

"They couldn't agree on who could pee further."

"What?"

"That's right, they couldn't agree on who could pee the farthest!"

"You're kidding me."

"No, they were in the day room watching TV, got into an argument, stood, dropped their drawers, and started peeing."

"Get their medication out and I'll be right there."

Walking over he thought, "Oh, boy, it's going to be one of those days."

## Chapter 26

Hoping the day would be an improvement over the previous one, Dr. Goldfarb grabbed Julius's chart to see if there had been any significant changes in his behavior and attitude during the night. The most notable annotation was that the night nurse threatened to not show if forced to cover his unit again.

Turned out that Julius was a whiny, demanding, royal pain in the ass who made her life hell, to the point wherein she toyed with smothering the little weasel. But then realized her feelings were getting the better of her. Afraid she wouldn't be able to contain her rage for one more night, she had pleaded to be assigned to another unit.

Though he wanted to explore Julius's feelings toward women, dealing with Ivan took center stage, as his feelings towards anyone wouldn't matter if he ended up stuffed in a pine box.

Though he didn't look forward to it, he checked in with Julius.

"How was your night?"

"It was probably the worst night I've ever had in my life."

"What happened?"

"This night nurse is the whiniest person I've ever been around. She should be fired. If she's on tonight, I want to be transferred to a new hospital. She was so bad I dreamt this attractive, smart attorney was coming to rescue me from her and Ivan."

"Sylvia Goldsmith's not coming to rescue you, Julius. Forget it."

Julius pouted.

After Dr. Goldfarb walked out he smiled, thinking that she might be going after Ivan, since she represented Gilbert.

Chapter 27

"Dr. Goldfarb, this is Ivan. Listen, doc, dealing with the little weasel is maddening."

Dr. Goldfarb thought to himself, "Tell me about it."

"So Mr. Schmidt, do you think there's a middle ground between your $500,000 and his $50,000?"

"Tell the little weasel if he cuts me a check for $300,000, I'll let him live."

"I'll pass that on Mr. Schmidt. Can you call tomorrow about this time?"

"You'll hear from me. And tell the little weasel this is my final offer. There's no further negotiating."

"I'll pass it on."

Walking into Julius's room, he was taken aback by the amount of food sitting in front of him.

"Did you order for five people?"

"No, just myself. I like a variety. Most of it I'll just toss."

"Isn't that wasteful?"

"Are you the garbage doctor or something?"

"No, though I do believe you should eat what you order."

"So that's your hang-up, not mine, I can afford it. So have you heard from Ivan?"

"I just got off the phone with him. He agreed to drop his demand to $300,000."

"Tell him to forget it."

"He said he won't negotiate further."

"In that case, tell him I'll take it."

"Are you sure?"

"Of course I'm sure, if it gets Ivan off my case, $300,000 is nothing. I thought of paying him $500,000, so I've saved myself

$200,000, but don't tell him. He gets a little nasty when he learns he's made a mistake. So when can I go home?"

"After we finalize things with Mr. Schmidt. I want to make sure you're not snuffed out over this."

"I'm getting bored of this joint, so hurry up."

"Mr. Schmidt might want a cashier's check. Can you arrange that?"

"I can. I want something in writing too."

"I'll have the hospital attorney prepare an agreement."

The next morning Dr. Goldfarb received a call from Ivan.

"Did numb nuts come to his senses and agree to fork over $300,000?"

"Mr. Schmidt, though my client believes your demands are excessive, he has agreed to pay $300,000 to settle this issue. I'm having the hospital attorney draft an agreement for you both to sign, so if you drop by the hospital this afternoon, I'll have it for your review."

"It looks like you're restoring numb nuts to sanity, Doc. I'll stop by sometime after four p.m."

"That's fine; in the meantime I'll have Julius review the agreement also. Let's try and get this wrapped up tomorrow."

"I'll be in touch."

The contract was straightforward. For $300,000 Ivan agreed to let Julius keep all his bones in place. They both signed, Ivan grabbed the cashier's check, and Julius marched out to get in his sports car, the one with the license plate "Julius" parked in a handicapped parking spot in front of the hospital. Though asked by the hospital many times to move it, he said he couldn't be bothered, as it was the closest spot he could find, not being aware that it was how Ivan's goons spotted where he was.

Chapter 28

On his way home from the hospital, Julius drove by Sylvia Goldsmith's office in the hopes he could catch a glimpse of her. Unable to, he headed to his apartment complex.

Walking into the office, he didn't say, "Hello, how are you?" or anything civil like that--no, not Julius, he barked at the manager instead.

"How many vacancies do we have?"

"We're full. We've filled all the units. Isn't that great?"

"I suppose so. Have we raised rates?"

"Sir, it's been so hard getting tenants I fear raising rates will result in vacancies like we had a month ago."

"You're obviously not management material. Otherwise you'd realize a full house means we're not charging enough."

"You've told us repeatedly you're the only one who can raise or lower rents. We've tried contacting you every day the past month but haven't been able to, it's like you fell off the face of the earth. Where have you been?"

"I had to get away, I was being extorted."

"You what?"

"Someone threatened to do me in unless I paid them a lot of money."

She thought, "Aha, so we're not the only ones that want to do that!"

"I had to pay a lot of money to be saved, so everyone's taking a pay cut here to make up for it."

"A pay cut. We've got a full house and it wasn't easy to achieve, as this complex has quite a reputation in town."

"Well, I'm about to improve it. You're fired!"

Once the staff heard this they shook their heads in disbelief, as she was the best manager they had ever had. Then they heard that Julius intended to send a memo stating their salaries were being cut because the manager used poor judgment by not raising rents.

Before walking out, Maria, in tears, said, "Oh, yes, we had one tenant move out."

"Who was that?"

"Sylvia Goldsmith."

Stunned, Julius asked, "Where did she go?"

"She gave no forwarding address, though directed her mail be sent to her office."

"Well, good, I've been trying to get rid of her for years."

Maria left and so did Julius. She went home while he drove by Sylvia's office again on the chance that he could follow her home to see where she had moved.

After he left, one of the staff said, "He talks despairingly about Sylvia, but constantly talks about her, to where you have to wonder if he's smitten with her?"

"I wouldn't bring it to his attention if I were you."

"Yeah, that'd be a sure pink slip."

The phone rang.

"Terra Del Sol Apartments. This is Monica, how can I help you?"

"Monica, this is Sylvia, is Maria there?"

"No, Julius just let her go."

"You're kidding me, she was terrific! Why did he do that? On second thought don't answer that, I don't want you getting in trouble, just give me her number and I'll find out from her."

Maria answered her phone in tears.

"Maria, this is Sylvia. Why in the world did he let you go? You're the best manager he's ever had."

"He said it was because I didn't raise rates when the complex was full. I reminded him that he made it clear only he can raise or lower rates, but he didn't want to hear that. I also told him we've tried for a month to reach him but couldn't."

"What did he say to that?"

"He said he's been unavailable as someone was trying to extort money from him."

"Extort money from him? Wow, I wonder what that's all about. When you left, did he give you a severance check?"

"No?"

"Did he say he's going to?"

"He said he's been damaged so might not."

"I'll get your money for you."

"I can't afford to pay you."

"Don't worry. Rattling his cage will be compensation enough."

"Oh, just so you know, he always talks about you. I think he likes you."

"You just turned my stomach. My letter will end whatever's echoing through his screwed-up head."

Chapter 29

Jumper was becoming horribly depressed, as his savings were depleting and he wasn't selling anything. The prospect of selling Hadley's house looked pretty remote, as Hadley was holding out for the full price, and buyers knew they could go elsewhere to get a better deal. So he felt stuck. Finally, he swallowed his pride and applied for food stamps, which turned out to be a wise decision, as he learned he also qualified for Medicaid.

So at least he'd have food in his stomach and health coverage if needed. He didn't tell any of the guys in the office about it, as he was too embarrassed. They'd think he was a total loser. If things didn't improve though, he might have to drop his real estate license and get a job. Though he wasn't a drinker, he was sure thinking about it.

Every chance he got and everywhere he went, he pushed Hadley's house. He figured the more people he told about the place, the better his chances were to make a sale. So you can imagine his reaction when he got Hadley's call.

Upset with having to sign the house over to Ivan, Hadley realized it was still listed with Jumper, which meant he had to pay a commission too. In no mood to do that, he called him to tell him of the change.

"Jumper, Hadley here. Listen, I've got some bad news for you. We need to cancel the listing, as I owe Ivan Schmidt money, and we've decided that the best way to cover it is if I transfer title on the house to him. "

"So you're selling it to him?"

"No, not really, I'm just transferring title. Maybe he'll list it with you."

"The contract calls for me being paid if title transfers."

"But it's different here. I'm not making any money. I'm just transferring title. How can you expect me to pay you a commission when I'm not receiving any money?"

"I've invested all this time promoting your listing, and now you're conveying it to someone else and want me to receive nothing? That's not right! I need to talk to an attorney."

"You certainly can, but be aware that if you start suing members of the Traders Club, you'll be blackballed and no one will do business with you."

Totally confused, Jumper hung up, not sure what to do. His only listing, the one he spent hundreds of hours promoting, had just been taken away from him. Real estate certainly wasn't as easy as he thought it would be. On the contrary, it was downright hard.

After losing the house to Ivan, Hadley was trying to figure out how to make up for his loss, when he ran into Norm.

"So, are you still being recruited to run for Senate?" Norm chuckled.

"No, that fell apart," he replied.

"So what happened, did they catch on to you?"

"Apparently some of the stories I've been telling got back to Buttercup, so she's not talking to me."

"You mean, some of those raunchy jokes did you in. You're probably lucky anyway, because had they become serious and got around to vetting you, you would have been toast."

"Maybe so, but I kind of liked the idea of being called Senator."

"If you would like me to call you Senator, I certainly will, if it makes you feel better," Norm replied.

"Stuff it!" Hadley retorted.

What Hadley didn't know was that Buttercup and Suzie Belle were terribly disappointed when word leaked out about his off-color jokes, because they were convinced that he was sure to be the state's next Senator. Even more surprising was who was behind the leak--Norm. Everyone suspected it was Gomer, but he had stayed as far away from the mess as he could, because God forbid that word get back to Buttercup that he was sabotaging her guy. He would never hear the end of it.

Norm saw real promise in getting old folks to Switzerland, so found out who the president of the conservative religious group was, and sent him an unsigned letter containing many of

Hadley's jokes, knowing full well it would scuttle his chances. Sure enough, it did. Rumor had it that the president had called a special board meeting, and invited Buttercup and Suzie Belle too.

All were aghast at what they read. Buttercup was so upset, Suzie Belle excused them and escorted her off to the bar where in short order they were downing Bloody Mary's, because the thought of drinking Vodka Martini's was too much for Buttercup to handle. They would remind her too much of Hadley.

Norm said, "Hey listen, instead of me footing the bill for infomercials, why don't we sell the idea to the insurance companies?"

"Terrific idea. It never crossed my mind. Listen, I've been up to my ass in alligators so haven't thought about it much lately, so I'm glad you brought it up."

"I'm sure they have marketing funds for that."

"I'm sure they do."

"But what if they don't go for it?"

"You mean, support the idea?"

"Right."

"If they don't, it certainly would be sad if word got out that they were the ones who floated the idea in the first place."

"You wouldn't do something like that, would you?"

"Of course not, and I would make it perfectly clear that we would protect them from that happening."

"I think you're onto something here. Let's give it some more thought."

"Listen, I need to let things settle down for a while anyway, what with my hassles with Julius, Jumper, and Ivan."

"Julius and Jumper are idiots, but Ivan's nasty. You don't want to mess with him. Did he get upset because you gave Julius a hand?"

"Yeah, it cost me the house because of it. Now I've go to make up for it."

"Maybe you can with this new idea."

"I hope so. Of course, forking the house over to Ivan sure beat the alternative, because what his guys did to Louie Safaroli was downright brutal. They broke both his arms and fractured one leg. He lost his house, job, and family over it. Did I tell you Ivan called the mortgage company holding the note on his house and told them that he got it through fraudulent means?"

"Yeah, you did. Did they call you because you put the deal together?"

"Nah, I've done too much business with them. They want me bringing them more deals, so they're not going to bother me."

"What are your plans for Ivan?"

"I'm going to leave him alone. I don't want to take a chance. He said the next time I mess with him, I'll end up like Louie, and I don't want that. I saw how Louie looked and what it did to him, so I'm staying as far away from Ivan as I can. Speaking of Louie, what are your plans for him?"

"I don't know yet, though with the direction we're going, perhaps we'll never need his services again. Any idea what he's doing?"

"He got a job working for a competitor, then got so discouraged thinking about what happened that he started drinking heavily, nearly lost his job because of it, got involved with AA, and even got himself a dog to fend off loneliness. And apparently it's helped. I know someone who works for the company, and they said he's got a brown dog people rave about because she's so fluffy. He takes her for a walk daily, which has been a boost to both of them. I guess he's even talking to his old lady again. Though it's unlikely they'll ever get back together again, there's a possibility they might reconcile. Anyway, that's the latest. If I run into him, what should I tell him?"

"Maybe I'm getting soft, but just say 'we believe he's fulfilled his end of the deal,' and leave it at that. Listen, maybe if we can get this new idea off the ground, we can focus on that and get out of what we're doing."

"Is that note still available?"

"No! There have been too many headaches letting people use it, in spite of the fact that I've done well. I don't need that crap. I'm just going to keep it."

"Listen, I've got to go. I'll talk with you later."

Tom Jorgenson completely forgot about Hadley and Louie for nine months. Then that changed when Louie called to tell him that he had carried out his responsibility for using the note by causing mayhem to someone. Figuring he was through with the mess, he wasn't, as he ended up being severely beaten himself.

Then, to make matters worse, someone notified their mortgage company that they had obtained their loan through fraudulent means, causing them to lose the house, which upset his wife enough to file for divorce. In the process, the mortgage company insisted that they share who had helped them to get their loan, so he told them, which caused Tom's sphincter muscle to tighten substantially. If he could have run away, he would have, but he had too many deals in the works. And then it dawned on him that his two Error and Omission policies might save his behind.

He felt sorry about Louie and his wife losing the house and splitting over it, then felt relieved that Louie wouldn't be calling anytime soon to buy another, as he didn't know what he would do if he did. Because Louie had a way about him where he would have you convinced that there was no one as capable as you to help him. And if you bought the line, you nearly became his prisoner. In short order, he would be chewing up your time, as once he grabbed on, he wouldn't let go.

As it turned out, the mortgage company never contacted him or the Arizona Department of Real Estate; instead, took the house back and left it at that. Relieved that he had avoided a bullet, he decided no more deals like that. No, he was going to follow the straight and narrow, even if it meant walking away from a deal. The Traders never saw him back at the club either, as he fully ensconced himself in residential sales, believing it was the safest route to go. Though he did toy with listing and selling mobile home parks after selling one for a client, he decided against it, as the market was dominated by a single practitioner who operated from home.

Chapter 30

Ivan, feeling good that he'd extracted $300,000 from Julius's hide, plus tired of Peety's bantering, decided that Peety needed something to amuse him when he was gone, so he headed out the door.

By happenstance, he came across a figurine that caught his eye, as it seemed to match his mood and mindset. Figuring that if he set it across from Peety's cage, it would remind him of him (Ivan), he bought it.

"I'll call him the 'Critter' for lack of a better name, as he's a cagey creature with a devilish smirk, long fingers, big ears, potbelly with a frog perched on his toe, who makes me think of the devil himself, which means he's my kind of guy!"

Ivan was excited, and Ivan never got excited. But he was seeing a mirror image of himself, which delighted him to no end. The smirk on the Critter's face made you know he was up to no good, though you didn't know what it was. Ivan thought, "Peety will have a field day analyzing him, which will keep him busy so he won't bug me."

The lady he bought the Critter from said he was a one-of-a-kind character who appeared to be an ideal match for him, whatever that meant! He had never bought a figurine before, but the Critter stood out as it made him laugh, which he never did. He figured the three of them would get along quite well considering one was a bird and the other couldn't talk, which was fine with him, as Peety talked enough.

Peety kept quiet when Ivan brought the Critter in, as he didn't know what to make of the goofy-looking creature. He was startled when Ivan said, "This is the Critter. Get used to him."

Peety was at a loss for words, which wasn't his norm.

"Do I just start talking, certainly there's no need to introduce myself, furthermore he's a damn figurine. A goofy-looking one at that, though the longer I look at him the more I see Ivan in him. They are much alike, though I see a substantial difference. I can tell him what I think and not have to worry about having my food taken away. 'Walla'--my own therapist! Free association here I come!

"I can share my inner conflicts and the idiot's not going to judge me; instead will just sit there with a smirk on his face so I don't have to worry about rejection. My mental health will improve. It's even possible I'll become so mellow I'll no longer needle Ivan. Well, that might be going too far, Ivan needs needling, furthermore I'm the closest thing he's got to a conscience."

Anxious for Ivan to leave so he could start his first session, he was disappointed to see him sitting there staring at the Critter. It was as though he was looking in a mirror seeing the devil himself, all the while loving the spark in his eye. Good grief, did that mean he was going to be sticking around more? I hope not. God forbid we should be competing for a therapist, especially one with a devilish look on his face.

Over the next couple of weeks Ivan devoted more time to the Critter than he did to Peety.

Filled with jealousy Peety, grew to hate the Critter, so taunted him, became an absolute bully for that matter. But no matter what he said, it didn't wipe the smirk off the Critter's face, which irritated him further, only to have it dawn on him that was what therapists were for. He was not really angry at the Critter. The Critter was a substitute for someone in his past.

Then it dawned on him that he'd held deep-seated resentment towards his mother for years for improperly nourishing him in the nest, and not adequately preparing him to live in a cage. His mother was at fault. "I feel better already," he said to himself. "The Critter's not my enemy, I love the Critter and his snarly smirk. He's my friend."

Feeling good about this new-found revelation, he strutted around the cage like a peacock, only to feel guilt set in when it dawned on him that his mother had brought him worms, taught him how to fly, and how to avoid predators. Then it dawned on him too that his father was often nowhere to be found growing up, because he usually flew the coop.

Though mom didn't say much about him, she did describe him as a horny old coot who wasn't much on responsibility, so kicked him out of the nest more than once. Mulling this over, Peety thought that maybe what he saw in the Critter was not his mother, but instead, his father. Looking at the smirk on the Critter's face, he thought to himself, "Son-of-a-gun! The little devil does remind me of that horny old coot." Feeling good about his newfound revelation, he dropped a load, which brought a sense of satisfaction. "Ivan will for sure think of me when he walks in the door now!"

Chapter 31

Ivan received a letter from Sylvia Goldsmith stating that Gilbert had arranged financing to pay off the liens he held on the three homes under renovation, which included the penalty for paying off the notes early. The letter went on to say that before the money would be dispersed, Ivan would need to prove that all tracking devices secured to vehicles and properties had been removed.

Ivan told Peety; "I could really screw with them if I wanted to, but after pocketing an unexpected $300,000, I guess I could be a nice guy."

Ivan called Sylvia.

When she answered, he said in a melodious voice, "Sylvia, oh, Sylvia, this is Ivan calling. So your boy found someone dumb enough to lend him money."

"Gilbert had absolutely no difficulty finding new financing. For that matter, he should have gone to this lender from the beginning, but had this crazy notion that he could work with you, only to find out that wasn't true."

"I'm heartbroken."

"For some reason, these new folks are charging less and not requiring monitoring devices on his vehicles and properties, including his home. Quite novel on their part, don't you think?"

"So they're idiots."

"They're not idiots; on the contrary, they're well-respected in the lending industry, something you're not."

"You're making me feel bad."

"As soon as you can prove the tracking devices are gone, we'll release your funds."

"I'll tell dip-shit where they are, and he can bring them to the Traders Club."

"My client's not going to do that. You're going to remove them yourself and make any repairs necessary from taking them off."

"I'll have someone get in touch with numb-nuts to take care of things."

"His name is Gilbert Humphrey, thank you. And one more thing. If you fail to remove all the tracking devices, rest assured we'll be in touch with you."

"Good luck collecting."

"I'm good at that."

Ivan hung up and turned to the Critter, saying, "These people don't know whom they're dealing with. I toss letters from attorneys in the recycling bin. They're idiots."

The Critter's smirk and Ivan's phone call prompted Peety to sing, "Hit the road, Jack, and don't you come back no more, no more…"

Ivan looked at him and said, "Keep it up and I'll get you an audition on American Idol."

Peety quit singing, whistling instead, as he knew that he was on Ivan's bad side.

"Damn," Ivan said. "Now I've got to find another place to put that money to work. Life sucks."

Peety kept whistling, as he wasn't about to say anything.

Ivan grabbed his hat and headed out the door.

The minute he was gone, Peety looked at the Critter and said, "I used to have fantasies about other birds, but those ended years back when I realized I'll never get any nooky locked in a cage. So why fantasize about some sexy bird when you can't do anything about it? Do you know how that makes me feel, you smirky little devil?"

The Critter looked straight ahead.

So Peety responded, "Why bother talking to a dumbbell like you? Talking to you is a waste of time. Here I thought I could get some concrete answers to complex problems and all you do is smirk. You're probably made of porcelain anyway, which means there is no way you can give me concrete answers. Why am I wasting my time talking to you, dingbat? There, I feel better now."

Turning away from the Critter, he tried to think of something besides his problems, because he heard that the more you think about yourself, the more unhappy you'd become. What a stupid statement to make to someone who loved focusing on himself. I get mad thinking about it. Maybe I'll think of someone else, though it's hard to do when there's no one more important than me.

Chapter 32

Gilbert was so happy to be out from under Ivan's clutches, he vowed that once the renovations were complete, he would ask Mindy to spend a day in Sedona with him. They could drive up in the morning and return that night.

He'd never bothered to ask her if she'd ever been there, as going to Sedona for him never grew old. The breathtaking beauty of the area was mesmerizing. He loved the red rocks. If Mindy wanted, they could take a jeep tour or go by horseback, though he preferred the idea of the jeep tour, as he didn't want to subject some poor horse to someone his size for very long.

If she wanted, they could get a couple of rooms to spend the night, then head to Antelope Canyon and Glen Canyon the next day, as both were worth seeing. Antelope Canyon was spectacular, with its shades of orange, red and yellow reflected from the smooth sandstone walls that had been sculpted by Mother Nature with wind and water over thousands of years. Equally impressive were Glen Canyon and the Lonely Dell historic site, along with scenic overlooks of Lake Powell and the Vermillion Cliffs.

All he had to do was get up the nerve to ask her.

He felt very comfortable with the way Mindy addressed issues; for that matter, had become quite smitten with her. Acutely perceptive, she quickly assessed malicious intent in others, in spite of their veiled sincerity. A disciple of the dogma, "It's more important to watch what people do then listen to what they say," she was very protective of those she represented. So Gilbert felt very safe with her, as he knew she'd level with him and put his needs above her own--not realizing that there was a seductive appeal to that. He trusted her, so felt comfortable around her, not realizing that comfortable feelings led him to think of her often.

Relieved that his problems with Ivan were behind him, he finally asked her out. Seated in their favorite restaurant, he said, "I spoke with Sylvia. She said I have every legal right to go after Julius, but if I do, I need to find a different attorney because of her relationship with him. She's learned that part of the reason he went after me is that he's infatuated with her, and became jealous to the point where he thought more was going on between her and me than just a client-attorney relationship."

"What's this I hear about him being extorted?"

"Sylvia said that's true, he was. And for a lot of money, which he paid. Apparently he forked over $300,000. She thinks if I sue I can get that and more."

"Will you?"

"I don't know. I don't like lawsuits, but at the same time, I'm not about to let him get away with what he did, but haven't figured out how yet."

"Gilbert, now that you have new financing in place on your properties, why not drop out of the Traders Club? Dealing with people like Julius and Ivan, you don't need that. Furthermore, you enjoy renovating property and are incredibly gifted at it, to the degree that people line up to buy your homes. You don't need to trade them, so give it up."

"I've thought of that," he replied.

"Another reason to drop out is that there have been some interesting postings on the Internet recently about the Traders Club. Your reputation is outstanding, but if people learn you're a member, it could come back to haunt you."

"I don't know what I'll do. There are some characters who attend for sure, but there are good people too."

"Well, give it some thought. A psychiatrist once said, 'The most important person in your world needs to be yourself. So that when you look in the mirror, the person facing you needs to be someone you look up to and respect, because if you don't respect yourself, it's hard to imagine others will.' You're a good person, Gilbert. You're very good at renovating properties. Your knowledge, desire to do things right, and your relationship with people will take you far."

"Thank you."

"Now I have an uncomfortable topic to talk to you about."

"What are you getting at?"

"I have a job offer from a builder to sit on-site at his luxury home subdivision."

"How did that come about?" he asked, with surprise and concern in his voice.

"I don't know. I never applied or anything, or expressed any interest. It turns out he came though an open house I held for you. He didn't identify himself, just started asking questions, and before long we were having quite a conversation, to the point that when he left, he told me he was very impressed.

"He didn't say what he was impressed with, just that he was impressed. I was disappointed that he didn't make an offer to buy your house, only to conclude later, after he came to my office a few days ago, that our chat was really a job interview. Someone in his office recommended that he talk to me. Apparently they had come through an open house too."

"What did you tell him?"

"I'm considering it. His offer is very generous."

"You're great at what you do. Why would you want to give it up?"

"He's offered a salary and commission plus it pays every two weeks, which would eliminate the feast and famine ways I've been living. Though you're very generous when you sell, there are times I don't have much income, which makes paying rent, car payments, and things like that a little rough."

"Well, the timing is ironic."

"Why is that?"

"Well, Whiskers and I want to submit you an offer too."

"What are you talking about?"

"I would love for you to find more fix-ups for me so as to lighten your financial burden. Whiskers and I would like to invite you to move in with us. As you know, we have the guesthouse, which is sitting vacant. It can be yours. That way you're not paying rent. See, I'm not very good at this stuff, but we kind of like having you around, plus we get a little lonely and think you would be the ideal person to solve that problem. We'll give you as much space as you want, so don't worry about that."

"Are you sure about this?"

"Yeah."

"I'm a bit taken back by this. I didn't expect it."

"Listen, I'm kind of a dunce when it comes to certain things, especially when it pertains to women, but I enjoy working with you because you're smart, ethical, and have a good heart, plus you steer me straight. And hey, I don't know where this is going, but I'm interested in giving it a try."

"Well, you've certainly given me something to think about. I didn't expect this."

"I know it comes as a surprise, and I know you have a terrific offer from the builder, so I wouldn't begrudge you taking it. But it just wouldn't be the same not having you track down properties for me, and stopping by to make sure I've eaten and things are going okay. I've grown to really rely on you. But listen, if you take the builder's offer, please keep in touch, because we very much want that as we really enjoy your company."

"Well, that being the case, I've decided which offer to take."

"You have?"

"I like you and Whiskers too, so if you really want to try this 'shared house bit,' I'm kind of a neatnik, so can I clean before I move in?"

A smile broke across Gilbert's face and he said, "You can clean to your heart's content. For that matter, Whiskers and I will step back and let you take control of everything."

"Are you sure you want to do that?"

"Good point. Why don't we be practical and give this arrangement a six-month trial run?

"I'm interested in doing that. I'll also need help moving."

"I've got a truck." They shook hands.

"I'll tell the builder I've received a better offer."

"You've made my day. By the way, have you ever been to Sedona?"

"I have, and I love it. It's beautiful."

"Why don't we go there after you move in?"

"I'd love to. I love going there. The red canyon walls, the changes in scenery depending on the time of day, the brooks and different colors. It's an incredibly beautiful area. I understand there are more millionaires living there than any other place in Arizona. It's my dream to own a home there, but they're so expensive I can't afford it, but maybe someday I'll win the lottery and that will change."

"I was going to suggest we drive up and return that night, but I have another suggestion instead."

"What's that?"

"We get a couple of rooms to spend the night, and when we're through sightseeing, we'll look for a fix-up. If we don't find one, we'll start running ads in the Sedona paper in search of one. I'm sure in time we'll locate one, and when we do, we'll plan on spending our weekends working on it and when we're finished, we'll hang onto it. How does that sound?"

"It sounds like I made the right decision by turning that builder down."

They stood, Gilbert stepped in front of her and said, "I like the direction our future is going," then gave her a big hug.

Chapter 33

Alone with the Critter and in a reflective mood, Peety decided to free associate about his past.

"I don't recall my early days in the nest, though do recall spending considerable time alone. My siblings were snatched early on by a hungry predator. How I escaped the ravenous rapture befuddled my mother, though she was happy I did. I felt guilty about it for a while, then decided it was destiny, believing my star was meant to shine.

"From early on I was a precocious bird. Of course, my parents had no others to compare me to, but that didn't bother me, as I knew I was special. In time I was most anxious to prove it by putting my wings to test. Though my parents were nervous watching me set sail, I showed them I was an able flier, though early on nearly got shot down by a pigeon unloading above me. I was fortunate to escape the massive load, and my parents knew I'd be able to escape most any predicament, which pleased them to no end.

"Soon I was flitting about to my heart's delight, only to have self-confidence get me in trouble. Convinced I could fly in and out of precarious areas, I never saw the trap I flew into. But wham, my days of freedom were over. Hauled off and put in a store for people to gawk at, I was mortified the day they clipped my wings, as from then on, all I could do was hop about. What a bummer. Filled with depression, I didn't respond well to people when they came to the store, but did manage to catch the eye of a couple who thought I'd be a good mate for their young son. Taken home I soon learned he was as lonely as I was, which helped us bond. In time we became the best of mates.

"It took a while for him to trust me, and though I'm not trained in psychoanalysis, I soon became his therapist, as I would hear him out no matter what he said, which delighted him to no end. His relationship with his parents was strained, and he had no friends, so he came to me to talk and I would oblige him by listening intently, sometimes for hours. He knew I could talk but never wanted to hear what I had to say, as he was too interested in himself, which proved to be his downfall. Had I been allowed to advise him, I would have steered him straight, but he would have no part of it. So I kept my thoughts to myself, listened instead, and nodded my head when it seemed appropriate."

The Critter, maintaining the smirk on his face, looked straight ahead but Peety didn't care, as he was too engrossed in himself.

"Had he listened to me, I would told him anger can be a cover-up for other feelings, explaining that sometimes it's easier to get angry than it is to admit we're afraid, or insecure, or whatever feeling might be masked by the anger. But no, he wouldn't listen, so I didn't try because he was deriving too much pleasure from being angry.

"See, its fun to be angry. For that matter, he enjoys it so much that he's constantly looking for reasons to get angry. Imagine that. I just had to make sure he didn't get angry with me. But thankfully, over the years he cut me some slack, as I get bored once in a while and am prone to irritate him. For that matter, I irritate him whenever I can.

"Did I tell you why he gets angry when I say 'Praise the Lord?' Well, maybe I won't go into it now. I'll tell you another time, 'cause I've been yacking too much, plus I'm tired so I think I'll take a siesta. In the meantime, you keep looking straight ahead with that smirk on your face."

Chapter 34

After Ivan ducked out the door, Peety told the Critter,

"I told you yesterday that I like to get under Ivan's skin by saying 'Praise the Lord.' See, he lent money to a church quite a while back and they caught on to his 'creative ways,' which he wasn't happy about. They severed ties with him, then repaid his loan so when he comes home I'll sometimes say 'Praise the Lord' to irritate him.

"See, once in a while I have a problem with anger. Did I tell you the story about the Cherokee grandfather? You're familiar with Cherokees, aren't you? Why am I even asking you this? You can't answer! Cherokees are a prominent Indian tribe with a long colorful history. Anyway, this Cherokee grandfather wanted to teach his grandson about human behavior, so said 'Inside every one of us a battle takes place between two wolves. An evil wolf who focuses on anger, hatred, retaliation, lies, and greed, and a good wolf who focuses on love, compassion, humility, and a concern for others. The grandson thinks about it for a minute, then asks his grandfather, 'Which wolf wins?' To which the grandfather simply replies, 'The one we feed.'

"Those wolves exist in me. Now, it's hard to imagine two wolves inside a macaw, but they're there. They're small, of course. Anyway, I digress. Though I try to listen to the good one, sometimes the evil one is more convincing, which gets me in trouble. So much so that I've missed many a meal because of my big mouth. People say big mouth, but in my case it's a beak. One would think I'd learn over the years, but sometimes when things don't go my way, I get angry and open my trap and that's when the proverbial you know what hits the fan. Oops, I think the door's opening."

Ivan walked in with a smug look on his face, looked at Peety and said, "Now that the bugs are out of Gilbert's house, I can't listen to him talk to his dumb cat anymore, which is too bad because you should have heard him complain about me. He went on about me as though the cat could do anything about it. What an idiot."

Peety wasn't going to say anything, just let him blabber, as he knew that once it was off his chest he'd drop the subject.

"I've got to find someone else to lend money to, as most are so happy to get it, they never read the fine print. Which for someone like me is a terrific source of pleasure, because it allows me to spy on them. They've given me permission."

Peety waited until he looked away, then shook his head. All the while, the Critter looked straight ahead with that shit-eating grin on his face.

Chapter 35

With the year coming to an end, the Traders held their annual recognition meeting, with all anxious to see who won the two most prestigious awards: Trader of the Year, and Most Ethical Exchanger.

For the fifth year in a row, Windy didn't represent anyone or close any transactions, so received the Most Ethical Exchanger award. Once again he felt honored to have his name etched on the award, then added that he had a suggestion for the club. Since no one wanted his job as treasurer, it should be outsourced to India. Not being sure where the idea came from, no one responded.

Trader of the Year award went to Gomer Gibson for saving the club from going broke. Norm Hickman boycotted the meeting after hearing Gomer was getting the award, though met Hadley Evans before to set up a time to discuss their insurance company idea.

After receiving the award, Gomer thanked the club, then bid farewell, as he had a doctor's appointment. (He didn't tell anyone it was with Dr. Goldfarb). What he really left early for though was to race home to show Buttercup his award. He couldn't wait for supper to show it to her, as he was sure she would be very impressed and want to see it right away. He just wouldn't be able to expound on the reason he received it. He'd have to tell Dr. Goldfarb too, though wouldn't go into details, figuring you don't have to tell your psychiatrist everything.

Tossing salt on his wound for losing his house, Ivan nominated Hadley Evans III for Mortgage Broker of the Year. Unaware of what was behind the nomination, plus afraid to do anything that would upset Ivan, the traders all concurred. Hadley accepted the award, uttering what a joy it was to be around such fine upstanding people, meaning he would qualify for Bullshit Artist of the Year Award too if they offered one. What members weren't aware of, though, was his toying with running for political office, but had they known, they would have been convinced he had the gift for gab.

Gilbert received the Renovator of the Year award.

Mindy Mort was awarded Super Sleuth of the Year.

Ivan didn't receive any awards, but didn't care as he had had a successful year, thanks to the contributions of Julius and Hadley.

 Jumper Gehrig dropped out of the Traders Club after his failed experience with Hadley. Real estate too. Since he didn't care if the Traders were upset with him or not, he hired Sylvia Goldsmith to go after Hadley for his commission. Nearly broke, he got his old job back at the feed lot, figuring that if he was going to shovel shit, he might just as well get paid for it.

Gomer marched through the front door of his home, proudly displaying the award he had received at the Traders Club. Buttercup feigned surprise and awe at his achievement. To think that he had been selected Trader of the Year made her suspect there was more behind it, but she wasn't about to inquire. Instead, she was content to say all the proper things one says when someone receives an award. "Ah, what an achievement! To think I'm married to the Trader of the Year--that's  really something! That's certainly going to look nice hanging in your office." (Thinking to herself, "'Cause you ain't hanging it anyplace else.") "You have every reason to be proud of yourself."

"Well, I must say I was surprised to receive the award, because there are so many more deserving people than I, but I'll take it nonetheless."

"You're just being modest dear, I'm sure."

"Listen, I've got a medical appointment, so I'll see you later."

With that, he was out the door.

Arriving at Dr. Goldfarb's office, he presented his medical insurance cards, then filled out a form identifying what medical issues he was dealing with, though this wasn't necessary, as Dr. Goldfarb had already had his medical history sent--compliments of the digital age. He knew what doctors Gomer was seeing, their diagnoses, and the medications they recommended. The bottom line being: his history was extensive, which was part of the reason he was referred.

Not sure what to expect from a psychiatrist, he soon felt very comfortable, as Dr. Goldfarb was pleasant, bright, and very professional. In short order, Gomer was explaining in depth his medical concerns, his personal concerns, his relationship at home, his role at the Traders Club, and his sense of self. Then he realized that he had been going on for some time, so asked, "What do you think, doc? Am I nuts?"

"That's a common concern everyone has who sees a psychiatrist, Gomer, and in your case the answer is no, you're not nuts. But let's take a look at some of the things going on in your life to see what kind of picture we come up with. You relayed that momma schedules your day, kind of controls what goes on at home, and that you rely on her quite a bit, am I correct?"

"Yes, it's true."

"Once a week you attend this Traders Club, but go as a bystander rather than a participant, because you're afraid you'll be taken advantage of. Is that correct?"

"Yes."

"Every day, except for weekends, you see a different doctor for a different ailment. Is that true?"

"Yes."

"Based on what you've told me, who would you say you spend the majority of your time thinking about?"

"What do you mean?"

"Who do you think about the most?"

"Nobody's ever asked me that before! But based on the questions you've asked and the picture you've painted, it kind of seems like the answer is me."

"Let's say that's true. Let's say that you have been the focus of your time and energy. How has that worked out for you?"

"What do you mean?"

"How has focusing on yourself benefited you?"

"I don't know how to answer that."

"Let's look at it another way. Has focusing on yourself brought you the happiness you hoped for?"

"No."

"So would it be safe to say that if you continue as you are, you'll stay unhappy."

"I never thought of it that way."

"Are you open to exploring ways that might bring you what you want, which is happiness?"

"By all means. Who wouldn't?"

"A psychiatrist I trained under years ago told me, 'The more you focus on yourself, the more unhappy you will be.' "

"I never heard that before. But I guess that kind of fits me."

"He also told me, 'The role of a psychiatrist is to serve as a mirror, reflecting back to people how they come across, because if people don't know how they come across, they can't change."

"You've pointed out to me things about myself I was not aware of. What would you recommend I do, because deep down, I'm not happy with the way I am."

"Let me make a couple of observations. You're a wealthy man. You don't need to work. So the question is, what can you do to change the focus from yourself to others, and if you do, might it bring you what you want? Which is happiness?"

"I've never considered thinking of others. I've always thought of myself. I was brought up that way. 'Watch out for yourself' was drummed into my mind. Now to think I might need to change that is strange."

"The way you were brought up, how has it worked for you?"

"I'm sitting here, aren't I?"

"Yes, you are."

Gomer then said, "You hear every day that the food bank needs help. Maybe I should volunteer there. Yeah, I'll do that. It can't hurt. Maybe it's worth a try. Maybe you've got something here, doc. I've always focused on myself. Never thought of others, didn't think I had to. But as you point out, I'm not as happy as I want to be, so maybe by helping others, I might help myself. What a novel idea."

"It's worth a try. There are many people who need help. And there are many successful, wealthy people who derive tremendous satisfaction from helping others. Why don't you see where this new thinking takes you? If you have questions or concerns, c'mon back and we'll look at what's going on."

"I think I'll do that. Won't my wife be surprised if she learns I'm volunteering at the food bank! It's worth the look on her face to do it."

"We'll leave that for another time, what do you say?"

Gomer laughed and said, "I think you've got a point there." They shook hands, then Gomer walked out and promptly headed for the food bank. He didn't know if it would help, but it was sure worth a try.

Julius Stern received the award for Property Owner of the Year for achieving 100% occupancy in his apartments. When his staff learned that, they shook their heads in amazement, then rattled his cage by telling him Sylvia Goldsmith called.

"What's that dingbat up to?"

"She's very happy, her practice is going well, she enjoys her new apartment, and her social life has improved. She's dating a doctor."

"What doctor in his right mind would date her? Who's the idiot?"

"A Dr. Goldfarb."

Julius nearly peed in his pants.

Then he got his cage rattled more when he learned, "Oh, yes, she sent you a letter too. It's on your desk."

After reading it, his stomach turned into knots, so he headed to the bathroom.

Returning to his office, Julius was jolted to find Gilbert waiting for him. Towering over him, Gilbert, asked if he could close the door.

Fearing the worst and expecting it wouldn't make much difference, Julius said, "Go ahead. What do you want?"

"We need to chat," Gilbert said.

Expecting to be pummeled, he said, "About what?"

"I understand you were concerned that my relationship with Sylvia went beyond the professional?"

"How could it not?"

"She's an attractive lady, no doubt, but our relationship was always platonic, always above board. She was and is my attorney, and nothing else."

"So why are you telling me this now?"

"Maybe you should have asked me that before you hired someone to rough me up. You could have saved yourself a lot of money and me a lot of aches and pains."

"So are you going to sue me over it?"

"No, I'm not."

"You're not, then what are you going to do?" Backing up, he feared he was about to get pummeled.

"I've thought long and hard about it, and decided I have two options. Deal with my anger, or forgive you, and I've decided to forgive you." Then Gilbert started to leave.

Julius didn't know what to think, so meekly said, "I'll see you at the Traders Club."

Gilbert stopped, looked at him, and said, "No, I've seen enough of what goes on there. I'm dropping out," then walked out the door.

Julius was shaken. Expecting to be beaten to a pulp, he was instead forgiven. He had never been forgiven before so didn't know how to handle it, so he went home to think.

In the morning after a sleepless night, he knew he needed to talk with someone. He couldn't call Dr. Goldfarb--for that matter could never return to him again because of his relationship with Sylvia--so that left only one person to consult. Rabbi Goldman.

Picking up the phone, he placed the call.

"Rabbi, this is Julius."

"How are you, my friend?"

"Not so good. I need to talk. Can I come see you?"

"I'm free now, Julius, if you have time."

"I'll be there shortly."

Rabbi Goldman didn't know what to expect, but sensed from the tone of Julius's voice a far different attitude than what he was used to seeing in him. The cocky, arrogant, self-assured Julius was, all of a sudden, subdued. This was confirmed when he walked through the door. His body language gave the appearance that he was very down. Inviting Julius into his office, the Rabbi closed the door for privacy, then said, "Something is heavy on your mind. I've never seen you like this. Please tell me what it is."

Julius talked for two hours in a way he'd never talked before. He talked about his experience with Gilbert, then discussed his fears, anxieties, apprehensions, his parents, Sylvia, Dr. Goldfarb, his wealth, his apartments, why he did some of the things he did, what he thought of himself, and anything else that came to mind.

Rabbi Goldman sat back, asked a few questions but for the most part listened, and in the process, saw a side of Julius he'd never seen before. Though he didn't expect profound changes because of their discussion, there definitely was a splinter of hope for the future.

Walking to the door, Julius thanked him profusely for taking the time to listen to him. Then asked if he could return again, because he had never revealed to anyone what he had just revealed to him, and as such, felt very exposed. Rabbi Goldman assured him that their conversation would be kept in confidence, adding that he looked forward to his coming back so they could talk some more, then surprised Julius by giving him a hug. He had never been hugged before. Rabbi Goldman then told him, "I'm always here for you, my friend. Salome."

Julius walked out the door a much-relieved man.

Julius headed to his apartment complex and caused quite a stir upon walking in by saying hello to the rental agent. So taken back by his pleasantness, she nearly fell out of her chair. He then approached the receptionist on duty and asked for Maria Gonzalez's personnel file.

She said, "It might take me a minute to get because I have

someone on hold."

He said, "Take your time, I can wait." Wow, she thought. "What's going on with him?"

It took longer than a few minutes, so she expected to be raked over the coals when she handed him Maria's file. Instead, he thanked her for getting it for him. She was so flabbergasted she didn't know what to say, so instead she said nothing and, and meekly backed out of his office.

Picking up the phone, Julius dialed Maria's number. She had caller ID, so assumed it was one of the gals she had supervised calling, only to be stunned when she heard his voice.

"Maria, this is Julius. I'm calling to apologize for how I treated you, and to ask you to come back as my manager."

Maria stammered at first as she didn't know what to say, then finally regained enough composure to say, " Can we talk first before I give you my answer?"

"By all means. Is tomorrow morning convenient for you?"

"I'll be there at ten."

"Great."

After hanging up, Julius thought to himself, "I'm doing the right thing, and I feel good about it."

Maria arrived early for her meeting with Julius, in hopes she could say hello to the gals she had supervised. Walking in the front door, she was greeted warmly by two of them. The third was answering phones, though turned calls over to the answering machine when she spotted Maria so she could give her a big hug. Afraid to speak openly, she whispered in her ear that Julius seemed changed, but to be careful. Maria mouthed that she would, then asked, "Is Julius here?"

"Yes, he's in his office. The door is closed, but he told us to send you in when you got here."

"It's good seeing all of you. I'll be talking to you soon."

She then took a deep breath, walked to the door leading into Julius' office, and lightly tapped on it.

"C'mon in," was the order from the other side, though there was something about the order that was different. It wasn't sharp and angry as usual; instead, it had a mellower side.

Entering his office, she was surprised to see him stand and offer his hand, because normally a gal extends hers first, not a guy. Seeing Julius offer his caught her offguard. She was on edge as it was, so to see him do this unnerved her a bit. At the same time, it spoke to some thing different about him. Maybe his attitude was different.

"Maria, please be seated."

When she was he said, "Thank you for coming. I'm sure my calling you came as a surprise."

"Very much so," was her response, "Especially in light of the fact that I've hired an attorney to get the money I felt I was due."

"Oh, that. Don't worry about it, you'll get your money."

"Thank you."

"We ended on a rather unfortunate note, which is why I wanted to speak with you. I should not have fired you for following my orders. I was wrong for doing it, which is why I want to offer you your job back. I've had a chance to do some thinking since you left, or after I fired you, and had a chance to consult with my Rabbi, who happens to be a wise man whom I respect greatly.

"During my conversation with him, he brought to my attention some things about me I'm not entirely proud of. My attitude hasn't been the best, along with my temper and overall demeanor. He helped me understand how I came to be the person I am, which I wasn't aware of. We don't need to go into what those factors were, but we're all a product of our upbringings, and I had a lot of issues from the past. Issues I hadn't resolved, so I kind of took it out on others, like you."

Maria sat listening and watching. She had learned early in life that it's very important to listen to what people have to say, but far more important to watch what they do, so she had her eyes directly on him to make sure his body language jived with what was coming out of his mouth.

Julius then went on, "I know things have been rather rocky between us, but you're the best manager I've ever had. I watch how you conduct yourself, how you interact with staff, how you treat tenants, and it's all top-notch. You're very good. For those reasons, I would like to see you come back. I put an ad in the paper for a manager and had all kinds of responses, which isn't surprising in light of the economy, but my preference is to have you return. How about it, do you want your job back?"

"I need to work; but I'm very afraid to work for you.  I don't
know how honest I can be here, because I don't know how
you'll take it."

"Probably better than I used to, but old ways are hard to change."

"That's what I'm afraid of…Oh, well, here goes.  You
micro-managed, were temperamental, volatile on occasion, we
never knew what to expect from you, to the point where we
walked on pins and needles around you.  You would blame us
for things we didn't do, find fault with things we did, never
complimented anyone, you probably sold more papers than
anyone in town, because after a short time working for you,
everyone here started looking at the want ads for another
job, including me."

Not knowing how he'd react to that, she watched him and waited
for a response.

"It kind of sounds like I wouldn't qualify for employer of the
year around here, would I?"

"I'm afraid you're right.  There was many a night I cried myself
to sleep because I found you impossible to be around.  But I
needed the job.  I needed to put food on the table for my kids,
and we needed a roof over our heads, and still do.  Though I
interviewed for another job I didn't get it, because they called
here for a reference but didn't get a very good one."

"That was before I spoke with my Rabbi."

"Well, someone else got the job, so it doesn't matter."

"I know you're afraid to return, Maria, and under the circumstances I don't blame you. I know how hard it is for a person to change. I've been a jerk to work for, so you have sound reasons to think that'll be the case in the future. But you have to admit, the previous guy, the guy I was, would never humble himself to admit his mistakes, or go so far as to invite someone back they had fired, so that's a change."

She nodded in agreement.

"Maria, you need a job, and I need the best manager I ever had to come back. If you will, I'll agree to meet with you every Friday afternoon to have sessions like we're having now, where we'll lay things on the line, speak frankly, and try to work through issues together. I'm not saying it's going to be easy, but I'm willing to try. I'll go a step further. In the event I fire you any time during the year, I'll pay you a full year's salary on top of whatever I've paid you to that point, and I'll put that in writing."

"That's very generous, and the offer is quite appealing. But because of what's happened in the past, can I give you my answer tomorrow?"

"I'll wait for your call."

She extended her hand to shake his. He put both of his over hers and said, "I hope you come back, Maria."

Maria went home and was soon on the phone to Sylvia. Sylvia was notably apprehensive. "Be careful Maria, he might be showing signs of maturity, but his irresponsible ways aren't that far in the past. Let me know what you decide and what you want to do about your back pay."

Maria then contacted the gals she supervised to share with them the conversation she had had with Julius, and the decision she had to make. All said Julius was better than he used to be, but they'd had no recent crises either, so weren't sure how he'd handle one if they did. They all said they'd love to have her back, but wouldn't guarantee they wouldn't keep looking, though if she returned they would feel much better knowing she was there to protect them should he change back to his old ways. Maria then called her mom to get her opinion. She also talked to her kids to get their thoughts.

In the morning Maria called Julius to say she'd be willing to give it a try. He expressed his appreciation and said he would have an agreement drawn spelling out what he had agreed to do. She said she would return to work at noon so he could go to lunch.

Chapter 36

Gomer had never worked so hard in all his life. His muscles ached from making boxes, putting food into boxes, unloading boxes from trucks, hauling boxes from one area to another, packaging up boxes and putting boxes in peoples' cars. No sooner had he arrived at the food bank than he was ushered back to the warehouse to start work. The gal taking him back thanked him profusely for volunteering, as they were behind in getting food out to the many folks standing in line, which Gomer saw when he looked out the door.

Though he was unsure what to do initially, he soon caught on, and in short order was involved in the process. Assigned to the fruit and vegetable area, he was told to toss any items that might show signs of deterioration in a trashcan, then take the trashcan to the dumpster. He had never lifted such heavy items before. A full trashcan was beyond his ability, so he kept them half-full.

When they were caught up in that area, he was taken to the sorting area, where he had never met such happy people in all his life. Retirees and others were working their tails off, but laughing and joking, which amazed Gomer to no end, as they were all working for free. Before long others started to leave, and Gomer looked at his watch and realized it was past five. Buttercup was likely waiting at the supper table for him, wondering where he was.

Looking down at his clothes, he realized he was a mess. The designer shirt and pants he had on were soiled to the point they were candidates for the dumpster, but he didn't care. He couldn't ever recall spending a more pleasant afternoon. On the way out, he was presented an application to sign, as they wanted information on those who volunteered. He signed, then was thanked again for volunteering. He was also asked if they could expect to see him back and he replied, "If I can get out of bed in the morning, I'll be here." Then he trudged out to his car where he sat down for the first time in three hours, simply exhausted.

As Gomer walked in from the garage at home, Buttercup looked at him in horror as he made his way to the dining area.

"My God, what happened to you? You look terrible! Look at your clothes. They're ruined. What have you done to ruin those nice clothes I bought you? This is not like you. What have you gone off and done? You look like some bum off the street. What would our friends and neighbors think if they saw you?

You're not fit to be seen in public. Go back and take those filthy clothes off. Jump in the shower too. I certainly don't want to sit across the dining room table looking at you the way you look right now. So what have you been doing to cause you to look like this?"

"Having one of the best afternoons I've ever had in my life!"

"And you end up looking like this? What in the world have you been doing?"

"Sorting fruit and vegetables at the food bank."

"At the food bank! Are you off your rocker? Maybe you need to see a psychiatrist!"

"I did, earlier today."

"Oh, my God, don't tell any of our friends or neighbors you did. They'll think there's something wrong with us. You for sure, and me for being married to you. Didn't you think of that before you acted so hastily? We'll never live it down. You need to go back and get out of those clothes, while I need a drink. You should have consulted me before going off to the food bank. I can see it now; people might have spotted you down there. We have our image to think of. We can't be just going off and doing stuff like this."

Gomer was tired, hungry, dirty, and pleased. If he had known that volunteering at the food bank was what it was going to take to get under the old lady's bonnet, he would have volunteered years before. Screw the image and their phony friends, he thought. He liked the people he had hooked up with at the food bank. Though he didn't really know them, they seemed downright genuine, which was a far cry from the folks they usually hung out with.

Shuffling back to his bedroom, he stripped, put his dirty clothes in the damper, turned on the shower, and stepped in, letting the water drench his tired body. After toweling off, he donned his bathrobe and slippers then headed to his closet to pick out the oldest clothes he could find, figuring he'd get in less trouble wearing them. Shuffling back to the dining area he passed Buttercup's bedroom, only to see the door closed. Sure she was on the phone to her friends, he lumbered down to the kitchen where his food was waiting for him. He was grateful that it was. Picking up the tray, he thanked their housekeeper for keeping it warm, wished her good night, then headed back to his room to eat.

In the morning, Gomer had a terrible time getting out of bed. Every muscle in his body ached. Making his way to the kitchen dressed in the old clothes he had set out, he immediately ran into a buzz saw.

"Under no circumstances do I want you leaving this house looking like that. I have your schedule printed out, and I have not scheduled any time for you to go back to the food bank. That was a terrible idea to go there in the first place. If your psychiatrist recommended it, I'd recommend you get a second opinion, because a man of your stature in the community doesn't need to be working at the food bank. It's way beneath you! Though I didn't put it on your schedule, you should plan to hang that nice plague on the wall of your office that you got from the Traders Club. That's more symbolic of the person you are than some guy tossing rotten food in a dumpster at the food bank."

She didn't give him much chance to speak, though it was pretty clear what her thoughts were. Maybe he would be making another appointment with Dr. Goldfarb. Stonewalling Buttercup might not be the right solution. It's possible he'd need professional advice on how to deal with her.

His coffee sure tasted good, though, as did the bagel and cheese. Keeping his mouth full might be better than opening it and inserting his foot, so he kept munching away, letting his mind free-associate about what he intended to do during the day. Putting in a full day at the food bank might be a bit much, as he had little experience performing manual labor, and could tell from the feedback he was getting from his muscles that he had better take it easy there.

Perhaps today he needed to appease his wife by changing from the clothes he had on into designer clothes, then fulfilling his list of chores. Once out of the house, he'd cancel his doctor's appointment in the afternoon to check his hemorrhoids, as they felt fine. Expecting a reaming from his wife, he'd head to a department store to buy clothes to wear at the food bank. He felt safe that he wouldn't be spotted going into a department store, because none of their friends or associates went to one.

At two p.m. when he arrived at the food bank, he was warmly received. They even remembered his name. One retarded gal who helped in the front office gave him a big hug. He was told they needed help sorting again, so he headed back to the sorting area where he found a group overwhelmed with work. He recognized some of them, though other than a "welcome back," he didn't hear much from them, as they were up to their eyeballs in work.

When 4:30 came, the crisis had been resolved and folks were

back to their jovial ways. Gomer could see that many had established long time friendships volunteering at the food bank. They were a close group. Thinking he'd better make it home in time for supper, he decided to walk out with others who were leaving. All were thanked and praised when they left, which made them all feel good.

When Gomer arrived home, all hell broke loose again, as Buttercup was none too happy that he had gone back to the food bank. And then to learn that he had bought clothes on his own, and had the audacity to shop at a department store, caused her to really unravel.

"We do not go to stores like that! Do you realize store cameras spotted you? What if our friends saw you there? What would they think? At least you're not as filthy as yesterday. You need to get out of those clothes, because I don't want to sit across the table with you dressed like that. For that matter, I'm so upset by the change in your attitude and behavior, I'm retiring to my room for the evening. Hopefully tomorrow you'll get over this foolish notion that you need to help others!" Then she stormed off.

After two weeks of getting ragged on by Buttercup, Gomer called Dr. Goldfarb's office to arrange an appointment to see him. Surprised to hear Dr. Goldfarb answer himself, he said, "Hey, doc, this is Gomer."

"Gomer, how are you?"

"Not so good."

"What's wrong?"

"My wife's been chewing on my ass ever since I started volunteering at the food bank, and to save what's left, I need your help figuring out how to deal with her."

Dr. Goldfarb laughed and said, "Let me grab my appointment book and see what we can set up for you. How about Thursday afternoon at one? I've got an opening at three also."

"I'll be there at one. Keep the three o'clock time open too, I might need it."

"Okay, Gomer, I'll see you then."

Chapter 37

Norm called Hadley to share a few ideas relative to the insurance companies.

"Why don't we ask the insurance companies to pay us for moving the 'dying process' up?"

"What a great idea," Hadley replied.

"We'll point out we're improving their bottom line and benefiting the economy too. If they ask how the economy's benefiting, we'll say 'we're taking the old folks off the social security rolls earlier than they might.' "

"The young bucks in this nation, once they hear about it, will love us for it because they're already complaining that they're paying too much into Social Security and Medicare. By our moving the dying process up, we're lightening the load on them. I think we're onto something here!"

"I've got another idea."

"What's that?"

"Wouldn't be a shame if old folks had no insurance, not even Medicare?"

"Where are you going with this?"

"If they had no insurance, going to Switzerland could be moved up sooner."

"You got a point there; of course, if they couldn't afford a doctor, how would they get the letter from a doctor saying they've got one foot in the grave, because the Swiss require that?"

"You know those folks who create documents for illegal aliens?"

"You're thinking they can create documents for us?"

"What with fewer illegals coming across the border, they're probably not as busy these days."

"Do you think we should patent this idea?"

"I don't know but keep your brain working; I'm getting excited thinking about this. We might be on to something. I'll call you next week."

After they hung up, Norm couldn't get the idea out of his head. One thing for sure they couldn't do was hire young, slick sales people. On the contrary, they would hire older people, some close to retirement or even retirees, as the sick and elderly would be more inclined to relate to them. During the training process, they would be taught how to listen, how to gain trust, when to talk about the past, when to talk about values, religion, how to play on their feelings, but--more importantly--how to make them want to transfer their properties to them.

The more Norm thought about it, the more excited he got. With the aging population of our nation, they could be sitting on a gold mine. If they were really successful, he might even consider paying Gomer back, then thought to himself, "Nah, Gomer doesn't need the money."

While ruminating about a marketing plan, a thought popped into his head. They'd need a catchy phrase because every successful company had a successful phrase. Perhaps theirs could be, "Fly first class; return in an urn," though he wasn't sure if that would catch on, as there was a finality about it that was rather cold. He'd have to think about it. Maybe they could use "The dignified last flight." There's a possibility, he thought. It's a nice, comforting statement. Those with one foot in the grave would feel quite good knowing their remains would be handled graciously.

They'd have to come up with a name for the company, one that projected a sense of compassion. Maybe "Final Affairs," or "Compassionate Traveler," or "Miracle Wings" would work. He wasn't sure. Each was a possibility. He'd have to think about it. He liked the way all this was falling into place.

Chapter 38

After a very trying week, Dr. Goldfarb attended Shul. His reasons for going were many, though one reason was to spend a few moments with Rabbi Goldman, whom he found a very wise man. After the service, Rabbi Goldman bid everyone goodbye while Dr. Goldfarb waited for all to leave. Rabbi Goldman saw this. So when he approached, Rabbi Goldman said, "How are you, my friend? We haven't seen you for a while. You've obviously been busy."

"I have."

"Your challenges are many."

"They can be."

"In spite of your professional talents, I'm always here for you if you ever want to talk."

"There are times I need someone to share my woes with too, so I appreciate the offer."

"Your job helping sick and at times dysfunctional people isn't the easiest."

"It has its moments, though I'm not investing as much time in my practice as I was, which has helped."

"What prompted the change?"

"An attorney!"

"You're not in trouble, I hope?"

With a smile on his face, he said, "I could be."

"In what way?"

"This attorney happens to be a gal I think of often."

Rabbi Goldman beamed. "Those are the kind of problems I love hearing about. They're the kind of problems the world needs more of. If I can help promote this problem, let me know." He put his arm around the doctor and walked him to the door. "Salome, my friend. I'm always here for you."

"Thank you."

Dr. Goldfarb felt relieved walking to his car, because talking to Rabbi Goldman was like talking to his father, whom he missed deeply.


Chapter 39


Windy heard a knock at his front door, so he looked out the peephole to spot his mother standing there, and let her in.

285

She said, "I haven't talked to you or seen you in a couple of days so wanted to stop by to make sure everything's okay. You look frantic this morning, what's wrong?"

"Nothing."

"No, something is wrong! You look exhausted. Haven't you been sleeping?"

"No."

"Why not?"

"I've got to quit my job as treasurer."

"Okay. What has that got to do with your looking worn out?"

"I don't want to get outsourced to India."

"What are you talking about?"

"I heard someone wants to strip owners and top executives of their U.S. citizenship if they outsource 50% of their jobs overseas, and I'm afraid that since I'm treasurer of the Traders Club, I might be included."

"I've never heard such a thing. Are you sure you're not dreaming this up?"

"Why do you say that?"

"That's the kind of thinking you have when you're off your medication. Are you sure you've taken it? Let me check...No, you haven't. That explains it. Here's some water, take your medicine."

Washing his medicine down, Windy said, "They're not going to send me to India?"

"Who's going to do that?"

"The government."

"No! Why would the government want to take your citizenship away and send you to India?"

"Because I said at the Traders Club that we should outsource the job of treasurer to India."

"So you think the Traders contacted the government because you said that?"

"Yeah, do you think the government will come after me?"

"Of course not! Thank god you're not president of the club! What do you think would happen then?"

"I'd be in trouble for sure," he replied.

"The government's not going to ship senior executives and owners overseas and take away their right to be a US citizen because they outsource half of their company's jobs overseas. That's just not going to happen. Anyway, I won't let it happen to you. Just promise me you'll take your medicine on time."

"I will."

"Let's go out for breakfast," she said.

Though his medicine was kicking in, he was also starved. A couple of days had gone by and he hadn't eaten, because he was too busy waiting for the government to show up to have time to eat.

## Chapter 40

Hadley called Norm early in the morning, as he wanted to run an idea by him. Rather than hash the idea out over the phone, they agreed to meet for breakfast.

After ordering Norm asked, "What have you got?"

"What do you think of Swiss Solutions, LLC?"

"My initial thought is that it says where they're going (Switzerland), but sounds like too much of a link to the drug industry. The idea of a solution going in someone's vein might turn many off so, nah, I don't like that one."

"What about Swiss to Heaven, LLC?"

"That's got potential. I'll have to think about it for awhile."

"I really liked and wanted to use Heavenly Endings, LLC but that name's been taken."

"Just keep working at it. You're on the right track!"

"As soon as we find a name we'll check to make sure no one else is using it, then set up an LLC. They're not expensive to do, or hard either. We'll need to notify the Corporation Commission and run an ad which will cost about $50.00. Altogether we'll be out $200.00, which isn't bad."

"So the key now is to pick a name?"

"Yeah, as far as I can see it is. I wish I could think of one right now because I'm anxious to get going, as I see real potential."

"Well, sleep on it. Maybe something will come to you in the middle of the night."

"That's it. You just named it."

"What are you talking about?"

"End in Sight, LLC. What do you think?"

"It's got possibilities. Is anyone else using it?"

"Let me check." He pulled his laptop out, hooked into the Internet, searched for a bit, then said, "Nope. It's available."

"Let's sleep on it overnight and talk more in the morning. You know, the name is kind of soothing. It lets people know their suffering is coming to an end. You might have a good one here, Hadley, old boy."

"Pass the tobasco sauce, will ya'?"

"You put tobasco sauce on your eggs?" Norm asked. "What in the hell is wrong with you?"

"We live in the Southwest, for God's sake, this is Hispanic country. We like hot sauce," Hadley replied.

"You might, I don't. It raises hell with my stomach."

"Now, let me get this straight. Mr. Multi-tattooed ex-football player has a touchy stomach, is that true?"

"Shut up. Let's eat."

"So, what do you think of 'End in Sight, LLC'?"

"I like it." Norm replied. "Let's go with it."

"Yeah, I agree. I can see it now, Hadley and Norm's 'End in Sight, LLC.' It's got a nice ring to it."

"Hey, wait a minute. My damn stomach's getting a little worked up here and I haven't even had any of that rotgut tobasco sauce. What about Norm and Hadley's 'End in Sight, LLC'? I like that better."

"Why don't we just leave it at 'End in Sight, LLC,' with neither of our names connected to it?"

"Yeah, you're probably right. No sense in getting in an argument over whose name goes first. As long as it's a fifty-fifty deal, who cares?"

Hadley started to say, "Since it was my idea…" but Norm interrupted him by saying, "Don't even go there, as my stomach's about to explode and so is my temper."

"Fifty-fifty it is then," Hadley replied. "You got two hundred bucks?"

"You want me to put the money up for the ad and the application to the Corporation Commission, don't you?"

"You got a couple more for breakfast too?"

"What a friggin' leach!"

"I like having you for a partner. Can we meet for lunch too?" Hadley said, laughing as he did.

"Let's get out of here before I take the cap off that tobasco sauce and stick the bottle someplace you won't like."

Chapter 41

Everyone could see that Windy wasn't himself. His eyes were glossy; he was preoccupied, extremely tired, and involved in a conversation with himself that no one else was privy to. One could sense that he hadn't slept in days. Worried he might do something irrational, everyone gave him space, but watched him out of the corners of their eyes, because they knew he was a card-carrying member of the NRA.

Of course, many were, but with him it came out of a strong conviction that people were out to get him (which, had they known his diagnosis, would have been true). The cylinders in his mind weren't aligning properly, which was confirmed when the president started the meeting and said, "Today's election day. Are there any nominations for president?"

"I nominate Windy," one said.

"Is there a second?"

"I'll second him."

"Are there any other nominations?"

 No one spoke up.

"I declare the nominations for president closed.  All in favor of Windy for president, say aye."

The majority said, "Aye."

"Are there any no's?"

Ivan wasn't in favor of Windy but wasn't going to say anything.

"The aye's have it.  Windy takes over as president at the next meeting."

"Windy, do you have anything you want to say?"

Windy stood, faced his mates, and announced, "Conservatives hang on to the Constitution the way children hang on to a security blanket."

Whoa, those weren't the words of a die-hard conservative, and Windy was a card-carrying member whom they had just elected president for the coming year. Their confusion grew when he continued,

"Many believe that if it's not in the Constitution, it doesn't exist, which explains the conundrum over abortion, gay rights, monkey shit, airplanes, and the Internet. As far as they're concerned, constitutional interpretation trumps common sense and good judgment. Of course, any restriction on their right to own nuclear weapons is deemed a threat to their Second Amendment rights, which will not be tolerated, because if you give rational people an inch, they'll take away BB guns, Uzi's, bazookas, and machine guns, and that's not going to fly."

Many sat with their mouths wide open, then shook their heads when he then said,

"Then there's the goofball that sees lasers replacing guns, and immobilizing replacing killing. Imagine, immobilizing arms and legs but not breathing and internal organs. How insane! The NRA would never stand for that. It would put them out of business!"

Whatever he was on, they weren't ready for his next salvo.

"A strict interpretation of the Second Amendment would only allow muskets, because muskets were what the gun-signers had when they penned the Second Amendment. But they're not taking my guns," and he pulled out his pistol, brandishing it about, causing people to dive under tables.

"No one's taking my guns. I'll die first, or shoot the bastard who tries." Seeing people disappear under tables was enough to rattle him into realizing that something was wrong. Then it dawned on him. "Shit, I forgot to take my medicine. I'm in one of my nutty stages." Alarmed, he raced out the door in a total panic.

"What the hell was that all about?" Jose Gallegos muttered. "The guy's off his rocker, and we just elected him president!"

He then turned to his buddy Joe Castro and said, "Thank god he didn't suggest prisoners be allowed to have guns, because that would have really proven he's nuts." Joe nodded in agreement.

"No, he's okay. He's just having a bad day. Probably drank too much last night," one of them said. "We've all done that. We need to cut him some slack. I'm sure he'll be better next week when he takes over."

Everyone was ready to buy into that, because if they kicked him out, someone would end up having to take over the books, as they forgot to elect a new treasurer and no one wanted the job. With that, the meeting ended, with everyone trying to work through their minds what had just taken place with Windy.

Windy wove in and out of traffic racing home, lucky to not be pulled over or involved in an accident because of his erratic driving. Consumed by fear that the club would toss him out for being nuts--which he was--he gobbled a double dose of medicine, which made him an absolute zombie in minutes. Stumbling to bed, Windy succumbed to a deep sleep that lasted a day. Filtering through his mind was the irrational thought that he had been elected president of the Traders Club, which proved once and for all that he was off his rocker.

Awakening him the next day, his mother said, "When I wasn't able to reach you I decided to check on you. You've been off your medicine, haven't you?"

He didn't say anything.

"You know what happens when you quit taking it. Your mind doesn't shut down and you walk through your house with your gun, fearful someone's going to break in. How many times have we gone down this road? Do I need to take you to the hospital to get your medicine adjusted?"

"No."

"You're not still thinking about being sent to India, are you?"

He responded with a blank vacant stare.

"I found your medicine bottles open on the counter. Did you take some?"

"I don't know."

"We need to get you back on schedule and get some food in your stomach. Your stomach's growling. I can hear it from here. Why don't you get cleaned up and I'll get you some food."

With that, Windy staggered to the bathroom.

After getting food in his stomach, he showed signs of coming to life, so his mother asked, "Are you going to make it?"

"I think so."

"Well, don't go anywhere until you're up to it. If you need anything you call me, and I, or your brother, will get it for you. Understand?"

"I understand."

"Do you want me to bring you supper tonight?"

"No, I'll be fine."

Then she left, though she called later to make sure he was okay.

A few days later, he became obsessed with fear that the Traders had caught onto his psychotic ways and would throw him out. So, wrapped up with that thought, he toyed with the idea of not returning, then reality set in, which sparked a sense of joy. "They'd have to find a new treasurer, so I'm safe. No one wants the job."

Chapter 42

Secret Meeting:

Jose Gallegos, Joe Castro, and Mark Ramirez called a special meeting of the board after Windy's off-the-wall comments about the Constitution and Second Amendment.

Jose addressed the board. "I know it's highly unusual to throw out a president after he's been elected, but Windy's nuts. He has to be. To say what he said about the Constitution and Second Amendment shows that he's off his rocker. His comments were not what you'd expect from a good conservative. Now I know Windy proclaims to be one, but he's goofier than a bedbug. We can't let him run the club!" Then he sat down.

"Jose's right," Joe Castro said. "Expecting us to give up our guns for muskets is downright insane. I'm with Jose. We need to elect a new president."

Mark Ramirez chimed in, "But if we do, how do we tell Windy? If he has his heart set on being president and finds out the board held a secret meeting to take the position away, he might walk out. And if he does, who's going to take over the books? None of us want the job, but one of us would get stuck with it."

Jose turned to the secretary and asked, "Did you take minutes of the meeting announcing Windy's nomination and election?"

"Well, yes, I did."

"Is it possible those minutes could disappear?"

"You mean like misplaced or erased?"

"Exactly!"

"If it's the board's wish that that happen, it certainly could."

"What if we decide today on a new president and put his name down? Do you think Windy would catch on? Should the secretary redraft the minutes and put the new president's name in?" Joe asked.

"If he does catch on, we could say that he must have imagined being elected president, because no one else recalls it," Mark chimed in.

"Do you think he'll buy that?" Joe asked.

"He might not, but we could counter that by telling him that he's such a damn good treasurer that we realized after electing him to the job of president, we had made a horrible mistake. Handling two jobs is too much for one person, and we want him to stay on as treasurer."

The retiring president said, "So we've got a real can of worms on our hands, don't we?"

Looking around the table he saw everyone nodding.

"So who among us wants to be president?" he asked.

Mark Ramirez says, "The one who realized immediately the error of our ways was Jose Gallegos. I nominate Jose."

"Jose, do you promise not to say nutty things about the Constitution and Second Amendment?" the retiring president asked.

"I do."

"All in favor of electing Jose, raise their hands."

"Jose, the job is yours!"

Final Chapter

A couple of days later, Windy walked into the Traders Club with a ready excuse for not having updated the books. Ready to bolt from the meeting if asked the status of their money, he was tremendously relieved when Jose Gallegos was introduced as president, because the focus was off him.

"Speech, speech!" the members cried when Jose took the gavel, all of them keeping an eye on Windy to see how he'd handle that.

"Ladies and gentleman, I'm much honored to be elected your president this year. And I know of no better way to kick off the year than by recognizing the greatest treasurer any club has ever had: Windy Wales!"

The members were on their feet hollering, whooping, clapping, and cheering.

The fear and apprehension Windy had felt when he walked in was overtaken by pure joy. A smile spread across his face, the likes of which people had never seen before. To be so warmly recognized for the job he had done meant the world to him. He would handle the books for them. For that matter, he would do almost anything if it meant that he was allowed to remain a member of the Traders Club.


THE END

The Critter

My sister made the critter for me. Watching me open the package brought the brightest smile to her face. As I pondered her work of art she laughingly relayed she had a lot of fun making it. From the moment I saw it I loved it and have relished having it ever since. I think of her whenever I see it. She was a delightful gal. Her infectious laugh charmed us and the goodness in her heart brought warmth and joy to our lives. Thus it was a sad day when she left us. We've missed her deeply since. Rest in peace Jan. Your masterpiece is now available for the world to see.

www.ingramcontent.com/pod-product-compliance
Lightning Source LLC
Chambersburg PA
CBHW071257170626
46809CB00001B/248